HEARTBREAK AND HONOR

Highland Heather Romancing a Scot,
Book Three

COLLETTE CAMERON

Blue Rose Romance®
Portland, Oregon

Sweet-to-Spicy Timeless Romance®

"All else matters naught.

I give you my pledge, as long as life's

blood flows through my veins, I shall love

you above everything else, upon my honor."

Highland Heather Romancing a Scot
Triumph and Treasure
Virtue and Valor
Heartbreak and Honor
Scandal's Splendor
Passion and Plunder
Seductive Surrender
A Yuletide Highlander

Check out Collette's Other Series
Castle Brides
Daughters of Desire (Scandalous Ladies)
The Blue Rose Regency Romances:
The Culpepper Misses
The Honorable Rogues®
Seductive Scoundrels
Heart of a Scot

Collections
Lords in Love
The Honorable Rogues® Books 1-3
The Honorable Rogues® Books 4-6
Seductive Scoundrels Series Books 1-3
Seductive Scoundrels Series Books 4-6
The Blue Rose Regency Romances-
The Culpepper Misses Series 1-2

Prologue

Dounnich House, The Blackhall Stronghold
Mid-September 1818

Tasara leaned far out the narrow window, peering into the room adjacent to hers. A beautiful young woman stared back at her. "I thought I heard someone over there today. I am Tasara Faas. Are ye held captive, too?"

Tasara and her young brother and sister had been held against their wills for weeks now. In truth, as the days crept by, she increasingly worried they'd die as prisoners of the Blackhall blackguards.

The other woman edged as close as the window would allow. Brushing her hair behind her back, she whispered, "I am Isobel Ferguson, and yes, I was abducted." She spoke in the cultured tones of a noblewoman. "They intend to force me to marry the war chief this evening. Although, they believe I'm someone else, and I fear for my life when they learn the truth."

Ah, then Isobel also knew the evil nature of their abductors.

The Blackhalls would have much to account for on judgment day.

Isobel patted the windowsill with her palm. "If I had a rope, I would use it in a blink. What about you? Why are you here? I saw a young boy earlier. Your brother?"

Her heart cramping with renewed trepidation, Tasara sent a swift glance behind her. "Aye. He and my sister are sleepin'."

"You have a *sister* with you, as well?"

"Aye. Lala's four. We were seized many days ago—almost three weeks now—when I took the children to collect the stray goats." Tasara glanced inside her room again. "I dinna dare try to escape with the wee ones, and I canna—*willna*—leave them behind. I suspect we are bein' used as blackmail."

But for what purpose?

She had no doubt fear shadowed her bruised and battered face. She'd suffered at the hands of the brutes below. Toying with the fringed end of the scarf tied around her head, she said, "I overheard one of the Scots mention somethin' about forcin' my tribe to help them."

Tasara couldn't guess what the Blackhalls were about, but if they didn't have a care, they'd start a war.

"*Help* them?" Isobel's winged brows swooped together. "With what?"

"I dinna ken. I havena seen this Scottish clan before." An idea struck Tasara, and before she could rationalize all the reasons it wouldn't work, she blurted, "I shall help ye escape. Then ye can send others to rescue us."

Isobel's eyes went wide, and she dashed a nervous

look to the ground.

Tasara tore the scarf off her head, and her ebony tresses billowed down her back. Pushing her hair over a shoulder, she turned her attention to untying the scarves at her waist. Once done, she held them up. "With these and the lengths of blanket, we can make ye a line to escape. I have a knife to cut the blankets with."

"I haven't anything with which to tie a rope in my chamber." Isobel shook her head, frustration turning her mouth downward. "The curs didn't even provide me a bed to sleep upon."

Uncertainty swept Tasara, and her attention fell to the narrow ledge connecting the windows before meeting Isobel's gaze again. "Can ye walk along the edge to my room? There is a heavy bed in here."

"Yes." Isobel inhaled a large breath and offered Tasara a wobbly smile. "I have a knife too. Start cutting the blanket into strips and tie the ends together. I'll do the same over here."

Isobel Ferguson was a verra courageous woman.

Tasara nodded before disappearing into her room.

Hurrying to the bed, her heart banging against her ribs, Tasara fought doubts. If they were caught…

Nae.

She wouldn't consider it.

She trembled with fear as she worked, but in short order had cut the blanket into strips and tied the pieces together. Standing on one end, she yanked each knot to tighten it. Stealing a frantic glance at her still slumbering siblings, Tasara dashed back to the window with the blanket's remnants.

She cast a worried glance at the sulky sky. Clouds pregnant with moisture drooped low. Isobel's escape would be that much more difficult.

Tasara poked her head out of her casement. "Isobel, I've tied mine off to the bed."

Face pale, Isobel appeared in the adjacent opening. "I'm done as well."

Tasara flung her rope over the sill. "See, almost halfway." Reeling the material up, she formed the length into a ball. "Catch."

She lobbed the makeshift rope at Isobel.

The wad fell short.

Isobel bit her lower lip and speared an anxious glance over her shoulder.

She was wise to fear the consequences if they were caught. Tasara refused to contemplate the cost for her part in aiding Isobel's escape.

Determination firming her jaw, Tasara compressed her lips and removed her bracelets. After looping a scarf through the clinking metal, she knotted the ends and heaved the line again.

Isobel leaned out as far as she dared and snatched the rope with her free hand as it unfurled.

Thank God!

Grinning, Tasara gave a little triumphant clap.

Isobel removed the bracelets, then secured the two lines together.

Tasara held her breath as Isobel lowered the makeshift rope.

Blast and bother.

At least ten feet remained between the dangling end

and the hard ground. Tasara angled her head, studying the situation. Once Isobel hung directly below Tasara's window, there would be a few more feet of makeshift rope hanging horizontally.

Not too bad, in truth—as long as Isobel managed without falling.

Isobel pulled the cord into her window, and Tasara dared to entertain a glimmer of hope.

"I'm going to change my shoes. What should I do with your bracelets?" Isobel held up the trinkets.

"Throw them out the window. They arena valuable, and if ye leave them in yer room, the Blackhalls will ken for certain that I helped ye." Tasara inspected the landscape and pointed. "Perhaps over there, in that tall grass."

Isobel nodded, her expression suggesting she'd rather lick Angus Blackhall's boots than creep along the ledge and descend using the line the two women had tied together. Giving Tasara a weak smile, she dropped a small bundle to the ground.

The lump landed soundlessly.

"Isobel, wrap the rope around yer back and underneath yer arms and tie it in front." Tasara demonstrated what she wanted Isobel to do. "Ye'll be more secure, and the line should be long enough."

Isobel swiftly secured the cord as Tasara had suggested.

Tasara swallowed against the nerves throttling up her throat on Isobel's behalf.

Isobel tossed the extra line over her shoulder and then clutched the sill with one hand. She shoved her gown above her knees before gingerly climbing onto the opening.

Tasara's stomach lurched, and she fought the urge to shut her eyes.

Turning sideways, Isobel eased through the crevice. The fit proved snug, and she was forced to wriggle herself free.

"You can do it, Isobel," Tasara assured encouragingly.

Surely, the women's thundering hearts had alerted all within five miles of her intent. The Blackhalls undoubtedly streaked to the back of the keep at this very moment.

Grasping the knot below her breasts with one hand, Isobel groped the craggy exterior with the other and inched along the strip, her attention fixed on Tasara.

"That's it." Forcing a smile, Tasara nodded. "A few more steps, and ye'll be directly in front of my window," Tasara promised. A few moments later, she touched Isobel's ankle. "I'll help ye inside. How does that sound?"

"Fine." The strangled croak Isobel forced past her stiff lips clearly indicated otherwise.

A minute later, she stood quaking inside Tasara's chamber.

Tasara's eyes swam with tears, and she embraced Isobel. "I dinna ken another woman as brave-hearted as ye, Isobel Ferguson."

"Bravery had nothing to do with it. Desperation did." Isobel wiped the sweat from her face with her forearm. "That is the most God-awful thing I have ever had to do."

Oblivious to the drama playing out beside them, the children slept on, their cherub mouths partly open.

"I dinna ken if I could've done it," Tasara admitted.

"Let's be about it, Tasara. I want to be well and gone before my disappearance is discovered. What about you? They will know you helped me when they see the rope."

Indeed, they would suspect she'd assisted Isobel.

"I can untie the rope and then drop it outside. If ye hide the line, they will have nae proof." Tasara darted an anxious glance toward her brother and sister.

Isobel smiled. "Yes, that will do. I shall hide it in the woods somewhere."

Tasara laid a palm on Isobel's arm. "I ken my father or others of my clan are near. Find them in the forest, and they will help you back to yer people."

A tear crept from the edge of her eye. She hoped this woman would escape. That she could send help to free Tasara and her little brother and sister. She brushed the droplet away. "Our troop is no' large enough, nor do we have the weapons to fight these... These *vafedi mush*, evil men. Perhaps ye ken someone who can help us?"

Isobel gave an enthusiastic nod. "My brother is Ewan McTavish, laird of—"

"Craiglocky." Hope fluttered in Tasara's middle. Ewan McTavish was Isobel's brother? "All the brethren ken of Laird McTavish."

The children started to stir from their naps, and Tasara hugged Isobel again.

"Ewan will help," Isobel assured her. "And one of

his greatest friends is England's War Secretary. Lord Ramsbury won't hesitate to assist my brother in any manner he is able to."

Tasara prayed there was true.

Once more, Isobel clambered onto the window ledge. "Are you sure you are strong enough to lower me? I suppose I could try to slide down the rope."

She didn't sound at all confident, however.

"Aye. I can do it." Tasara already busied herself, wrapping the crude rope around a bedpost. "I'll use the post for leverage."

Hers and Isobel's gazes locked.

Neither voiced the obvious.

All of their lives depended upon Isobel's escape.

Dounnich House-Blackhall Fortress, Scottish Highlands
Later that day

Agonized screams and raucous shouts penetrated the stout door Tasara pressed her ear against.

Did friend or foe attack her Scottish captors?

Had Isobel Ferguson been successful in getting help?

Tasara hugged the arched entrance closer, straining to hear. The wood scraped her face, and her unbound hair tumbled forward, snagging on a splinter. Her drumming pulse and the blood whooshing in her ears further muffled the skirmish below.

Fear-induced sweat dampened her underarms and palms, yet also dried her mouth. She exhaled brief, hard-earned pants, barely sufficient to be considered breathing at all.

Calm yourself this instant, Tasara Faas. Highland travellers are made of sterner stuff. Hysterical, you're of no use to anyone.

She licked her parched lips.

So thirsty.

Only a partial mug of stale water remained. She must save it for the *tikni* ones sleeping in the bed. Pressing her forehead against the rough panel, she drew in several calming breaths, counting to ten each time she inhaled and exhaled.

"That's better."

Not by much.

A mouse cornered by a starving lion had a slower heartbeat.

How many minutes had passed since the first cry alerted her to the invasion?

Five?

Fifteen?

More?

Impossible to tell with terror thickening her blood and scrambling her thoughts.

She'd hung over the window casement in an effort to catch a glimpse of the attackers. Yet, her chamber faced the castle's rear, and only contented Highland cattle, one lone stag, and a pair of curious pigeons perched on the keep's ledge returned her frantic perusal.

Sliding a glance to her sleeping sister and brother, she dug her fingernails into the door's coarse timber, afraid to hope. Might they actually leave this hellhole alive and unharmed?

For their sakes, she must keep her wits about her.

Tasara had despaired of any rescue attempt and feared for their virtue and lives. After over three weeks of captivity, had their salvation finally arrived?

Only the threat of death had kept her captors from

ravishing her after the first night when two hulking, *reeking*, Highlanders pinned her to the floor and attempted to have their way. They lay buried and rotting, their necks brutally broken with one powerful wrench by the war chief, Angus Blackhall.

He wanted her virginity intact, claiming he knew an English gent willing to pay handsomely for an untouched wench.

The devil must inhabit such a monster, for while Angus protected her honor, at every opportunity, he mashed her breasts, mauled her buttocks, and rudely forced his thick tongue in her mouth, his fetid kisses gagging her.

Right in front of Lala and György too.

Tasara's other jailors did the same. Bruises dotted her flesh from her attempts to spurn their rough molestations.

Flinching as wild, unhuman screams penetrated the stout door, she tightened her grip on the jamb and winced when a fingernail tore to the quick. Stifling a curse, she squeezed her throbbing finger.

Even now, did her father and the other Highland travellers fight the Blackhalls?

She'd seen what those Scots did to their enemies.

To each other, for that matter.

Dread knotted her stomach, and she squeezed her eyelids shut against the horrific images of mangled bodies and glassy, sightless stares. She would never forget the sickening sound of bone crunching as Angus snapped her assailants' necks.

Surely, if the travellers attacked, they'd recruited

help. Perhaps Isobel's brother? Acting alone, the gentle Scottish gypsies proved as ineffective as a bee stinging an enraged bear.

They would be massacred as easily too.

Oh, God.

A torrent of dizzying terror slammed into Tasara, and she pressed her hand to her forehead. *Nae.* It didn't bear contemplating—that her family risked death because of one mad, land-greedy Scot.

Shoving her long hair behind her ears, she cringed when the oily tresses coiled around her fingers. Catching a whiff of herself, she wrinkled her nose. She stank almost as bad as her captors.

Never had clean clothes and a thorough scrub been more coveted, even one in the icy streams she'd often complained about as a child.

Warm bubble-filled baths in a tub of some sort flitted across a distant corner of her mind.

I must've dreamed that.

A child stirred, and Tasara dashed to the bed containing their wee forms. She didn't want them waking. She sucked in a shuddery breath and drew the ratty blanket higher, covering her slumbering sister's and brother's ears.

The thin fabric wouldn't stifle the battle raging elsewhere in the keep. *Nae,* the blessed, deep sleep of childhood and an empty stomach protected the children far more than the raggedy length of grimy cloth.

The need to do something, *anything*, to keep György and Lala safe overcame her. Tasara withdrew the bone-handled dagger sheathed in her boot and, for the hundredth time, searched the room's shrouded corners for apparitions.

Evil permeated the very stones of Dounnich House.

Beyond the narrow, mullioned windows, the fading light couldn't disguise the stark chamber's dinginess.

If she'd been alone, she would've attempted to escape from the upper story prison, but with *bairns*, one four and the other but seven years old, she'd considered the option and tossed it aside as easily as a gnawed chicken bone.

If need be, she would die protecting them.

At least she'd been able to help Isobel Ferguson flee the castle, mere hours ago.

Isobel and the man rescuing her vowed to send Tasara help. Perhaps they had, and that's what caused the ruckus below. A powerful laird in his own right, Ewan McTavish would seek vengeance for his sister's abduction.

Twilight cloaked the sky in deep violet-gray and darkened the tomblike chamber further. Tasara hadn't a candle to light or firewood either. She shivered and firmed her lips against her empty stomach's painful contractions.

No one had ventured to their chamber since a timid maid delivered cold, lumpy porridge and stale dark bread this morning, further testament to the mayhem within the keep.

The Blackhalls were mad, the entire, uncivilized lot.

Should she waken the children and tuck them into a corner in case the renegades sought to use them as hostages or living shields? She could pull the bed before the door, but given her hairy captors' size, two or three hefty pushes would send the cumbersome piece of furniture skidding across the floor.

Wiser to let the wee ones sleep and pray to God, no one entered their room until her father or another traveller banged upon the door.

If that's who fought below.

If not...

Please, God, let it be them.

Lala turned over, flopping one small arm above her head and murmuring something unintelligible in her sleep.

An almost undetectable scritching rasped at the chamber's entrance.

Tasara switched her blade to her left hand.

Who lurked in the corridor?

Not a Blackhall.

Those particular Scots plowed into the room, all barbarous bravado and cocksure swagger, bellowing vulgar threats the whole while.

The door latch wiggled.

Not *Dat* or another black tinker either.

They would've called her name or the children's.

Oblivious to the bedlam downstairs, her vulnerable brother and sister slept on, their small forms dwarfed by the immense bed, the blanket's folds nearly hiding them.

The unspeakable, vile things the Blackhalls threatened to do if the clan's blackmail demands weren't met echoed like an unholy, perverse mantra inside Tasara's head. How men could suggest the obscene things those scunners vowed...

A revulsion-borne shiver shook her.

Clutching the handgrip of her knife, she crept on tiptoes across the stone floor. Flattened against the wall, she squinted at the lever.

There.

It moved again—the merest bit.

And again.

The tiniest of jiggles.

Metal scraped metal, and her lungs cramped.

A key?

Swallowing her fear, she tightened her grasp on her dagger. Only the Blackhalls held the key to this chamber.

Tasara dried one damp palm, then the other, on her skirt.

Could she truly stab someone?

To protect her sister and brother, she would, by God.

A *click* announced the lock giving way.

Creaking on unoiled hinges, the door edged open, inch-by-cautious-inch, and as it did, the brutal sounds from below filtered into the chamber. Light from the passageway's primitive torch-lit brackets illumined a sinister, black-clad form.

A disheveled man paused at the threshold, his coat unbuttoned and a pistol protruding from his waistband. In one hand, he held a sword at the ready, and in the other, he brandished a dirk. Legs braced, he stood at the entrance like a buccaneer balancing atop a ship's pitching deck.

A pirate in the Scottish Highlands?

Tasara blinked, slapping aside the ridiculous notion. Lack of food and sleep made her imagination run amuck.

For a tormenting instant, she'd feared the ethereal body was Satan himself. Except she doubted the devil possessed flaxen hair and required blades to inflict mortal damage.

Fallen angel seemed more apt for the apparition illumined within the doorway.

She strained to see the man's face. The dim interior hid his features except for a well-defined profile and a chiseled jawline.

A scowl notched her forehead and pulled her lips taut.

Evil men weren't supposed to be attractive.

Stance wide and her hand lifted to bury her knife, she waited for the intruder to move away from the door's protection.

She must defend the children, no matter the cost.

"Tathara?" Lala's plaintive cry filled the chamber. "*Piuthar,* where be ye?"

The man's head whipped toward the bed.

The bedding rustled and Lala, her voice tear-clogged, whimpered, "Me be afraid. I hearded fightin'."

Advancing farther into the room, the intruder looked this way and that. Light from the passage spilled across the threshold but failed to reach the bed or the room's outer edges.

"A child? Might've told me," he muttered in a clipped British accent while sheathing his weapons. "No matter, I suppose. A female's a female."

My God, what did the debauched knave intend?

The same loathsome things the Scots had threatened time and again?

Not as long as Tasara's heart pumped, he wouldn't. She shifted, ready to spring. A wee bit farther and she'd have a clear target. He would taste her blade before he laid one finger upon Lala.

The man faced the bed and extended his arms. "Come along, sweeting. Let's be about it then. I'm in a bit of a hurry."

How dare he, the loathsome degenerate?

Tasara made an inarticulate noise.

He whirled, his body tense and alert.

"Tathara!" Terror resonated in Lala's high-pitched cry.

Tasara lunged, swinging the blade in an arc intended for his neck. "Depraved sot."

Ducking, he leaped away, and her dagger sliced air instead of flesh. Half-crouched and keenly alert, he regarded her.

"Ah, the gypsy wench I was expecting." Straightening, and unperturbed at practically being skewered, he pointed at her knife. "I do believe you tried to impale me. Most ungrateful of you, I must say."

"Tasara?" György's sleep-thickened voice mixed with Lala's sniffles.

"By Jove, *not* another one?" The specter inclined his head in the bed's direction, his penetrating gaze riveted on Tasara. "How many are there of you in here, for God's sake? An entire clan?"

"Who are you?" Tasara circled him until she stood between him and the bed. What are you doing here?"

The gentleman retreated a couple of paces, and his pleasant chuckle took her aback. He clicked his booted heels together and dipped his head. "The Duke of Harcourt, at your service."

"**D**uke? What's a ruddy English duke doing sneaking into a Scottish keep's chamber?" Tasara flinched. She hadn't meant to speak aloud.

"Why, rescuing you, of course."

Did he wink?

Cocky fellow, wasn't he?

But then, he *was* a duke.

The attitude came with the title, no doubt present from birth. Probably had his noble bum and snotty nose wiped with the finest linen or silk. Astonishing that he would deem to exert himself enough to muster a sweat.

Didn't nobility have servants do everything for them?

Muted shouts and calls echoed from somewhere in the keep.

She tilted her head, attempting to recognize a voice.

The horrific shrieks and roars of minutes ago had ceased, although an occasional shrill cry yet rang through the stone passageways, raising the hair along her nape.

"Ye be here to rescue us?" Holding Lala's pudgy

hand, György knelt on the bed, his ebony eyes wary and likely sprinkled with a dab of excitement too.

In the muted light, Tasara couldn't be certain. Lads fantasized about adventures of this sort.

"I am, indeed, young sir." His grace smiled, his teeth gleaming in the half-light. "Whom do I have the pleasure of addressing?"

György shook his sister's grip loose.

Jamming her thumb in her mouth, she toyed with the curls tumbling atop her left shoulder. Her gaze wide and distrusting, she stared at the duke.

After scooting from the bed, György gave a handsome bow. "György Faas, Yer Highness, and these be me sisters, Tasara and Lala."

"It's *Your Grace*, György, not Your Highness."
I think.

Tasara's attention swung between the duke and her brother. Harcourt undoubtedly *had* been treated like royalty his entire life.

"*Grace*? Are ye sure, Tasara?" György pulled a silly face and snickered. "That be a lass's name."

The duke chuckled again, the rich timbre resonating from his chest. "So it is. Most embarrassing, I'll admit. But I'm afraid someone started the ridiculous tradition far too long ago for me to change things now. I'm just grateful they didn't select Chastity or Prudence."

"*Aye*, me too, *Your Chastity*." György clutched his belly in glee and laughed harder, unaware of his impudence at addressing a duke so informally. "*Dinna* ye have a given name?"

"Indeed, I do. Several as a matter of fact. I'm

named Rochester after my father, though I prefer to be addressed as Harcourt or Lucan, which is part of my middle name, Lucan-Ashford."

His agreeableness irked Tasara. No doubt, he could charm the fur from a fox and have the creature thanking him for the honor of losing its hide.

"Pray, tell me, why is an English nobleman helping to free Scottish Highland travellers?" Tasara flung a glance to the entrance, unwilling to lower her dagger until a familiar face appeared. "And where the devil is everyone else?"

The duke leveled the children a guarded glance. "The others are either dealing with the... ah…remnants of the ugly business downstairs or searching chambers for more hostages."

The whoosh of doors opening and then banging closed carried into the chamber, while footsteps thudding on the stone floors verified their rescuers searched this wing of the keep.

"I don't believe there are other captives." Tasara partially lowered her knife and shoved her hair behind her ear again. "Isobel Ferguson fled this afternoon. The Blackhalls mistook her for someone else. I know of no others being held."

"Yes, the wretches confused her for my cousin." His deep voice soothed her fraught nerves. "Your father witnessed Miss Ferguson escaping and raced to inform her brother."

"He did?" Tasara's prayers answered at last. She'd *known Dat* watched the keep from the forest. "My father is here?"

"He is." The duke motioned toward the door. "Along with a slew of other gypsies and McTavish clansmen."

Isobel's clan.

"Is your cousin Scots, then?" Absurd how pleased the knowledge Scottish blood might run in his ancestral lines made her.

"Yes, Lydia's the daughter of Laird Farnsworth of Tornbury Fortress, my mother's second cousin. Or mayhap it's third cousin once removed. I cannot get the extended relative rigmarole correct. I just know we share a common ancestor somewhere in our tangled family tree." The duke pointed at her knife. "You can put the blade away. I mean you no harm."

She frowned, still not trusting his conviviality.

The guards carried an enormous key ring. The metal loop wouldn't fit inside a coat without leaving a noticeable bulge. His grace's pocket—if he truly was a duke—contained no such telltale lump.

Mayhap he wasn't who he claimed. Wary, she adjusted her clasp on her dagger. "How did you get the key to open the door?"

"I didn't use a key." He withdrew a narrow piece of metal from inside his jacket. "I picked the lock."

Having never seen a lock pick before, it might've been an oversized toothpick or nail cleaner for all she knew. Tasara gave a short nod. Curious, that—a duke carrying around a lock pick. What other peculiar habits did he have?

Never mind. She didn't want to know.

Strolling to the room's center, he buttoned his

jacket. Several dark blotches marred the fabric and his pantaloons.

Blood.

A shudder rippled through her, and her focus involuntarily drifted to his sword. Had he killed someone during the rescue?

Possibly, given the violent nature of her abductors.

Why would he risk his life for strangers? Highland travellers, to boot?

Society—principally the snobbish English—never withheld their contempt of the black tinkers, lumping them in the same inferior category as the persecuted Roma. Each a people scorned and shunned worse than lepers because their customs and traditions differed from what Polite Society deemed acceptable.

"So, why are you here?" Tasara waved her hand in an arc.

"I had just arrived at Craiglocky to visit my cousin when this disagreeableness began. Miss Ferguson's brother is a long-standing friend of mine, so naturally, I insisted upon helping." The duke did wink this time and grinned too, the boyish actions sending her fitful pulse cavorting again.

Aye, a ruddy dangerous man, he was indeed. Hazardous to simple, gypsy maidens unused to a rakehell's practiced wiles.

"Besides, I'd grown a bit bored." He struck a dramatic pose. "And what could be more invigorating or honorable than rescuing a beautiful damsel in distress?"

Comical and glib of tongue too. Slick and sly, like most bluebloods tended to be. However, he'd seen to their freedom and, as such, deserved her gratitude. Regardless of her misgivings, a smile tugged one corner of Tasara's mouth.

"Damthel in a dreth?" Lala spoke around her thumb while flapping her grungy skirt back and forth. "Me have a dreth."

"Indeed, you do, fair maiden." The duke bent low in an exaggerated bow. "And I shall see you safely delivered to your father."

Lala smiled, her thumb securely anchored between her small teeth.

Tasara pulled in a long expanse of air and fought back tears of relief. Their ordeal had finally ended. She'd not been as brave or strong as she would have liked, but she hadn't crumpled into a worthless, sobbing, quivering mass either. Travellers were resilient and sanguine despite their hardships.

She bent and slid her blade into its sheath inside her boot.

Harcourt, smooth and silent as a Scottish wildcat, ambled to her. A ray of corridor light bathed his face as he gazed downward.

Her traitorous heart gave an excited tremor. He was so different from the shaggy-haired, broad-faced men of her clan.

His sharp hewn features, high cheekbones, a square jaw, surprisingly black-lashed eyes and dark eyebrows, all bespoke an aristocratic heritage, no doubt many generations old. His sculpted mouth spread into a knowing smile, revealing square teeth and a charming dimple in his right cheek.

She wanted to touch the indentation.

Verra attractive and verra dangerous, indeed.

Angelic? Or devilishly handsome?

Which better matched the man's character and personality?

"What say you, a trifling reward for my efforts? I'd ask for the honor of a waltz, but we're not likely to have the opportunity. Perhaps a kiss instead?" He dipped his head, his lips mere inches from hers.

She'd never been kissed.

"A kiss? Ye *canna* kiss her." György's tone turned belligerent. "Ye *dinna ken* each other, and ye *nae* be wed."

Harcourt grazed her lips with his, a butterfly wing's wispy touch, no more.

"How dare you?" Tasara stiffened her spine and thrust her chin out. Mindful to keep her voice tempered for the children's sake, she glared at him and fisted her hands. "What, because I'm a traveller, you think I'm fast and free with my favors?"

"No. Never free," Harcourt murmured for her ears alone while trailing a finger over her lips. "If you lived closer to London . . ."

Did he suggest he would *pay* for her favors, the conceited, insulting bounder? A scarlet haze of rage momentarily blinded her. Tasara jerked away from his touch and let fly with a solid punch.

~*~

Lucan's grunt of pain and the impact of Tasara's blow

resonated loudly in the chamber. The wench had walloped him in the face. Damned hard too.

"Thithter, why ye hitted the man?"

"'Cause he is a duke, that be why," György sneered. "*Gentlemen* should *nae* be forcin' kisses on unwillin' lasses like these Highland whoremongers did to our sister."

"György." Tasara shot her brother a stern look. "Watch your language in front of your sister, young man."

Had Tasara been accosted?

Bloody hell.

Lucan should've assumed as much. He touched his already swelling flesh in disbelief. He'd have a deuced difficult time explaining the discolored eye. He heard the hoots and snickers already. Unless he convinced the others, his injury resulted from fighting the Blackhalls.

Yes. Just the thing.

No one should suspect anything else. He'd fought a battle, hadn't he? Even if the scuffle ended almost as quickly as it began. Still, hand-to-hand combat might give a chap a bruised eye.

Pulse careening, he sucked in a deliberate, tempering breath. Tasara riled his temper, further piquing his desire to taste her lips.

Most women of his acquaintance simpered and fawned in his presence, mistakenly thinking he preferred compliant, biddable ladies. A wise man trod warily around their deceptive kind, not vixens speaking their thoughts and planting men facers.

He doubted Tasara capable of subterfuge.

György—wise child—had hit the mark, straight on.

Lucan didn't go round stealing kisses, but then gypsies didn't go about clobbering dukes either.

Posture rigid, she retreated until the back of her knees collided with the bed.

Lala scrambled into Tasara's arms, and György—glowering at Lucan—scooted to her side.

Noble little lad.

Quite an age difference between the three. Tasara must be in her late teens, and the youngest couldn't be more than, what?

Three? Four?

Lucan probed the tender flesh with his fingertips and winced.

You bloody well deserved it.

He had, dammit.

Propositioning women, especially ones who'd undergone the distressing ordeal she had experienced these past weeks, was beyond the pale. But when she'd gazed at him, her eyes luminous and mouth parted—the tempting honey-spot near her lower left lip taunting him, begging to be kissed—he'd lost his last vestiges of reason.

His senses, already highly attuned and stimulated from fighting, swiftly transformed into sexual arousal. Not typical behavior for him and most disconcerting. He prided himself, above everything, on being a gentleman. Instead, he'd been an imposing cur, and chagrin chafed his conscience.

In truth, Lucan adored women.

He enjoyed playing the gallant and the flirt—

enjoyed complimenting aging dames, shy spinsters, and plain wallflowers as much as he did confident, pampered beauties. And he enjoyed dancing, which made him a hostess favorite since they relied upon him to coax the shyest of maidens onto the dance floor at least once.

He'd been set on securing Tasara's freedom, and once they returned to Craiglocky, drinking himself senseless to obliterate the faces of the two men he'd killed storming the keep. This to rescue a woman he'd never met and wouldn't ever see again.

Well, not only to free her but also to assuage Sethwick's rage and reap vengeance on the Blackhalls for stealing his friend's sister away. Insult Sethwick and you insulted Harcourt. Plus, the barbarians had designs on Lydia. Their interest in his cousin bore further investigation. Why the Blackhalls had held the gypsy lass prisoner, he hadn't the faintest notion.

The three forms, huddling in the dimness, stared at him.

What color were Tasara's eyes, anyway?

By God, why did he care?

Still probing his swollen eye, he sighed. "That was abominable and unpardonable of me, and I must beg your forgiveness, Miss Faas. Please, let me assure you I'm not in the habit of imposing myself on women."

"Hmph." She jutted her dainty chin up a degree, and Lala, thumb firmly planted in her mouth, rested her head against her sister's shoulder. "Handsome is as handsome does."

He couldn't see Tasara's eyes clearly, but Lucan didn't doubt they skewered him. Better not turn his back, or he might find her dagger buried to the hilt somewhere on his person.

3

"Tasara? Wee ones?"

Upon hearing Balcomb Faas, Lucan stepped into the hallway.

The gypsy rushed along the passageway.

A group of sweaty, rumpled travellers and Highlanders followed in his wake, including McTavish, better known as Viscount Sethwick in England. Several men sported split lips, cuts, and bruises, as well as bloodied and torn clothing.

"My children are there, Yer Grace? Are they safe and well?"

A wicked abrasion marred Balcomb's cheek, and he limped in his haste to reach the chamber. A crimson-streaked slice along his thigh revealed the cause of his uneven gait. The diminutive man had fought with the fury of a dachshund downing a badger.

"*Dat. Dat.*"

A joy-filled smile stretched across the traveller's thin, haggard face when Lala bolted on her short, chubby legs from the chamber. He knelt and then gathered his daughter against his chest.

Not far behind her, György threw himself into Balcomb's embrace. "*Dat*, I've missed ye." His scrawny arms encircling his father's neck, the boy whispered into the gypsy's shoulder.

Tasara edged by Lucan, her eyes downcast, yet proud defiance in the set of her shoulders and angle of her head. Bedraggled and exhausted, her colorful clothing hung loosely on her slender frame.

Had the Blackhalls intended to starve them, for God's sake?

Still, his first view of her in full light stole his breath.

Her ebony hair hung in waves past her narrow waist. A pert, upturned nose graced her heart-shaped face. Fine brows swooped into arches above her eyes, the color undecipherable as she kept her lashes lowered. Twin cherry spots glowed upon her ivory cheeks.

Several bruises—some vivid in their newness and others older and fading—marred the slender column of her throat and below her elbows. Her lower lip, split and swollen, revealed she'd been struck recently.

Gutless bastards.

Tasara possessed an unusually delicate countenance and bone structure, especially for a Highlander. The hearty Scots generally bore strong familial and clan features and claimed a sturdy stockiness she lacked. Come to think of it, elements of her speech rang with unexpected refinement too.

Perhaps her parents were educated.

"The Blackhalls?" Lucan canted his head toward the noises filtering upstairs and exchanged a significant look with Sethwick.

Sethwick's gaze rested on each of the Faas children in turn before meeting Balcomb's closed expression. "Dealt with."

His curt answer revealed what he wouldn't in front of the little ones. The carnage Lucan witnessed before sprinting upstairs wouldn't soon be forgotten. Hopefully, the worst of the gore would be cleared away before they descended.

Sethwick's attention fell on Lucan's eye, and his lips quirked into a half-smile. "Harcourt, your pretty face is going to sport a dandy blackened eye." Several men chuckled, and Sethwick slapped Lucan's shoulder. "But if that's the extent of your injuries, I'm most grateful. We've a few men who didn't fare as well, I'm afraid."

No need to correct Sethwick's wrong assumption.

György poked his tousled head above his father's shoulder and glared. "He shouldna tried to kiss my sister."

The crowded passageway grew tomb-silent.

Every gaze but Tasara's

focused on Lucan. Hers seemed permanently affixed to the floor, her black lashes fanning her pinkened cheeks as she fidgeted with a clasp at the front of her embroidered shirt.

Heat scorched Lucan, culminating on his face. Devil take it, blushing like a lad in short pants caught sneaking a bonbon.

Well, her lips were a sweet treat of sorts.

He wanted a taste of her mouth, but not until it

healed. Damn and blast, he might've hurt her if he succeeded in stealing a real kiss. Might have done, even with the gentle sample he'd snatched.

Humor glinted in more than one knowing male gaze, and Lucan fought to maintain eye contact with the smirking Scots. The gypsies, their faces bland, peered at him accusingly. A specimen at Bullock's Museum or a medical laboratory received less intense scrutiny.

Lucan snagged Balcomb's attention.

The tinker scowled, disapproval creasing his weathered face and stretching his mouth into a single condemning line. He held his peace, although his dark regard chastised severely.

Did fear of confronting a duke prevent him from rightfully defending his daughter's honor?

The notion left a sour taste in Lucan's mouth.

Another inequality brought about by status.

A duke could do no wrong, a gypsy no right. Preposterous and unjust. He'd witnessed far more unscrupulous behavior amid the upper ten-thousand than amongst commoners and those lowly born.

Lala pulled her thumb from her mouth. "Thithter hitted the preddy man."

She pointed at Lucan before ramming her thumb home between her rosy lips.

A few muffled guffaws and choked-off laughs—even amongst the travellers—greeted the announcement, but Tasara's sweet mouth firmed into a thin ribbon as color swept her face once more.

Sethwick's incredulous expression earned a twitch of Lucan's lips. Reverse the situation, and he'd be laughing his arse off.

A muscle in Sethwick's jaw worked, yet he remained mute.

Rarely did something render Craiglocky's lord speechless. In fact, Lucan couldn't recall a single time his glib-tongued, diplomatic friend didn't have precisely the perfect thing to say.

A jot of censure hovered in Sethwick's eyes.

Go ahead, say it.

I'm a lout. Scoundrel. Reprobate.

The worst sort of knave.

Balcomb stood, Lala clinging to his neck and György to one leg.

"Ye'd *nae* right." Fists balled, György glowered at Lucan. "Ye're *nae* better than the others."

No. I'm not.

"György, hush dear." Tasara awkwardly embraced her father around the children. "I'm thrilled to see ye. Can we please go now? I've had quite enough of this place."

"*Aye*, lass. Are ye unharmed?" Balcomb asked far more with the discreet question.

She gave one, short nod. "*Aye.*"

"I'm proud of ye." He smiled and tenderly touched her shoulder. "Ye kept yer sister and brother safe."

"They were *verra* brave." She patted Lala's head and winked at György.

Balcomb's smile grew into an enthusiastic grin. "I did think my heart would stop when I saw ye lowerin' Miss Ferguson from the window, though."

"Yes, well, we hadna many other options." Tasara

laughed, low and melodious, happiness shimmering in her gaze. "None, truthfully."

She shoved her mass of curls behind a shoulder. "Miss Ferguson is the bravest woman I've ever met."

Utterly lovely.

One eye swollen shut, Lucan examined every inch of Tasara with the other. A desperate need grew to commit each angle of her face, every curve of her form, the lilt of her voice, and the music of her laughter to memory.

Absurd. Illogical. Ridiculous.

Yet, Lucan drank in her presence, uncaring that a moon-eyed beau gawked less.

Sethwick elevated a raven brow, his inquisitive gaze vacillating between Lucan and Tasara.

Lucan's friend was too bloody, damned perceptive.

With a final probing look, Sethwick turned his attention to her. "I'd say you are every bit as brave as my sister, Miss Faas. Please permit me to introduce myself. Laird, Ewan McTavish, or if you prefer my English title, Viscount Sethwick." Beaming, Sethwick bowed. "I'm forever in your debt for helping Isobel escape."

Tasara curtsied, refusing to look in Lucan's direction. Neck bent, she fingered the worn leather belt at her waist. Coppery highlights glinted on the crown of her head and flashed off the earrings dangling from her ears. Hard to believe this subdued goddess had done her best to render Lucan a human pincushion a few minutes ago.

Just how proficient was she with her blade?

He'd offended her mightily, and his conscience pelted him in the ribs every bit as fiercely.

I ought to be horsewhipped.

He never would have voiced such a loutish innuendo to a lady.

Why insult the gypsy lass, then?

Blister it if he knew what maggot squirming in his brain possessed him to act the arse.

Your brain's not to blame.

Look to your cock for the cause of your stupidity.

That hit the mark.

"If you"—Sethwick's regard swept Balcomb and the other travellers—"ever have need of anything, you've only to ask. And please know you are always welcome on McTavish lands."

"Thank ye, yer lairdship." Balcomb shifted his daughter higher upon his hip before shaking Sethwick's extended hand.

Sethwick cocked his head, his attention focused on Tasara. "Miss Faas, you bear a remarkable resemblance to an acquaintance of mine in London."

Who?

He turned to Lucan and gestured toward her. "Doesn't she look like Bridget Needham?"

Tasara flitted a glance Lucan's way, but as swiftly lifted her perfect little nose in the air and looked away.

Well, I'll be hell-fired.

Her eyes are as unique as she is.

It didn't altogether surprise him. Nothing about this woman met his expectations.

Her wounded, gold-flecked violet eyes had seared

his with accusation, and guilt scraped his conscience. Precisely why he acted the cavalier around the ladies. He preferred chivalry's mantle to uncouthness's raw chafing.

"Uncanny. Even her eyes." Sethwick scratched his nose. "Do you not see the likeness, Harcourt?"

"Yes, their coloring and features are quite similar. Miss Faas could pass for Mrs. Needham's daughter. However, I've been told I resemble Brummell." Lucan pointed at his chest. "And I assure you, there is no relation there, thank God." He smirked and lifted a shoulder. "Not quite sure they meant it as a compliment, in any event."

"Perhaps those making the comparison weren't referring to appearances but another characteristic." Sethwick pulled on his earlobe, his mouth quivering suspiciously.

A raised voice ascended from below, and a shadow flitted across Balcomb's face. He turned abruptly, thrusting Lala into Tasara's arms, then bending and scooping György into his. "Excuse us, sirs, but we must be off. I'm sure ye *ken* my wife be anxious for the return of our *bairns*."

"Of course, Balcomb." Sethwick nodded and smiled. "Remember what I said. If you ever need anything, please don't hesitate to seek me out. I am forever in yours and Miss Faas's debt."

"Thank ye." Balcomb hustled the corridor's distance, speedily ushering the girls before him. "Move along. *Nae* time to dally. We've a ride ahead of us."

Their voices blended in low conversations, the

travellers and Scots trailed after them, recounting the short battle's highlights.

Only Lucan and Sethwick remained before the chamber's open door.

Would Tasara look back?

I hope she does.

What did it matter?

Does there have to be a reason?

Lucan would never see her again.

Shouldn't bother me, but it does.

He'd return to his world and she to hers.

More's the pity.

Lucifer playing a harp in heaven or Prinny remaining faithful to his wife seemed more probable than Tasara crossing his path again.

Fascinating—*annoying*—what a chance encounter could do to disrupt a structured life.

Lucan touched his puffy eye, now swollen worse than the time he'd been stung by three bees, and winced. He mentally shrugged and released a short sigh. Things would settle to normalcy again—as soon as he left the Scottish Highlands for England's genteel familiarity.

The *haut ton's* strict adherence to protocol proved beneficial at times. It left little room for surprises, which suited him fine at the moment. When his father had died unexpectedly, he'd learned that surprises escalated into full-fledged fiascoes.

God, he wasn't dredging up *that* unpleasantness right now.

The subtle sway of Tasara's hips as she sped along the passage, sleek and agile as a feline, her swinging hair teasing the crest of those supple mounds, caused his groin to contract and swell.

Confound it.

Most unexpected and unwelcome.

Before she whisked around the corner, she peeked over her shoulder, her gaze meshing with his for a poignant instant in eternity. She buried her face in her sister's hair and disappeared from his life.

A giddy smugness—for surely that's what he felt flitting through his chest—encompassed Lucan.

She'd felt a connection too.

Sethwick stared after her, consternation etched upon his face. He cut Harcourt a sideways glance. "How old do you think she is?"

Lucan smothered a wave of unjust jealousy. Sethwick was blissfully married. So revoltingly happy, in fact. If they hadn't been chums for a decade, Lucan would have been hard-put to not gag and poke fun.

"I don't know." Lucan rolled a shoulder. "Eighteen? Nineteen?"

"Think she might be as old as one and twenty?" Sethwick turned in the stairway's direction.

"Perhaps, but Faas would have been a very young father. Not impossible, though."

Harcourt eyed a lopsided portrait, the canvas torn and curling at one corner. *Ugly, hairy brute—*

He squinted.

Egads, that's a woman?

The Almighty hadn't been kind to the Blackhalls.

"True. How old do you think Balcomb is?" Sethwick sidestepped a dead rat.

"Cannot be above forty." Neatly avoiding the foul-smelling rodent, Lucan held his breath. "And I would guess he's younger. Closer to eight and thirty."

Descending the stairs, he flinched as his stiffening muscles protested the exertion he'd put them through. A hot bath and a finger or two of Scotch—perhaps an entire bottle—wouldn't be amiss.

"Why? Aren't they the same travellers who visit your lands annually? Surely, Sethwick, you've seen them before."

"*Aye*, they are, and I have." Sethwick gave a sharp nod as they maneuvered a bend in the narrow stairwell, their boots clacking atop the slabs. "But I don't make it a habit to spend extensive time in the black tinkers' encampments."

Cobwebs hung from the windows, and a layer of dust, thick enough to plant vegetables in, lay upon the casements.

Lucan stifled a sneeze.

Dounnich House needed a good scrub.

"You have to remember, until two years ago, I spent most of my time in London." Sethwick knitted his brows. "And I vaguely recollect a conversation with Mrs. Needham about a niece who went missing about eighteen years ago."

4

Familiar sounds and smells—a crackling fire and sizzling meat—teased Tasara awake.

Coffee and bacon and wood smoke. Mmm.

She snuggled deeper into the comfortable bedding. Once slumber had claimed her last night, she'd slept dreamlessly and deeply, awakening in the same position she'd drifted to sleep in.

Falling asleep had presented a bit of a challenge.

Bit of a challenge?

No, it had been a dashed clash of exhaustion and lingering fear wrestling with newly awoken awareness.

A certain handsome, blond-haired, silver-eyed duke kept impolitely plowing his way into her thoughts. His grace wasn't the man she'd dreamed of previously, though. That young man had possessed moss-green eyes and golden hair, the shade of wheat at harvest time. And he always laughed, not scowled or tried to steal kisses.

She lifted her hand and flexed the fingers. Her bruised knuckles protested. She'd never punched anyone before, and her uncharacteristic violence horrified her. But the pompous oaf had suggested—had essentially called her a promiscuous strumpet.

The gall.

Somehow, she'd assumed he would prove different from the other gentry and lords who either visited the encampment or solicited the gypsy women when they ventured to a town or a city.

The duke hadn't been the first to make such a crude insinuation, and sure as wintertime snow fell in the Scottish Highlands, he wouldn't be the last.

Memories intruded of the Blackhalls' groping and pinching, grinding their groins against her buttocks and stomach, hissing the vilest filth imaginable...

She shuddered and drew the blankets closer.

It's over. They're dead. You're safe.

For now.

Until some other man fancied her.

Dat had rebuffed suitors and less honorable men on her behalf since shortly after she'd turned fifteen. Tasara would like to marry someday, but other than Rígán, who'd disappeared four years ago, no man had caught her interest.

She'd captured plenty of theirs, however, and more than one had extended her a dishonorable offer.

Idly rubbing her knuckles, Tasara tried to soothe the soreness.

Her disappointment in the duke made no sense. She didn't know the man. Why did his character flaws grate and chafe?

Perhaps because the elite thought they could buy whatever they wanted, and when something couldn't be bought, half the time they took it anyway, as though entitled to whatever fleetingly snared their interest.

Thank God the duke didn't seem to have a vengeful bent, or she might even now be jailed for striking a peer, though she'd been defending her honor. Instead, the gypsy encampment safely ensconced her.

The travellers had moved their camp during her absence. After an hour's ride, she and the rest of her family had finally reached the new site. Hugged and kissed until she squirmed and begged for a reprieve, Tasara ate her fill of savory rabbit stew before bathing, scrubbing her hair, and crawling into bed.

The black tinkers lived a humble existence, absent of luxuries, but she wouldn't trade her life for privileges and wealth. Nothing remotely pretentious could be claimed about her kin—humble and honest Highland folk. Generous and caring to a fault, they lavished on one another the thing they claimed in abundance.

Love.

She breathed in the tangy scent of dried herbs hanging from grapevine hooks above her head. Dawn's welcoming, pinkish-peach ribbons teased the sky through the bow tent's parted opening.

Lala and György, their sable heads barely visible above the woven blankets piled atop them, slept on.

Her father and stepmother had risen already, no doubt enjoying a strong cup of coffee beside the fire as they often did. Long ago, Tasara began lingering abed to give her parents a few moments of rare and cherished privacy.

She reached for the book normally tucked beneath her pillow.

Nothing.

Flopping onto her back, she sighed. She'd been too tired to put the worn volume there last night. *Dat* had insisted she learn how to read and write—quite unusual for a gypsy, let alone a woman.

Several years ago, a scholarly fellow married one of the tinker women and had taught Tasara. He'd also schooled her in basic geography, mathematics, and a smattering of French.

She'd not been the most accommodating pupil, preferring to run shoeless through the meadows or ride horses bareback. However, reading became one of her greatest passions—along with playing the violin— though books were expensive and hard to come by.

A smile played around the corners of her mouth. The low murmurs of her parents' voices soothed and wrapped her in contentment. More than once while captive she'd feared she'd never see them or the gypsy clan again.

"Balcomb, ye must consider Lala and György, and the rest of the clan. Jamie be concerned about retribution too."

The band's leader?

Tasara's eyes flew open at the urgency in Edeena's whisper.

Plump, kind, and perpetually smiling, her stepmother epitomized cheerfulness, and her earnestness unnerved Tasara.

"What of Tasara?" *Dat*'s question came from a greater distance.

He likely paced about their campsite. He always

wandered when upset.

"If what ye say is true, Laird McTavish already suspects somethin' is afoot," Edeena said. "Jamie fears the tinkers will be blamed."

A pan clanked, and the sizzling eased. Only nine years Tasara's senior, her sweet-natured stepmother seldom argued with *Dat*.

"And she struck an English duke." Edeena fairly hissed the final word. "Ye *ken* the hatred the *Sassenach* have for all things Scots, but especially we travellin' folk."

Ah, *Dat* had shared that unpleasantness.

Tasara pushed her hair from her face.

Should she interrupt them?

Let them know she'd awoken?

She didn't want her parents to think she deliberately listened to their private conversation.

"I *ken*, Edeena, but she thinks she's my daughter."

Tasara bolted upright, her hair swirling around her shoulders. Impatiently, she pushed the wavy mass behind her.

"She was younger than Lala when my first wife found her wanderin' in the woods."

Dya died twelve years ago, giving birth to a stillborn son. Tasara had adored her mother, and though she loved Edeena, *Dya* would always be the mother of her heart.

Dat's voice broke. "We'd never camped in the glen before, but a woman went into labor and was havin' a rough time birthin' her *bairn*. Forba went in search of fairy flax to ease her pain. I've always thought God had his hand in her findin' Tasara that day."

On her knees now, Tasara peered through the opening at the two shadowy forms near the fire.

"We didna dare seek the authorities for fear of bein' accused of stealin' the lass." *Dat* spread his hands, palms upward. "Ye *ken* gypsies have been accused of such many times with harsh repercussions."

True.

Only a few years ago, a clan had been sacked, their tribe members wounded and killed, and their possessions destroyed, when a couple had been arrested for abducting an infant.

The babe's mother had accidentally smothered her child in her sleep, and terrified of her husband's wrath, she'd buried the poor thing, claiming passing travelers had stolen the infant.

Neither the decimated gypsy clan nor the falsely accused couple received an apology or any restitution.

"Hmph, as if takin' in abandoned and discarded children out of the goodness of our hearts is criminal." Edeena shook her head and clucked her tongue while sliding the bacon onto a plate. "The *gadjo* steal our *tinkas* and peddle them into indentured servitude. Or worse, sell them to brothels or medical laboratories. Have ye forgotten poor Rígán?"

What does Rígán have to do with this?

Casting a wary glance around the encampment, Edeena tempered her voice. "Nae one wants to say it, but we are all thinkin' that's what happened to him."

Tasara dug her fingernails into her thighs.

Too much.

She wasn't a traveller.

Dat wasn't her father.

For eighteen years she'd lived a lie, and Rígán—

God.

Had a medical laboratory been his fate?

Scalding tears pricked her eyelids, but she refused to let them fall. Crying—nothing but a self-indulgent, useless waste of energy.

Miss Faas could pass for Mrs. Needham's daughter.

Was that a coincidence? Providence?

Checking the children—they'd tunneled further into their blankets—Tasara crawled closer to the entrance.

Dat knew something and reluctance kept him silent; she would swear it.

He'd acted most peculiar at Dounnich House when Laird Sethwick and his grace remarked on her likeness to their acquaintance. *Dat* had practically shoved her through the hall and into the night after their offhand comments. In truth, he'd also remained unnaturally quiet during the ride to the encampment.

Tasara had assumed him weary and lost in his musings, and perhaps weakened from his minor leg wound. Instead, might he have been mulling over the gentlemen's conversation and alarm prompted his hasty departure?

Perhaps *Dat* had hidden something and was afraid.

Had he and *Dya* committed a crime or been involved in a plot of some sort?

An image of a smiling, green-eyed man skirted around the misty fringes of Tasara's memory before fading into nothingness. Again.

She had never paid the specter any mind before, nor the two dark-haired women she dreamed of every now and again—one sweet-smelling and quiet, and the other gentle and loving and who liked to sing. She'd always assumed they'd been members of another gypsy tribe.

"Why was a *bairn* in the woods, far from any town or estate with a gash to the back of her wee head, Edeena, unless someone meant her harm?"

Hands braced on his hips, her father faced the rising sun.

Tasara crammed her fist against her mouth.

Good question. And one she didn't particularly want to know the answer to. Nonetheless, a tiny part of her couldn't help but be curious.

"Ye have to tell her, Balcomb. If ye willna, then I shall. She has a right to *ken*." Edeena's voice rose in frustration. "At least now ye have a hint of her origins, and it no' as though we are castin' her from the clan."

"Edeena, it will *seem* that way to Tasara."

Edeena set aside her coffee. With a sigh, she stood and stared at *Dat* for a moment and then hurried to him. She touched his cheek.

"I love Tasara too. I *dinna* want to see her hurt, but we *canna* risk the entire band's safety. Her people can protect her far better than the travellin' folk." She tucked into his side, resting her head against his shoulder, and he wrapped an arm around her waist.

"Didna ye say Laird Sethwick promised ye could ask him for anythin'?" Edeena tilted her head to look at *Dat*. "Ask him to find Tasara's real family. If I were her,

I'd want to *ken*."

"I have an idea who they might be." *Dat* kissed Edeena's forehead.

Tasara plunged through the tent's opening. "Who am I, then?"

5

Tasara shivered as much from nervous anticipation as the cool morning air.

Her parents whirled to face her.

"Tasara…?" *Dat* cast his wife a pleading glance before striding to Tasara, limping on his wounded leg. He tried to embrace her, but she backed away and tightly hugged the blanket she'd thrown across her shoulders.

It wasn't terribly brisk this morning, but her teeth chattered nonetheless. She shook her head, clearing her thoughts and quieting the cacophony rioting in her mind.

Not a traveller.

Not a Faas.

Who am I? Am I even Scots?

Good God.

Never say she was English. A *Sassenach*. Wouldn't that be a cruel twist of providence?

"I dinna understand." She flinched at the raw pain coloring her voice. "How could ye keep such a secret from me all these years?"

Cupping his nape, *Dat* tucked his chin to his chest. "At first, it was out of fear and then out of love."

Her heart cramped at the sincerity in his words.

He raised his head and dropped his hand to his side, his eyes glinting with tears. "I couldna bear to lose ye, because though ye might no' be the daughter of my loins"—he patted his chest—"ye are the daughter of my heart."

This must be tearing him apart too. He'd acted out of love and a desire to protect her. That she understood. She'd have done almost anything to keep György and Lala safe.

He sucked in a ragged breath. "Nothin' and *nae* one will ever change that."

The sun inched higher on the horizon, casting everything in gilded tones as though nothing had changed.

Tasara glared at the cheerful orb.

How dare the sun do what it always did and would always do, while her world tilted and wobbled before tumbling to an abrupt halt?

"Tasara." *Dat* gestured to the tent. "Get dressed, and then walk with me while we have our coffee. I have somethin' to show ye."

Lala, blinking sleepily, stumbled from the opening, her thumb stuffed in her mouth as usual.

Father scooped the groggy child into his arms.

After giving Tasara a sleepy smile, Lala laid her tousled head against his chest, closing her eyes once more.

Fresh tears pooled in Tasara's eyes.

Nae crying.

Edeena scooted past her and gave her a kind, but

unsure, half-smile when she ducked beneath the canvas. A moment later, she emerged carrying an armful of blankets and clothes while steering a half-asleep György before her. She inclined her head toward the canvas. "I shall have breakfast waitin' when Balcomb is done speakin' with ye."

Ten minutes later, Tasara sat beside the only father she'd ever known on a fallen log before a rambling brook paralleling an oak grove some distance from the encampment. Birdsong filled the air, the familiar trills soothing. Several travellers sent them curious or speculative glances, but none intruded, as though they knew what transpired beneath the stately trees.

Truth be told, they probably did.

The tinkers didn't hold to secretiveness amongst their own, and *Dat* and *Dya* keeping a confidence of this magnitude proved worrisome.

Dat held a bundle atop his lap and sent her a sidelong look accompanied by a pained tipping of his lips. "I've kept these, despite the risk."

"Risk? Why would there be a risk?" Tasara's attention dropped to the bag.

He'd pulled it from a hidden compartment beneath their wagon. She hadn't even known the secret compartment existed.

"This is yer heritage, and somehow it seemed wrong to destroy them." He patted the rough sack. "The clues to yer real identity are in here."

He passed her the parcel.

"I'm no' sure I want to ken." Curious, yet leery, she stared at the lump. She met his warm brown gaze. "This changes everythin'."

"No' the way yer family or the clan feels about ye. Ye'll always be part of us, *nae* matter where life takes ye from this point onward." *Dat's* eyes misted, and he looked away for a long moment. He audibly swallowed several times, his Adam's apple bobbing.

Her eyes also filled with moisture, but she blinked the dampness away. For certain, knowing her true identity would be a good thing, and Edeena had been right. Now that Tasara had learned she wasn't a traveller, she did want to know the truth.

"I suppose I always suspected this day would come." He flicked his calloused fingers at the bag. "And that is why I kept them."

With some effort, Tasara untied the cord cinching the opening. The bag smelled musty, and the cloth stuck together, protesting being pried apart after so long. She withdrew a yellow, lace-edged satin gown, obviously a costly garment.

"Ye were wearin' this when Forba found ye. She wrapped ye in her shawl so *nae* one would see the garment's quality. She was convinced somethin' foul was afoot when she stumbled upon ye. Had the sixth sense, she did." He quirked his mouth at one side and scratched his jaw. "She said she opened her arms, and ye ran into them, no' the least afraid."

"*Dya* always made me feel safe." After setting the dress between them, Tasara rummaged in the bag again. This time she exhumed a china doll with frizzled brown ringlets.

"Mary," she whispered, trailing her fingers across

the doll's cracked face and then fingering the familiar pink leather coat the toy wore. Almost perfect, except for a missing shoe.

She met *Dat's* keen gaze.

"I remember her. I think . . ." Tasara shut her eyelids, and the green-eyed man's face appeared. He had a freckled nose. "I think my father might've given her to me."

Glancing around, *Dat* nodded encouragingly.

"It is good ye remember somethin'." He pointed at the sack. "There is more."

Tasara found a pair of shoes, stockings, and a yellow hair ribbon, stiffened with age and marred by a bloody patch. Feeling around the bag's bottom, she grazed a piece of metal. She lifted the pendant, then held the gold locket before her. The oval dangled from a fine gold chain, and a carved rose surrounded by scrolls decorated the front.

She flipped it over and let loose a short gasp.

~*~

Alexa Love M & F

~*~

Tasara traced the engraving with her forefinger. "Alexa?"

"Alexandra. Ye told us yer name was Alexandra." *Dat* took the locket and pressed the latch. It didn't open until he wedged his thumbnail between the closures, and they slowly separated. "The middle name we gave ye, Alesta, is Gaelic for Alexandra."

"How thoughtful of ye." Forba and Father wanted her to retain a morsel of her heritage, yet they'd made no effort to find her real family. The insight gnawed disturbingly.

Tasara bit her lip as *Dat* spread the sides apart before laying it in her palm, revealing miniature portraits of a man and woman. An ebony-haired, violet-eyed lady and a gentleman with honey-colored hair and sage green eyes stared back at her.

"I dinna remember them." She tightened her clasp on the locket. "Except for his eyes. I've dreamed of him, I think."

Dat pointed at the young woman. "And ye have her eyes."

"I never told ye my last name?"

Tasara furrowed her brow, trying to remember. How could she have lived an entirely different life and have no recollection? Just fleeting glimpses through blurry windows, impossible to distinguish from dreams and fanciful imaginations.

"How old was I when *Dya* found me?"

"We think ye were around three, but ye were *verra* wee, and we couldna be certain." He folded the dress and tucked it back into the bag. "As for yer last name, ye called yerself Alexandra Addlebirdie."

"*Addlebirdie?*" She chuckled and passed him the shoes and doll, which he hurriedly stuffed back into the bag. "Guess I couldna pronounce my name. Sounds like a demented or crazed fowl."

"Tasara…?" Her father laid his hand atop hers. Scrutinizing the glen once more, he stiffened.

Jamie strode in their direction, a determined expression upon his face. The black tinkers' leader eyed the bundle as *Dat* casually placed it behind the log.

Dat's eyes clouded, and he leaned nearer, murmuring in her ear. "I think ye were tryin' to say Atterberry. Ye'd been with us for five years before I heard someone mention a Dowager Lady Atterberry in Edinburgh."

"Surely, there are many Scots with the same name." Tasara lifted a shoulder, unimpressed by the connection. "If that's even what I was tryin' to say."

Why did her father look anxious and keep peering about as though afraid they'd be overheard?

His behavior made her jittery as well. Almost upon them, Jamie's bearing sent a frisson skittering across her shoulders.

Dat's face settled into a grave expression, worry crinkling the corners of his eyes. "How many have a stepdaughter, an heiress, who disappeared?"

"You think *I'm* her? The heiress?" She laughed, unconvinced.

Wouldn't that be something?

"Shh, speak naught of it." He nodded as Jamie reached them. "Jamie," he greeted cordially and calmly as he and Tasara had been discussing nothing more important than the weather.

Tasara's breath caught at the coolness the band leader's usually jovial gaze held when he swept it across her.

"Balcomb. Lass." Arms crossed, Jamie fixed her father with an intense stare. "Ye've told her then? That she must leave the tribe today?"

6

Chattsworth Park House
Three days later

Lucan stepped from the carriage and then indulged in a wide yawn and exuberant stretch.

Despite the coach's plush squabs, his arse ached to hell and back from the lengthy two-day trip and the bouncing and jolting through every possible hole in the roads from Craiglocky Keep to Chattsworth Park House. Damn lucky he hadn't chipped a tooth during the last miserable stretch from Derbyshire.

He yawned again.

Once inside, did he dare request coffee?

He far preferred a cup of strong, rich coffee to tea.

The swill he'd drunk since Craiglocky—or rather, attempted to drink doused with copious quantities of milk and inferior sugar—didn't deserve the honor of being called *café*. A jigger's worth of whisky in his favorite Turkish brew wouldn't be amiss either.

The carriage pushed the bounds of enclosed spaces Lucan tolerated. He rolled his shoulders and flexed his spine, his tension-tautened muscles protesting as much from underuse as anxiety.

He would have preferred to ride, but Achilles had gone lame before the entourage returning from Dounnich House reached Craiglocky Keep. He might've borrowed a horse, but when the skies deposited sopping sheets of rain in an unending deluge, even the conveyance's cramped compartment held a shallow degree of appeal. The blasted rain ceased late this afternoon, and he'd finally been able to open the windows and breathe a mite easier.

Lucan appreciated Scotland's rustic charm and bucolic inhabitants—one fascinating gypsy lass in particular—but the year-round cooler temperatures and wetter weather he could well do without.

England's cold and dampness already stretched his tolerance for inclement weather.

At this time three days past, he'd been planted a facer by a tempestuous Scottish gypsy, and her arresting features remained etched in his mind.

Too bad, mere weeks ago, he'd given his mistress her *congé* for cuckolding. Except for a single dalliance with an eager maid at Craiglocky, he'd been reduced to a monkish existence. Unless he tended to the task himself, there'd be no easing the ache in his loins until he secured a new paramour.

Made him damned cantankerous, it did.

He heaved a sigh and rubbed his sore bum. Not a single woman came to mind whom he would consider offering the position to, although many had made known their interest in sharing their favors.

Tasara's fiery gaze nudged his memory, and a fresh wave of guilt assaulted him. She'd belted him soundly for trying to steal a simple, innocent kiss. Well, mayhap not wholly innocent, but he couldn't have done more than brush her lips with children looking on, now could he?

If he'd hinted that he had seriously entertained the slimmest notion—no matter how fleeting—that she would make a splendid mistress, she'd splay him wide open and leave him as buzzard food.

After she used her dagger to relieve him of his ballocks.

He touched the bruise framing his eye and winced. The inn's cloudy looking glass had revealed the purplish-red ring had acquired a revolting shade of puce around the outer edges.

Mother would have a fit of vapors when she saw his damaged face. He daren't tell her he'd been rescuing abducted gypsy lasses and fighting a remote clan of barbaric Scots. She'd cock up her dainty toes—in the most elegant fashion, of course.

Although always possessed of a delicate constitution, after his younger brother Harvey had died of a gunshot wound, the remotest hint of violence sent her into a dither—calling for smelling salts and clutching her chest before collapsing into a swoon— always within easy reach of a fainting couch or settee.

Lucan gave a nascent smile.

Duchesses didn't collapse into undignified heaps upon the floor, even when overcome.

Twilight teased the horizon, and he flicked open his

pocket watch. Not quite a quarter past seven. He'd arrived home in time for dinner. Mother didn't keep country hours and insisted soup be served at the stroke of eight.

He fingered his stubbly jaw.

If he made haste, he'd have time for a bath and shave first.

She'd be miffed if he dared to dine in his current state. Oh, she wouldn't say a word, just lift a faultlessly plucked eyebrow. Her reproachful, pale steel gaze and silent disapproval spoke quite loudly.

More on point, he hated disappointing her. As far as mothers went, she was nigh on perfect. When he'd come into his title at sixteen, she'd been his desperately needed rudder, leading and guiding him with encouragement and keen intelligence.

She need never know Father expired in the arms of his latest lover. Lucan had seen to that. Thank God, he'd been who Father's mistress sought when his sire had died. By Father's directive, no less, the paramour had claimed.

Quite a noble sire, old Rochester—burdening a youth with his father's indiscretions. Perchance the man thought himself honorable, sparing his duchess betrayal's heartache. Paid well to keep her silence and make Paris her permanent residence, the mistress quietly disappeared.

To this day, Lucan's sweet mother remained blissfully unaware of her husband's infidelities and the reason why Lucan never favored being called Rochester. She'd loved the man until the day he died, and Lucan, naively, had once believed his sire felt the same for her.

Brilliant actor, the duke.

Doting husband. Devoted father. Considerate employer.

Adulterous liar and cheat.

Smythe stepped from the carriage, a valise in each hand. The valet guarded Lucan's toiletries and shaving gear as though he toted the crown jewels rather than a strop, brush, and razor. "I shall see to a bath for you at once, Sir."

"Thank you. I thought that very thing myself." Smythe had an uncanny ability to read his mind—one of the reasons Lucan retained the man. Never mind the valet's real name was no more Smythe than his was Bathsheba. The black servant's accent, as well as his scarred face and body, spoke of his suffering as an escaped slave.

Where Smythe acquired his shaving and valet skills, Lucan never asked. And Smythe never volunteered how he'd made it to London. However, when he'd offered to use his ratty shirt to shine Lucan's shoes for a piece of bread and then gave the loaf Lucan bought to a pair of skeletal children, Lucan had engaged him on the spot.

He'd never regretted the decision.

As he snapped his timepiece closed, a movement across the expanse of green caught his attention. A rider, heavy-handed on the whip, cantered his horse through the meadow adjoining Lucan's property with the neighboring estate, Aldecot Vale.

Frowning, he rubbed his brow and yawned again.

Odd.

The place had been closed tighter than a banker's vault for almost a decade—ever since the owner, Viscount Renishaw, shot Lucan's brother, Harvey, in a duel. Then, like a cowardly serpent, Renishaw, aided by his brother, Maurice, escaped punishment and justice by fleeing the continent.

Scurrilous bastards.

Perhaps the viscount had let the place, or one of the myriad other Renishaw rabble had moved in. No short supply of that riffraff, more was the pity. Lucan would have bought the place years ago, if not for its entailment.

He climbed the front steps and grinned when the door swung open.

Tibbs teetered inside the entrance, so stooped, the ancient butler's shock of white hair nearly touched his knees.

Egads, would the man never retire?

He was ninety, if he was a day.

"Hello, Tibbs. Splendid to see you."

Upright and *still breathing.*

Tibbs squinted, wrinkling his nose and forehead until his features squished together like a newborn's. He worked his tongue in and out of his mouth, across almost toothless gums.

Ought to get him some spectacles— and false teeth.

His tailcoat fastened askew, and one side of his breeches falls undone, a blob of jam clung to the butler's sloppily tied cravat.

Hell, Tibbs needed his own valet. *Or nursemaid.*

The butler's features screwed tighter as he strained to identify the new arrivals. "Young Sir, is that you?"

"Indeed. It is." Lucan waved Smythe ahead. "Smythe, please take my things to my chamber and see to a bath at once."

"And a bracing cup of coffee with a dram of whisky for your constitution too, I should think." Smythe gave a sympathetic nod, his large, black eyes understanding.

Few people knew of Lucan's fear of enclosed spaces. However, the valet shared Lucan's dread—Smythe had stowed away in a barrel crossing the Atlantic—and they'd found a degree of comfort in sharing the cause of their mutual phobia aggravated by the miles of enclosed travel within the carriage.

Lucan's fear originated after accidentally becoming locked in a trunk while playing hide-and-seek. He'd nearly suffocated, and although the event took place two decades ago, irrational terror seized him whenever he found himself enclosed in smallish, dark places.

"How did you get the missive so soon, Your Grace?" Tongue peeking from the corner of his mouth, Tibbs angled his head to peer at Lucan as he shuffled beside him into the grand entrance.

With a hand to the butler's bony elbow, Lucan steadied the rickety man. A strong breeze would lay Tibbs flat or carry him off.

"We didn't expect you for at least another day or two." Tibbs turned, and after three grunting pushes—each of which Lucan feared would either send the wizened man into heart failure or onto his scrawny arse—managed to close the door.

Almost.

Like a hound waiting for his master's approval,

Tibbs grinned at Lucan, revealing the two remaining teeth at the front of his mouth.

Definitely pursue the false teeth business.

How did the chap manage to eat?

On second thought, Lucan didn't want to know.

"Your hat, Young Sir?" Tibbs extended a quaking hand. "Lady Montgomery sent the note round to you just yesterday."

Lucan paused in handing the majordomo his hat and gloves.

"Note? I've been in Scotland, not London, and came straight here from Craiglocky Keep." He passed the items to the butler while scanning the entry. "I'm afraid I haven't received a letter from my sister, and what's Genevieve doing here anyway? I thought she was lying in for another week."

She'd birthed a second daughter four weeks ago. If ever a woman was meant for motherhood, it was his sister.

"Lucan, I'm glad you're here." Genny, the picture of health, other than vague shadows beneath her pewter-gray eyes, sped along the corridor, her arms outstretched. Her navy and white striped gown swished about her ankles, and her shoes clicked rhythmically on the marble as she rushed to him.

After embracing Lucan for a long moment, she angled away, a tremulous smile on her mouth. Her eyes rounded when her gaze lit upon his face. She tenderly touched the corner of his discolored eye. "Whatever happened?"

Smythe ducked his head differentially. "His grace's

attempt to befriend a Highlander met with a degree of distrust."

Truthful, yet not as humiliating as having Genny know a slip of a girl planted him a facer.

Lucan sent the valet a grateful smile.

After a partial bow, his black eyebrows cocked in a superior manner, Smythe turned and marched up the grand curved staircase. Couldn't fault the servant for being confident of his worth and position.

"Not agreeable of the Scots fellow, was it?" Genny looped her arm through Lucan's.

He inclined his head in answer. "I saw a rider at Aldecot Vale. Has the place been let?"

"No." She pursed her lips and then sighed, her shoulders slumping. "You might as well know. Maurice Renishaw returned a fortnight ago. Leonard died in a duel over some woman's honor, and now Maurice is the viscount."

"The devil, you say!" Every muscle in Lucan's body contracted. How dare the knave return to England, and most especially, Aldecot Vale? He probably thought his new title protected him.

Not from Lucan, it didn't.

"No, and Lucan, there have been a few peculiar mishaps since he returned." She brushed a hand across her forehead, fine fatigue-borne lines forming at the corners of her eyes.

In his joy at seeing her, he'd missed the subtle signs of weariness she displayed. Unease nipped at Lucan's anger. "Such as?"

"Mr. Yeager has found fencing damaged more than

once. A few sheep and cattle have gone missing, and a haystack burned Saturday." She leaned nearer a fraction and tempered her voice. "He's expressed concern the incidents may not be a coincidence."

Honest and competent, Chattsworth's steward, Charles Yeager, didn't speculate idly.

Lucan nodded. "True, such occurrences might've happened naturally or have been helped along. I shall speak with him tomorrow."

Just like Renishaw to play vengeful, childish pranks. As a boy, he used to do the same, frequently at the expense of some unfortunate animal.

"That's not all," Genny said while eyeing a tottering Tibbs. "Yesterday, Jeremy escaped his manservant and wandered to Aldecot's stables. Franklin eventually found him, but I'm afraid he exchanged harsh words with a groom. And then Renishaw took it upon himself to call here afterward."

Gentle, sweet-natured, and two years Lucan's junior, Jeremy suffered physical and mental crippling due to complications during his birth. Their parents refused to sequester him with a family in a remote village because, through no fault of his own, providence rendered him a pair of unfortunate blows.

Genny set her jaw, her eyes hard as slate. "That fiend called Jeremy a drooling imbecile and threatened to have him arrested and imprisoned if he ventured onto Aldecot's lands again."

Renishaw would, the blasted cull.

"Why is Jeremy bent on venturing to Aldecot?" Not like his brother at all. He feared new places.

She shut her eyes for a second. "According to Franklin, Jeremy's meandered over there several times of late. Hound puppies were born a month ago, and he desperately wants a dog. With Renishaw's return, I fear for our brother."

Lucan didn't underestimate the threat for an instant. He had half a mind to storm over to Aldecot and give Renishaw an earful. Or punch him to a pulp, except Mother would ring him a peal if he did.

Sucking in a calming breath, Lucan unclenched his hands. In his rage, he hadn't realized he'd fisted them. He'd have time enough to confront the cur later—either here or in London.

Yes, wiser to attend to the task in Town.

Mother wouldn't know and become agitated or have one of her spasm spells, and he would have time to temper his anger and construct a plan.

"I shall see to engaging an additional companion for Jeremy."

Would two more guardians be a better idea?

Perhaps a couple of local fellows would be interested in the positions. Best see to hiring a few when he spoke with Yeager the next day. Jeremy wouldn't survive a day in prison.

Perhaps Lucan ought to put a word in the local magistrate's ear about the odd goings-on and have the stable hands patrol the estate's borders too.

"Come along, I shall take you to Mama." Genny's voice hurtled Lucan back to the present.

"I hoped to bathe and rid myself of travel grime before seeing her. You know she's a stickler for appearances."

"But, Lucan—"

He patted Genny's hand. "Twenty minutes at most, and I shall meet you in the drawing room for a glass of wine before we eat. Then you can tell me why you're here and not at home recovering from Sarah's birth." He touched her cheek. "You look tired, Gen."

A pinched expression settled upon her features, and she drew her reddish-blonde brows into a tense line. "No, Mama knows you've arrived and insists upon seeing you at once. She sent me to fetch you. You know how stubborn she can be when she's set her mind to something."

"Where are your husband and the girls?" He searched the corridor again. "And Jeremy?"

"Veronica and Sarah are in the nursery, and Langley, bless my husband's kind heart, took Jeremy for a walk to the stables."

The Earl of Montgomery likely wanted to take a gander at Lucan's newest stallion too.

"There's a litter of kittens there." She crossed her arms as if chilled. "We thought the cats might distract Jeremy. You know how dependent he is on Mama, and he's been most upset that he's not allowed in her chambers at present."

Lucan frowned and rubbed his nape, gone stiff from the awkward angle he'd slept in the carriage. Or perhaps poking his head out the window, rather like a hound enjoying a cart ride, had caused the crick.

"Why isn't he allowed? Mama always permits Jeremy to visit her sitting room." This didn't make sense. "Why the sudden change?"

"I don't want her agitated." Genny urged Lucan along the passageway. "Doctor Philpott says her heart is quite fragile and advised against upset until she is stronger."

"Her heart?" Lucan immediately advanced toward the winding marble staircase. His bath would have to wait. "Has she been ill?"

Genny hesitated and glanced at Tibbs hovering nearby, wringing his gnarled hands. "Tibbs, you may have your tea now. Take your time. No need to rush. We have things well in hand."

"Thank you, Miss Genevieve." He wobbled the passage's expanse, his gait as unstable as a week-old puppy.

"My God, why does Mama permit him to act as the majordomo?" Lucan suppressed a yawn. He needed his coffee.

She waited until Tibbs left their sight to answer. "The poor dear has nowhere to go. Last month when Mama suggested he might stay here without duties, he cried, arguing he wasn't a charity case."

"Well, I'm hiring another butler to make sure Tibbs doesn't hurt himself doddering about the place." Lucan winked at his sister. "Now, what's this about Mama?"

Apprehension clouded Genny's eyes. "Lucan, she suffered a serious seizure. Something about her heart. I think the doctor called it angina, whatever that may be."

"Has to do with chest pain, I believe." He waited for her to ascend the stairs before him.

"She's been asking for you." Genny touched his forearm. "Lucan, we came very close to losing her."

7

Craiglocky Keep
A week later

"What do you think they're discussing?" Tasara, her arm looped through Seonaid Ferguson's, halted in the kitchen courtyard to nip a few sprigs of mint. "Laird McTavish said he would summon me when he and *Dat* finished."

Try as she might, she couldn't quell the anxiety ebbing and flowing through her, hence the mint. She thought to brew some tea to calm her stomach, though sipping lavender tea might prove more beneficial for her fraught nerves.

For more than a week now, she'd been a guest at Craiglocky Keep. If that was what her position here could be called. The day she left the gypsy encampment, Father had given her a scant moment to kiss and hug Lala and György before he insisted they leave for Craiglocky Keep.

Jamie and several other band members stood by as she and *Dat* rode away.

Tasara had assumed they would call on the laird, tell him her tale, and then she would return to the traveller's camp until matters were settled. But after a brief, private word with his lairdship, Father had pecked her cheek and hurried on his way, leaving her with strangers and no explanation why she wasn't returning to the tinkers.

Her belongings, other than her knife always sheathed in her boot, and the moldy bag containing the items she had when Forba found her, remained with the travellers. She hadn't even been permitted to take her violin, her most cherished possession except for the locket she now wore about her neck. The instrument had belonged to Forba, but after she died, *Dat* had given it to Tasara.

So much for Edeena's claim that Tasara wouldn't be cast from the tribe.

What else would one call this banishment?

The injustice pinched severely. Left alone, abandoned without a word of explanation from the man she'd called father most of her life, Tasara didn't have an inkling what to expect or what her future held.

Perhaps she ought to ask Seonaid if she had a premonition in that regard.

When Tasara had asked her about the unusual gift, Seonaid had lifted a slim shoulder. "I've always had the second sight, but I have no control over my visions. Sometimes I know things in advance, and other times, I am as surprised as everyone else. Don't fret. All will be well." Seonaid gave her a reassuring smile. "Ah, Fairchild comes to get you even now."

She regularly did that, knew things before they happened.

A trifle disconcerting, but never frightening.

Tasara twisted round to comb the kitchen entrance.

"Miss Faas." The butler stood framed within the door's opening. "His lordship requests your presence."

Seonaid gave Tasara a brief hug. "I shall wait outside the study, and when you are done, we shall enjoy mint tea and shortbread."

A few minutes later, Tasara sank into a well-used leather wingback chair facing Laird McTavish's desk. She pulled her fringed shawl tighter around her shoulders, then fingered the fine cream muslin of her borrowed gown to calm her jitters.

This gloomy room, with its dreary stone walls and ancient weaponry, made her uneasy. The urge to peek inside the suits of armor to assure herself no ghosts or skeletons of long-dead McTavish ancestors hid within overwhelmed her.

Folding her hands upon her lap, she slid *Dat* a sidelong look. She'd never seen her father this anxious or unsure.

Jaw taut, he sat rigid and tense, his attention directed straight ahead. He seemed to avoid her gaze.

Silly. Of course, he's not doing any such thing.

Laird McTavish relaxed against his chair, drumming the fingertips of one hand on his bent knee. His expression solemn, his gaze wavered between Tasara and her father.

If she knew what had transpired before her summons, she might put aside her disquiet. Thank goodness for Seonaid. Slightly younger than Tasara, the sweet girl took an instant liking to her and became her almost constant companion, easing Tasara's loneliness and confusion.

Not that she spoke of her feelings. Baring her emotions or burdening strangers with her troubles served no purpose. Neither did complaining, but Seonaid seemed to know what bothered Tasara without being told.

The epitome of kindness and hospitality, everyone at Craiglocky tried to put her at ease. Seonaid had gone so far as to lend Tasara clothing and, even now, waited outside the study as promised.

Tasara looked directly at *Dat*, but his focus remained on Laird McTavish. She didn't know if she'd be permitted to go home today. His lairdship had sent for her father and, once he'd arrived, straightaway sequestered them in the study for an hour before inviting her to join them.

She crossed and uncrossed her ankles, then huffed an impatient little breath.

Come on. Out with it.

Why didn't Laird McTavish say something?

She cleared her throat.

Neither man spoke.

Oh, for heaven's sake. What are they waiting for?

"My laird, do you believe me this person my father thinks I am? This Baroness Alexandra Atterberry?" she finally asked. She made a point of saying you rather than ye as Seonaid had advised her.

Another dashed thing to remember.

She twisted her mouth in irony.

Was baroness right?

Why the Scots insisted on calling a titleholder equivalent to an English baron a Laird of Parliament boggled the mind. Who concocted such poppycock? Keeping the title balderdash straight proved nearly impossible.

Tasara crossed her ankles again. She needed to stand and move about. When agitated, sitting never served her well. "Well, do you, Laird McTavish?"

"Quite possibly." Smiling, he straightened and picked up a letter. He raised it for her inspection. Rows of neat writing covered most of the page. "This came in today's post. Hugo and Bridget Needham—I suspect she is your maternal aunt—will be arriving any day."

No longer able to sit for another moment, Tasara stood. "And then what happens?"

"They'll confirm or disprove your identity." He leveled her father a telling glance.

She frowned slightly.

Something else went on here.

Her whole life had turned topsy-turvy—*so blasted confusing*—which agitated her all the more. She'd never been this lost and unsure, not even when held prisoner those three weeks. Yet, at least at Dounnich House, she'd known *who* she was.

Inhaling a soothing breath, she resolutely squelched her dismay. She must put her emotions aside and face this situation with logic and reason. "And if I am this Alexandra Atterberry?"

"Well, I suppose that depends on you." Laird

McTavish tucked the letter into a drawer. "Although, turning your back on a title and fortune seems ill-advised, particularly since your father has given me to understand the Scottish travellers would prefer you resume your prior life."

If he'd struck her, Tasara wouldn't have been more wounded or astounded. She whirled to face Father.

Chagrin darkened his swarthy features.

"Is that true? Is that why Jamie and the others made me leave?" Her voice caught, and she spoke past the painful lump in her throat. "Have I somehow brought shame to the travellers? I was an innocent child. How am I to blame?"

Dat opened his mouth, but before he answered, a series of short, sharp raps sounded upon the stout door. An instant later, it flew open, banging against the armor behind it and sending a jarring clang throughout the chamber.

Seonaid, Lady McTavish, a young woman, and a middling-aged couple surged into the room.

Hugo and Bridget Needham, Tasara would wager.

"Where is she? Where's my niece?" The woman spun to search the room, her violet pelisse swirling in her haste. Upon spotting Tasara, she froze and blanched, her hand at her throat.

The young woman released a chirrupy shriek and slapped a gloved palm to her mouth. Her eyes wide with excitement, she hopped on her half-boot clad toes and pointed at Tasara, emitting happy little squeaks.

At any other time, the man's flabbergasted expression, sagging jaw, and bulging eyes would have been comical.

However, Tasara couldn't breathe. Couldn't move. Couldn't think.

An older version of herself gaped at Tasara from across the stone floor as if glancing into a time-forwarded looking glass.

"Oh, my God." Bridget Needham sent the austere man an exuberant glance. "Hugo, do you see? It's truly her. It's our Alexandra."

~*~

No.

Tightness seized Lucan's chest, and his heart faltered for a beat. Mother couldn't die, not so young. He hadn't married nor fathered children yet. Mother was as much a doting grandmamma to Genny's daughters as she'd been a loving mother to him, his sister, and their brother. Lucan's children couldn't miss knowing their grandmother.

Except—he hadn't planned to marry in the near future. And had no plans to marry in the intermediate future either. Several years from now—perhaps a decade or more—seemed reasonable.

Mayhap he'd seek Genny's and Mother's counsel on suitable prospective brides when the day finally came.

Certainly, he desired love, but he didn't require the emotion for a good match. In fact, he might be better off without the encumbrance. Father's perfidy had left Lucan jaded and pessimistic toward the institution of marriage altogether. Apparently, even the most perfect unions held dark, painful secrets.

So, why hope?

A few weeks, months, perchance a year or two of marital contentment—if God blessed him with exceptional good fortune—before he descended into a hellish state for the remainder of his life.

Besides, any woman he wed must accept Jeremy. Too many denizens of High Society whispered and pointed at his unfortunate brother, one reason Mother stopped venturing from Chattsworth Park.

And, by all that's holy, Father seized the opportunity like a stag in the rut.

What had Father imagined?

Had he thought if Mother didn't know of his unfaithfulness that it exonerated him? Or perhaps, his father encouraged Mother's over-protectiveness and took advantage of her reluctance to expose Jeremy to ridicule by sequestering him at Chattsworth Park House.

Lucan would never know.

Moments later, he stood outside his mother's chamber. Funny, how he still felt the minuscule rush of anticipation he experienced as a child when summoned to her room.

Forcing a tranquil mien to his appearance, he rapped lightly upon the door. It wouldn't do for her to detect his concern. She'd fret and work herself into a nervous state. Easily done when in good health and not to be considered with a fragile heart.

The carved panel swung open almost as though someone waited on the other side.

Genny glided to the immense bed straightaway and, after kissing their mother's cheek, straightened the already tidy bedclothes.

Always a fusser, Gen needed something to do with her hands. She'd knitted enough blankets to keep the children of The Foundling Hospital he sponsored in bedding for a good while.

"Welcome home, Your Grace." Mrs. Wells dipped into an arthritic curtsy, a grimace tightening the abigail's mouth when she bent.

He'd bet his forgone bath his mother's lady's maid had hovered near the door waiting for his knock.

"Thank you, Wells. No need to curtsy as I've told you many times before." Grasping her elbow, he helped her upright. "After all, you used to catch me hiding in the wardrobes and beneath the beds."

Before I locked myself in that infernal trunk, that is.

"Don't forget behind the curtains where you snuck bonbons and biscuits." She chuckled, her cheeks balling like miniature twin plum puddings, and pointed a plump finger at him. "You were quite the little rapscallion."

Lucan had always possessed a particular fondness for sweets.

He sought his mother and nodded toward the bed. "How is she?"

"Resting comfortably, but she's excited you're home." Mrs. Wells motioned him onward, murmuring out the side of her mouth, "Try to keep her calm."

"Lucan, darling?" His mother, a pale form in a swath of rose, cream, and lace, attempted to rise.

"No, Mama. You mustn't exert yourself." Genny

stilled their mother with a hand to her shoulder. "Wells and I shall prop you with pillows if you wish to sit up."

"Indeed, we shall." Like a protective mother hen, Wells charged to the bedside, tsking and clucking the whole while. "You let us assist you, Your Grace." She wedged a pair of pillows behind his mother. "Remember what the doctor said."

"Pshaw, that old windbag. Doesn't know what he's talking about." Her voice thin and reedy, Mother gave a weak wave of her hand. Only a few strands of silver tinted the lank flaxen hair hanging about her shoulder and splayed across the light pink satin pillow. "With his dire predictions, he'd have me selecting my funeral gown. How's a patient supposed to recover with such a gloomy bat scowling at them?"

"Nonetheless, you must do as Doctor Philpott says." Genny offered a tense smile and moved aside when Lucan reached the bed. She fidgeted about the room, straightening this and that while casting them furtive looks. She turned to Wells. "Would you please check on Mama's dinner? Her tray should've been brought by now. Oh, and send a maid to the nursery to ask Nurse how the girls are. It's almost Sarah's feeding time."

The lady's maid nodded as she waddled to the door. "Yes, I want to make sure Cook prepared the liver the way I requested."

"Liver. Phah." Mother pulled a face and gave a dainty shudder. "Why should an invalid be forced to eat liver?"

Wells paused at the entrance. "Because the doctor advised you to. To strengthen your heart."

"He also wanted to bleed me, to draw out my ill humors. I cannot think that's too beneficial to my heart." Mother closed her eyes, her fair lashes dark against her cheeks' pallor. "A warm, creamy custard would have me mending much quicker."

Wells grinned, her chins folding like a well-used fan. "Perchance, that's dessert."

She winked and pulled the door closed.

Lucan sat upon the mattress's edge. He bent to kiss Mother's forehead and then took her hand. So frail and cold. He gave her thin fingers a gentle squeeze. "What mischief are you embroiled in now, young lady?"

"It seems my heart has been damaged from my spasms and will weaken as time passes." She opened her light slate eyes, so like his, and tipped her mouth into a wan smile. "Doctor Death and Gloom says I might only have a few months to live."

Alarm knotted Lucan's stomach, and he curled his toes in his boots to keep his distress from showing.

Genny came to stand beside the bed. She placed a comforting hand on Lucan's shoulder. She'd had days to digest this news. He'd had but minutes.

"He also said with proper care and attention to your health, you might very well live much longer." She gave Lucan's shoulder a brief squeeze. "Many years, in fact."

Always the optimist, thank God. If Genny disintegrated into a blubbering mess, he'd be hard-pressed to retain his composure, male stoicism be damned.

Lucan rubbed his thumb across the back of Mother's blue-veined hand. Not yet fifty. Too soon. "I shall consult with Europe's finest physicians. We'll not let one antiquated country doctor determine your future."

"Your eye is bruised. Later you must tell me why." She patted his cheek before letting her hand flop across her middle. Her eyes drifted shut again. "You need a shave, dear, and you smell of cabbage and corned beef." Her delicate nostrils quivered. "And onions."

His midday meal.

Her breathing shallow, Mother winced and covered her heart.

Lucan exchanged a worried look with his sister.

Did Genny's eyes glisten?

What exactly had the doctor said?

First thing tomorrow, he would discover for himself.

"Lucan?" Mother's hand twitched within his.

He turned his attention back to her. "Yes, Mama?"

"Promise me you'll find a wife before I die." She gripped his hand with surprising strength, determination replacing the resigned look in her weary gaze.

"Mama, I—"

"Genevieve has Montgomery and the girls, and they've already said they want Jeremy to live with them." She drew in a shallow breath. "I want to know you have someone too. That when I die, you're not alone."

"Let's not talk of this now."

Or ever.

Lucan sent Genny a desperate glance.

Turning her head, she wiped a tear from the corner

of her eye with her bent forefinger.

He patted his mother's hand. "We can discuss my future when you are stronger."

Egad, he couldn't promise to seek a wife. Not now. No eligible women lived nearby, and only the need to find a knowledgeable physician would force him from Chattsworth Park House. Besides, rushing into—

"Mama?" Alarm sharpened Genny's voice.

Mother went deathly still and just as ashen, except for a bluish tinge edging her lips.

"Promise me, Lucan." Her pain-glazed eyes fluttered open. "Promise me. By Christmastide."

Genny gasped when their mother's eyes rolled back in her head. "Mama!"

Hell.

Lucan closed his eyes. "I promise."

8

Wedderford Abbey, Scotland
Late September 1818

Tasara—no—Alexandra Bridget Clarisse Atterberry, *The Right Honorable Lady Atterberry*, settled against the claret-colored squabs of the Needhams' plush carriage. That title business still flummoxed her. For God's sake, why did a female baroness hold a Laird, *Lord*, of Parliament title?

What nincompoop came up with that?

She shifted, unused to the stays practically thrusting her breasts to her chin. More on point, what pea-wit decided a woman needed all the trappings she now wore?

Aunt Bridget had insisted upon a frenetic shopping excursion in Edinburgh to outfit Alexandra with clothing befitting her new station. Unaccustomed to the smooth fabric of her primrose pelisse or the fine kid gloves encasing her fingers, Alexandra idly brushed a hand across her lap.

I shall always be Tasara Faas, a simple gypsy lass.

She veered a glance out the window, finding the quiet within the carriage taxing.

Her gypsy family sang as they traveled, the tinkers laughing and joking, calling to one another along the caravan's length. Such a simple life she'd lived till now. Nonetheless, Edeena's words to Father echoed worryingly in her mind.

Ye must consider Lala and György, and the rest of the clan too.

A bruised heart and heavy spirit weighed heavily upon Alexandra. Father hadn't even remained at Craiglocky Keep long enough to meet her aunt and uncle. When Aunt Bridget, at last, released her from an exuberant hug, he had already slipped from the study.

Before journeying to Wedderford Abbey, Alexandra had wanted to stop by the encampment one last time, but Laird McTavish dashed that hope.

"The travellers have moved on, Alexandra." He kindly broke the unpleasant news to her. "Balcomb thought it best. To give you a fresh start."

The excuse didn't satisfy in the least. The tinkers hadn't wanted to say farewell. Precious Lala and György wouldn't know what to think, wouldn't understand why Alexandra had left them.

Betrayal lanced her, creating a wound that wouldn't soon heal. Still, she couldn't bear the guilt if the folk or Father suffered for helping her, and deep inside, she understood their reasons for fleeing.

"Laird Sethwick assured me no one would think to bring charges against my father." She searched her new uncle's face. "Do you think he's right? I'm concerned that my disappearance as a toddler might be blamed on him."

Across from her, Uncle Hugo adjusted his position, no doubt as stiff as she from days of traveling. "I see no reason for anyone to do anything of the kind. After all, Mr. Faas didn't abduct you, and he likely saved your life."

"All these years he cared for you, my dear." Aunt Bridget's eyes grew glassy. "And he went to his lordship straightaway when he suspected who you might be."

The latter wasn't altogether true, but Alexandra and *Dat* thought it prudent to keep silent regarding what Balcomb had overheard in Edinburgh.

And about her thumping a duke in his handsome face.

Laird Sethwick had swiftly reassured Alexandra that the Duke of Harcourt held no grievance against her, and she'd nothing to fear from him.

Easy for his lordship to say. He was rich and powerful.

Her heart gave a curious wobble.

So am I now.

"I must say, however, I am a trifle surprised at Mr. Faas's eagerness to claim the reward for your return." Aunt Bridget fiddled with a loose thread in her cuff's lace.

Uncle Hugo turned from watching the passing scenery and smiled at Alexandra. "Yes, took me aback a mite as well."

"But I imagine the life of a Highland traveller is fraught with hardship, and a sizable sum will go far to ease their discomfort." Katrina, Alexandra's cousin, offered the sensible reassurance.

"Reward?" Alexandra licked her lips, suddenly feeling sick. "You paid it?"

"But of course, dear." Aunt Bridget cast her a fleeting glance before resuming her perusal of the delicate tatting. "We didn't hesitate for a jot, did we, Hugo?"

"Indeed, not." He gave Aunt Bridget an indulgent smile. "I would have gladly paid more."

At another time, their devotion to one another would have charmed Alexandra. However, at present, she fought not to be ill about what she'd just learned. She swallowed. "How much?"

No wonder the clan, *Dat,* and Edeena eagerly toddled her off to Craiglocky.

"One thousand pounds." Uncle Hugo nodded sagely. "That should tide them over nicely for a long while."

A veritable fortune to a humble traveller.

The crack in her heart grew wider. She'd been betrayed and deceived for profit by those she trusted the most. What was it about money that caused people to throw aside common decency as easily as hearth ash?

A crazed Scot mistook Isobel Ferguson for another woman, and to gain valuable lands, had intended to force her into marriage. To coerce the travellers into helping the Blackhalls with their land-grabbing scheme, she, Lala, and György were captured. Angus Blackhall planned on selling Tasara's virginity to some debauched knave, and now, her clan and family had deserted her.

All for wealth.

Integrity and honesty disintegrated in the face of a bulging purse, it seemed.

Shutting her eyes against the pain of the travelers' perfidy, she found the carriage swaying strangely lulling. The rocking reminded her of her gypsy family's wagon.

When would she see them again?

Did she want to after the nasty revelation of a moment ago?

Of course.

György and Lala had played no part in the deception.

The duke's noble features pushed their way into her mawkish musings. The bothersome man continued to plague her conscience and dreams. How could one unfortunate encounter leave such a lasting impact?

An unnerving thought smacked Alexandra.

Would she see the nobleman in London?

Undoubtedly.

Her aunt intended to present her long-lost niece to Society. The next few weeks would be spent preparing Alexandra for that awfulness. She hunched further into the carriage corner.

Perfectly wonderful.

Something else unpleasant to anticipate. Paraded before the *ton's* elite, as awkward as a donkey in a poke bonnet at a ball.

She might just do something outlandish to see their responses. It could prove amusing.

A welcome as warm as Napoleon might expect

from the Prince Regent seemed probable. In her experience, the British didn't trust Scots, and truth to tell, except for her uncle, Alexa held the same opinion of *Sassenachs*.

Alexandra cracked an eyelid open.

Wedderford Abbey sat, majestic and imposing, in the distance.

She'd never imagined such splendor, let alone that she would ever own something of this magnitude. The mansion more closely resembled a smallish castle than a grand manor. A great sprawling gray-brown building boasting turrets, numerous chimneys, and three enormous wings lay encompassed by a vine-covered wall on all but one side.

Craiglocky Keep epitomized medieval magnificence, but Wedderford Abbey—well, an ancestor, or two or three, must've claimed a flair for lavishness. The place exemplified garish wealth and station.

And she, the late Baron Steafan Atterberry's eldest daughter, owned the estate and everything that accompanied the title including—according to Uncle Hugo—a sizable fortune.

She fingered the locket at her collarbone.

One day a poor Highland traveller, and the next a well-heeled, titled heiress. Unbelievable. The stuff from which fairytales and fantasies were birthed.

She shook her head and then promptly ceased, fearing the elaborate bonnet she wore would lose a feather or flower.

The monstrosity wouldn't be worse for it. Heavy

and cumbersome, the hat obstructed her vision, but Aunt Bridget had insisted as she applied lemon juice to Alexandra's freckled nose, "All proper ladies wear bonnets."

Alexandra suspected this proper lady falderal would be a profound annoyance. The rigmarole required to dress daily—often thrice or more—strained her composure and the bounds of her patience.

"Is this real?" She pinched her thigh, not confident she wasn't dreaming. "*That's* where I was born?"

"Yes, Alexandra," Aunt Bridget said. "Very real, and yes, you were born at Wedderford." Melancholy darkened her eyes and laced her voice. "Steafan was proud of his estate, proud of everything Scottish, for that matter. If the man possessed a fault, it was that he loved his country and his land too much. I've always wondered if he would have married Lyette if she hadn't been Scots."

"There's something to be said for marrying a Scottish lass." Uncle Hugo teased his wife. "Life is never mundane."

Aunt Bridget beamed.

She'd retained a constant smile on her lovely face since the moment she'd tearfully enfolded Alexandra in a suffocating, lilac-scented embrace.

If ever Alexandra doubted this woman was her relative, the uncertainty vanished the minute she looked into her aunt's violet eyes and saw an older version of herself mirrored there. No wonder Laird Sethwick noticed the likeness.

Only a blind man would deny the relation.

"Quite so." Uncle Hugo tapped his wife's hand, giving her a doting smile. "We were both present. Naturally, Bridget insisted on being with her twin when Lyette gave birth."

Aunt Bridget chuckled, a husky, musical sound while she rummaged in her reticule. "That's how I knew about your birthmark. I was the first to hold you after your mother and father. You'd wet Steafan's shirt, and I helped to change you."

Alexandra's face heated. A strawberry-sized, tulip-shaped birthmark marred her left buttock.

"But even without the mother's mark to confirm your identity, anyone who ever laid eyes on Lyette would know you are her daughter." Melancholy weighted her aunt's words. "I wish she'd lived to see you grown into the beautiful woman you now are."

Few children claimed the blessing of four mothers, two of whom Alexandra couldn't remember except fleeting, dreamlike glimpses. "What happened to my mother?"

After a pregnant pause, during which Aunt Bridget struggled for composure, Uncle Hugo answered.

"A fever took her when you were eighteen months old. Your father didn't want you raised motherless, so six months later, he married a young Scots widow. Wholly unexpected, given his devotion to your mother."

"*Humph.* I'll say. Took us all aback." Aunt Bridget's astringent tone and sour expression spoke volumes. "Minerva bore a daughter *soon* thereafter. In a wretchedly cruel scheme of providence, two months later, Steafan died—tragic riding accident—leaving you in the care of Minerva. And then… Then you went missing days later. Some at Wedderford suggested you'd wandered off searching for your papa."

Disapproval cinched Aunt Bridget's mouth, and she wrenched her reticule closed a mite harder than necessary.

Perhaps she didn't like her father marrying soon after her sister's death, or perhaps she didn't approve of his choice of a wife. Or…did she think it too coincidental—Alexandra vanishing on the heels of her father's death?

The unsettling thought crawled to a corner of Alexandra's mind and wedged itself there—a constant, uncomfortable reminder—like an annoying pebble in her slipper.

"Now, my love, don't get flustered. Steafan saw to all that business in his will. He was no fool. Let's see your pretty smile." Uncle's charm cajoled a partial bending of her aunt's mouth.

"So, I have a sister?" Peculiar. Alexandra had almost ceased thinking of Lala and György as her brother and sister, and yet still thought of herself as a traveller.

"Oh, dear." Katrina suddenly became intent on the scenery outside.

Her aunt and uncle regarded one another for a tense moment.

Finally, Aunt Bridget shrugged. "She might as well know. The truth will come out soon enough. She'll be better prepared this way."

"I suppose you're right." Uncle Hugo's

countenance became contemplative as he eyed Alexandra. He seemed to choose his words with care. "Shona came into this world five months after Steafan married Minerva. She couldn't be his daughter."

"Oh. Does she know?" How horrid if she didn't. Alexa knew the awfulness of discovering you weren't who you thought you were.

Aunt Bridget sighed and slumped against the seat. "We have no idea what Minerva has told Shona. We shall have to tread carefully until we know what they are about. The letter of the law is on your side, however."

"You were declared legally dead after seven years. I believe it's called death in absentia." Uncle straightened his hat then crossed his long legs. "Per your father's instructions, his attorney put the estate into abeyance and your inheritance share in trust. However, I don't know the particulars."

"Abeyance?" Alexa scratched her nose. The dratted gloves prevented her from doing the job properly. "I'm sorry. I don't know what that is."

Uncle Hugo folded his arms. "Simply put, abeyance is when there isn't a direct male heir. Daughters inherit equally until one submits a petition asking the title be granted to them. There must be no doubt as to their pedigree."

"Wise on Steafan's part, that." Satisfaction shone in Aunt Bridget's eyes. "Until she is of age, Shona cannot petition to claim the title herself, and with your return, Minerva would be most imprudent to attempt that deception and petition on Shona's behalf."

Seriousness sharpened the planes of Uncle Hugo's

face. "Besides, upon your return, there's a rebuttal presumption at common law—"

"In layman's terms, if you please, dearest." Aunt Bridget's sweet smile tempered her admonishment.

Hugo grinned, his mustache twitching. "The law recognizes Alexandra is alive."

"How astute since she's breathing and walking about." Her aunt's droll reply lacked sincere humor.

"Rather unpleasant for them, all this, don't you think?" Alexandra looked between her aunt and uncle. "I cannot help but feel compassion, and an iota of guilt, for causing their plight."

"They've been provided for, Alexandra. Mama says Uncle Steafan was a generous, kind-hearted man. They have not gone without." Katrina slipped her hand into Alexandra's.

"You've nothing to feel guilty about," Aunt Bridget reassured Alexandra. "We're overjoyed you've returned to us unharmed. It's nothing short of an answer to prayer. A miracle, in truth."

"Alexandra, your parents called you Alexa. How would you prefer we address you?" Gazing at her expectantly, Uncle Hugo brushed a finger across either side of his mustache.

Clever fellow. He'd successfully changed the subject to something less troublesome. A plain man, except for his warm, chestnut eyes, he exuded patience and kindness. Not characteristics one typically expected from a successful banker.

Her aunt and Katrina wore eager expressions too. His ploy had worked.

"Truthfully, I'm having a difficult time answering to Alexandra." She rolled a shoulder and gave a short laugh. "I answered to Tasara for so many years, it is hard to stop thinking of myself by that name. Alexa sounds more like Tasara—"

"Alexa it is then." Uncle Hugo smiled and winked. "I supposed as much."

"I imagine this is overwhelming." Katrina pressed Alexa's hand and tilted her bonneted head, indicating the house they approached. "Perhaps a little frightening too."

Katrina hit the mark square on. More than a little frightening, however. Outright terrifying, in a good, adventurous sort of way. Everything was unfamiliar and new.

Alexa closed her eyes for a moment.

I'd rather be traveling with the tinkers. At least I know who I am with them.

She breathed out a silent sigh. No sense reminiscing or wishing for what couldn't be. Destiny plopped her here, and she'd make the best of her good fortune. That was what travellers did.

The coach turned onto the manor's long, immaculate pathway, and her stomach constricted. A stepmother and young woman awaited her arrival.

Friends or foes?

"Yes, I'm sure it is a bit much to take in, but rest assured, your identity and birthright are irrefutable." A steely note crept into Aunt Bridget's tone.

"Indeed." Uncle Hugo nodded and chucked his wife's chin. "No need to get your feathers ruffled, my dear. As Steafan's only issue, Alexa's claim is indisputable. I'm sure Minerva and Shona will do their best to put her at ease."

"And don't forget, she has the locket and doll." Katrina grinned and patted Alexa's knee. "Your doll is like mine, except for her attire. I named mine Jane, and her coat is green. She sits atop my bedchamber shelf still."

Alexa grinned back.

She liked her outgoing, cheerful cousin, and was grateful her aunt insisted Alexa stay with them while in London. She needed a confidante and a friend. Seonaid's parents had agreed to allow her to visit the Needhams during the Season too. She would arrive at the end of October, and with Katrina and Seonaid as companions, Alexa felt more self-possessed about venturing into society.

"Hugo and I gave Alexa the doll for her second birthday." Aunt Bridget retied her bonnet's ribbons, then brushed a speck of lint from her whisky-colored skirt. She seemed edgy all of a sudden and exchanged speaking glances with Uncle more than once.

What could Alexa expect at Wedderford Abbey? She lacked her aunt's and cousin's sophistication, and her deficiencies in formal education or schooling in niceties proved awkward. Despite Aunt Bridget's assurances that she would tutor Alexa in decorum, qualms still fluttered in her belly.

While dining at Craiglocky, she had no idea which fork or spoon to use. Why provide three or four when one sufficed? And why deliver the meal in courses? It created more work for the servants and dragged dining out for hours. Serve the food, eat it in a timely manner, and be done with it, for pity's sake.

And that was another thing.

How could she become accustomed to people waiting on her when she was capable of doing things for herself?

Her first night at Craiglocky, a fresh-faced maid had tried to help her bathe, of all things. Were the privileged so lazy or supercilious they couldn't soap and scrub their nether regions?

Well, that's one task I'll see to myself, thank you.

"I cannot tell you how thrilled I am to have a cousin near my age. Less than four months separate us." A pout upon her lips, Katrina grasped Alexa's hand. "Studious older brothers consumed with rows of numbers and calculating figures are no fun at all."

A hush fell within the coach as the conveyance drew near the manor house. Aunt Bridget had told Alexa the Needhams hadn't been to Wedderford Abbey since the authorities discontinued looking for Alexa a month after she and her nurse had disappeared. Except for finding a doll's shoe beneath a willow, no other signs were ever uncovered.

Her aunt and uncle had continued searching, even hiring investigators. After two years passed without uncovering another clue, they too had resigned themselves to Alexa never returning. Though Uncle Hugo still placed flyers about Scotland every now and again on the off chance someone might come forth with new information.

With a creak and a jolt, the conveyance rolled to a stop, but no one made an effort to leave the carriage. Nor did Wedderford's front door swing open in welcome.

Aunt Bridget leaned forward and touched Alexa's knee. "We shall make this visit short, a day or two at most, to give Minerva and Shona time to adjust to their new positions in the event you choose to reside at Wedderford Abbey after the Season ends. I'm not sure what the marriage settlements between her and Steafan stipulated, but you're well within your rights to ask them to move to another residence or the dower house if you choose."

"I think it would be wise to get to know them before I make a decision. I'm sure this has come as a shock." Alexa looked at her uncle. "Should I be prepared for any opposition?"

His pensive expression didn't encourage her. "I've learned many things in my years as a banker, my dear, one of which is that those with the most to lose or gain are capable of the greatest treachery. My advice is to be on your guard, be watchful, and listen." He tapped the door with his cane. "In short, be careful whom you trust."

9

The entry, a yawning cavern leading to the unknown, now stood wide open, and a chill juddered from Alexa's neck to her waist.

Once her identity had been validated, notice had immediately been sent to Wedderford that she lived. What a jolt it must've been to Minerva *and* Shona—after so long, to discover their monies and everything they thought they owned now belonged to another.

Rather awkward, that business about taking up residence, or asking Minerva and Shona to leave.

By-the-by, seems I'm the rightful heir, although I've been gallivanting around the Scottish Highland with black tinkers these past eighteen years. Do take yourselves off now that I've returned from the dead.

Proof?

But of course, I have proof.

Want to see my bum?

Not that Tasa—er—Alexa intended to turn anyone out. Wedderford Abbey had been their home long before she arrived. She felt like the intruder, even if the estate and title legally belonged to her. Alexa couldn't blame her stepmother and sister for acting a mite put upon.

"What if they refuse to believe who I am or accept my claim?" That abeyance business was more than a trifle confusing, but Uncle Hugo promised her the solicitor had everything well in hand.

Aunt Bridget harrumphed and patted her hair one last time. "Not to worry, Alexa. Hugo has everything necessary to prove your identity and rightful position."

That included a written declaration from a physician attesting to her birthmark—gads, that had been a mortifying examination. *Dat* had provided a sworn statement detailing how and where she'd been found, and her aunt and uncle would give their oaths confirming the kinship, as well as having gifted the doll.

Would that be enough?

Aunt Bridget cast her husband an indirect glance. "Although, I'm sure Minerva will take one look at you, and she'll know the truth of it as we did. You are the image of Lyette."

The coach door swung open, and a muscular footman offered a polite smile before lowering the step. Once he assisted the women from the carriage, he hurried to the boot to help another footman with their luggage.

"Let's be about it then." Aunt Bridget squared her shoulders and jutted her chin skyward. "Into the dragon's lair."

This didn't bode well. Not at all.

"Just so." Uncle Hugo gave a mocking growl deep in his throat.

Neither seemed any more excited to enter the house

than Alexa. Only Katrina exuded a morsel of anticipation, evident in her fidgeting and sparkling eyes.

No one waited at the entrance except for a ramrod stiff, sober-expressioned butler. He was a rather formidable fellow. Highly doubtful his lips had creaked upward in the last two decades.

Hmm, make that three.

What would he do if Alexa broke into a Highlander's jig or started singing a bawdy ditty?

As disapproval fairly radiated from the majordomo already, he'd likely expire on the stoop at such antics.

She released a pent-up sigh. What had she expected? Her stepmother and sister to hurtle down the stairs and thank her for disrupting their lives? Nonetheless, a warmer welcome would have been nice.

Did they hide behind the chartreuse velvet-lined windows, glaring daggers at her? The beveled diamond-shaped panes reflected the sun, making it impossible to tell if anyone peeped from within.

Alexa turned and gave her aunt a warm smile. Venturing into this new chapter of her life without their support was unthinkable, and the knife hidden in her belongings was of little use in this situation or in the *ton's* fashionable drawing rooms.

However, despite Alexa's reluctance, Aunt Bridget had insisted after a brief visit at Wedderford Abbey, that they continue on to London to prepare for the Season.

Season. *Bother and blast. Season.*

How in the world would Alexa endure weeks of pretending to be something she wasn't? For certain, she would say or do something ignorant and stupid.

She didn't know how to waltz, flirt, apply rouge, or arrange her hair in the latest complex fashion. She could no more carry on a polite conversation about mundane matters than use a fan or parasol properly. What's more, she didn't want to learn those things.

Aunt Bridget nudged Alexa's elbow. "Come along, my dear. I promise, they won't bite. If they try, I shall use this on them."

She wielded Uncle Hugo's silver walking cane and didn't appear to be jesting. Hadn't Uncle mentioned the cane concealed a short sword?

Aunt Bridget adjusted her grip upon the handle.

Definitely *not* a good sign.

Alexa faced the entry once more. Not a spent blossom, twig, or fallen leaf marred the ornate gardens paralleling the house's sides. Perhaps she'd been allowed to frolic in the manicured lawns as a toddler. Or play hide-and-seek beneath the dangling branches of the willows standing at attention along the drive.

Had her doll's shoe been found below one of them?

She clasped her hands around her reticule. "I don't remember any of this."

"Of course, you don't." Katrina swooped in for a sideways hug. "You were scarcely more than a babe. Good heavens, I don't remember a thing from my early years except for a yellow blanket I toted everywhere. Whatever happened to that blanket, Mama?"

She gave her mother an accusing look. Nevertheless, the impish smile teasing her mouth revealed her humor.

"What blanket?" Aunt Bridget regarded her

daughter blankly. "Oh, that ratty—" She chuckled. "Never mind."

Uncle winked and wiggled his mustache before taking Aunt Bridget's elbow. "Forward ho, my dears. Armor on and swords at the ready?"

Good God.

Just *how* heinous was Minerva Atterberry?

Arms linked, Alexa and Katrina followed her cousin's parents. Well, more aptly, Katrina towed a reluctant Alexa up the wide risers. Her stomach tightened, and she swallowed. She'd been braver facing the Blackhalls, for pity's sake.

"Welcome, Mr. and Mrs. Needham." The butler dipped his head deferentially. He turned his passive gaze on Alexa and Katrina, and a smile of delight erased his intimidating countenance.

Alexa blinked at the transformation.

"Miss Katrina." He gave her a courtier's bow. "It's a pleasure to see you again."

"Thank you, Squires." Katrina bobbed a quick curtsy and gave him a saucy smile. "You're every bit as tall as I remembered."

He crooked a black brow. "I should hope so. Wouldn't do to gradually shrink. Why, in no time, I'd disappear entirely."

Katrina giggled. "Indeed."

Squires's keen gaze assessed Alexa, and his expression softened.

"Miss Atterberry, may I be the first to extend a warm welcome from the staff? They await you in the entry." He smiled, and friendliness sparkled in his hazel eyes. "Our delight at your return cannot be expressed with words."

Alexa's astonishment at his transformation couldn't either.

He stepped aside and gestured for them to enter.

Alexa took a deep breath and crossed the threshold into a magnificent entry, half the size of Craiglocky Keep's great hall.

Good Lord.

The place stole the air from her.

Had she slid across the ebony, gray, and white tiled marble floor or hidden behind the towering Grecian pillars and giant potted plants when playing?

What fun a child would have, chasing the myriad of miniature rainbows the crystal chandelier sprinkled atop every surface. The sprawling dual staircase banner tempted one to slide its gleaming mahogany length even as an adult.

A neat row of smiling servants lined one side of the lavish entrance, except for a long-faced middling-aged woman wearing a severe black gown, white cap, and chatelaine—the housekeeper, no doubt.

A rail thin, striking older woman, a pretty, rather plump, sable-haired girl, and a man—who might at one time have been handsome, but a life of dissipation left him paunchy and sallow—huddled on the other side.

Upon Alexa's entrance, the woman gasped and clutched her throat. Russet-brown eyes wide, a trembling smile touched her mouth.

"Alexandra." Tears streaming from her eyes, she flew across the floor, her aqua and peach gown floating behind her. She wrapped Alexa in a fragrant embrace.

Alexa's lashes brushed her cheeks.

Rosewater and lemon. Her stepmother had always smelled thus.

Minerva leaned away a fraction and gave a trembling smile.

"When I received Mr. Needham's letter, I was afraid to believe it was true." She sent him a contrite glance while wiping at her eyes with a lace scrap of cloth she'd retrieved from inside her sleeve. "I thought someone played a horrid, cruel, twisted joke, or sought to impersonate you, but…" She tenderly touched below Alexa's right ear. "It's really you. You have the scar from when you took a tumble from the swing."

"I remember your perfume, Minerva." Alexa blurted the first thing that popped into her mind.

Minerva's smile faltered, but she forced renewed enthusiasm to her upturned lips. "None of that silliness. You must call me Mama like you used to."

Rather than agree, Alexa sought her aunt. "I used to have dreams of a wonderful smelling woman, and one who liked to sing. Also, a green-eyed man."

Her expression cautious, Aunt Bridget nodded while removing her bonnet. "Lyette had a lovely voice, and your father's eyes were green."

"Shona, come meet your half-sister." Minerva kept an arm about Alexa's waist and beckoned her daughter.

So, Minerva *was* portraying Shona as an Atterberry.

Rigid disapproval radiated from Aunt Bridget. If she were a cat, she would have arched her back, bared her teeth, and hissed her displeasure.

Alexa slid Uncle Hugo a covert glance.

Now what?

He gave an almost indiscernible shake of his head and mouthed, *shh.*

Aunt Bridget's lips pursed tightly as if she'd recently sucked a lemon, and Katrina's wide, blue eyes reflected her troubled musings.

With a bent finger, Minerva signaled the man, his hip perched against a table. "Harrison, I'm sure you remember Alexandra."

"Of course." His lazy gaze trailed over her.

"He's my stepbrother, Harrison Peterson," Minerva offered for Alexa's benefit. "He came to live here shortly after Steafan's passing and has been my steward and man of business ever since. I don't know what I would have done without him all this time."

Alexa resisted the urge to cover her breasts from his snake-like perusal. An uncle shouldn't leer so lasciviously.

Mr. Peterson straightened and, with his hand extended, approached Uncle Hugo. "Needham. Haven't seen you since last Season. At the theater, I believe it was."

Uncle hesitated for the briefest of moments before clasping Mr. Peterson's hand. "Yes, quite so."

"Please call me Harrison, ladies." Mr. Peterson bowed to the women, belching as he leveled upright. He patted his paunch, the cumbersome lion-head ring on his little finger glinting with the movement. "Pardon me. Too many kippers this morning, I fear."

Aunt Bridget's winged eyebrows wrestled with the

curls framing her forehead as she snapped her drooping mouth shut.

"Alexandra, your resurrection from the dead has taken us aback, I must say." Mr. Peterson gave her a thin-lipped smile before focusing on Uncle Hugo once more. "Naturally, we shall need to *see* the proof you claim you possess verifying her identity."

Someone smothered a gasp.

If Mr. Peterson thought Alexa would bare her behind for him to take a gander at her birthmark, he could munch on fresh horse biscuits.

"You have eyes, don't you?" Aunt Bridget visually impaled him. "What other proof do you need? Shall we inspect her blood under a microscope? If she's not Alexandra Atterberry, then you're a mermaid."

Shona erupted into giggles but slapped her hand across her mouth and tucked her chin to her chest at her mother's and uncle's censured looks.

Alexa busied herself with removing her gloves and bonnet. Tension oozed from everyone, including the servants.

"Many people bear a strong resemblance to each other, as I'm sure you're well aware, Mrs. Needham." Harrison's chilly reply sent a fleeting shudder through Alexa. "We cannot have some beggar or bit o' fluff off the streets impersonating Lady Atterberry, now, can we?"

Cheeks apple-red, Shona choked on another giggle, earning her an inquiring glance from Katrina.

"If you have the evidence you claim, then there is no need for concern, is there?" He smiled, more of a sneer than a show of humor, his lecherous gaze ogling first Alexa's behind and then Katrina's.

Reprobate.

He didn't believe she was Alexandra Atterberry.

"Hush, Harrison." Releasing a nervous titter, Minerva made a shooing motion with her hand. "There's time for that disagreeableness later. Right now, I'd like to reacquaint myself with Alexandra."

Glancing at the assembled servants, Minerva hesitated.

"Must we do this now, Squires, when she's just arrived? I'm sure Alexandra would rather wait to be introduced to her official duties. They are ever so tedious, after all." She procured a sunny smile, clearly expecting him to concede.

"Very well, *Dowager.*" Squires gave the merest slant of his head toward the staff. "The *mistress* of Wedderford Abbey will greet you later."

Did Alexa imagine it, or had he emphasized the titles, and had Minerva's false cheerfulness faltered a mite?

"Not mistress yet." Harrison's face contorted into a scowl, which did nothing to enhance his already dour appearance.

"I'm sorry. I do want to make your acquaintance." Alexa offered the servants an apologetic smile. "I'm afraid I don't remember any of you."

Several gave her friendly smiles, but the elderly housekeeper glowered at Harrison and then at Minerva as the staff obediently filed from the entryway.

Interesting.

It appeared everything was not affable at Wedderford Abbey.

"I'm sure you would welcome a spot to eat. Come along. Squires, please have tea and sweets brought round to the drawing room." Before the butler acknowledged Minerva's request, she looped one arm through Alexa's, the other through Shona's, and propelled them down the hall's stretch, leaving Alexa's family to follow at their own pace.

Alexa glanced behind her as her stepmother towed her, willy-nilly, along. Aunt Bridget spoke quietly to Uncle Hugo, and poor Katrina, looking anything but pleased, reluctantly took the elbow Harrison extended.

Alexa tried not to gawk at the ostentatious display of wealth, from the gilded paintings covering practically every inch of the silk-covered walls to the assortment of marble-topped tables, Empire style chairs, lamps, vases, and valuable whatnots lining the corridor.

"Mrs. Eades has your chamber prepared." Forced enthusiasm tinged Minerva's voice. "Such a lovely room too, in different shades of yellows. You'll quite like it, I'm sure."

Alexa opened her mouth to thank Minerva, but her stepmother prattled on.

"Do you prefer a tray in your chamber, or will you come below to break your fast? If I remember correctly, you're quite fond of marmalade and stovies. Do you favor tea or chocolate in the morning? Or coffee, perhaps? I do hope you are still partial to cats. We have three. They're prowling around somewhere in the house. Your luggage will be taken above stairs and unpack—"

"That's most kind of you, but we won't be staying long. Just a day or two." Gracious, the woman carried on an entire conversation by herself.

"Oh? Whyever not?" Confusion creased Minerva's brow.

Alexa hurried to explain. "Aunt Bridget is anxious to return to London and begin preparations for the Season."

"Mother says we shall both have our come-outs this year. I was…*unwell* last winter, and prior to that, I was too timid. But with your company, I do believe I shall get on famously." Shona gave Alexa a shy smile. They reached the floral drawing room's entrance, and Shona slid her uncle a wary look. "He insists at your age, you must find a suitable husband at once."

Alexa forced an affable curving of her lips.

Planning her future, were they?

They'd best prepare for a rather abrupt upset then. She had no intention of abdicating her newfound independence for the constraints of matrimony and submitting to a husband's will just yet.

"I confess, I've no intention of seeking a husband for some time."

Eyes widened in disbelief, Shona sent her uncle another furtive glance, then bent toward Alexa. "Oh, but you must. Uncle Harrison has already contacted several eligible gentlemen on your behalf." She lowered her voice. "Though, it's supposed to be a secret."

Not anymore.

"That's quite enough, dear." A chagrined flush swept Minerva's cheeks as she ushered them into the grand drawing room. "She does get things confused sometimes."

Her lips forming a petulant pout, Shona shook her head. "But, Mama, don't you remember? Uncle said at supper last evening he'd already received an acceptable offer for Alexandra's hand."

10

Chattsworth Park House

My God, how many husband-hunting women did his mother and sister know?

Lucan took a gulp of coffee, burning his tongue for the second time in five minutes. He swore viciously beneath his breath. Perusing the piece of foolscap Genny handed him a moment ago, he pushed aside his plate of hot eggs and ham, his need for food having flown.

What he did need, however, was a lady of breeding and quality. More on point, one with whom he could anticipate an amicable future for several decades.

Fidelity would be a nice bonus.

The latter might prove the more difficult of the qualifications he required—insisted upon, in truth. He hoped his family would accept his chosen bride and that she would mesh well with them. If they adored her, so much the better. If not…

Oh, well.

Lucan mentally shrugged.

He'd have to make sure he selected someone they

got on well with or keep them apart. Not an ideal arrangement.

Tibbs's clanging around at the sideboard echoed the cacophony of thoughts jarring in Lucan's head. Commitment prodding him, he ran his forefinger down the list of eligible misses the meddling females in his family contrived with the force and speed of an avalanche once Mother's health crisis passed.

She'd made a most miraculous recovery in the past ten days; so much so, he might've become suspicious if he hadn't spoken to the doctor himself. However, she would never again be completely healthy, and the knowledge pricked annoyingly, like a thorn in his arse.

Sending Lucan a sympathetic glance, his brother-in-law took his customary place at the table. Lord Montgomery sniffed appreciatively as he placed two sausages on his plate, followed by a mound of scrambled eggs, a slice of ham, and a piece of toast.

"Are you quite sure you didn't forget anyone?" Lucan asked drolly, shaking the list and giving her his most sardonic raised eyebrow expression.

Genny chuckled naughtily and tapped the foolscap before taking a seat and spreading her serviette.

"Those are merely *suggestions* to help you get started, Lucan. Mother and I wrote a few close friends to see if there are any more eligible women on the social scene we're not acquainted with."

"Wrote more than a *few*, old chap. My deepest condolences," Montgomery muttered as he chewed a bite of buttery toast. "Had my fill of damsels contriving to become my countess. Sorely glad it's you and not me this go-round."

"Hush, darling." Genny waved him silent with a vague flutter of her ringed fingers, her attention lingering on Lucan. "We've already received a couple of responses, and I've added their names."

Bloody hell. There are more?

"Tea, Miss Genevieve?" Tibbs pattered to her chair, holding the tea and coffee pots at precarious angles.

Lucan held his breath as the wavering butler prepared to pour the hot beverage.

"Leave the pots, please, Tibbs. I can pour for Lord Montgomery." She bestowed a brilliant smile upon the butler. "I'm ravenous this morning and shall require several cups of tea while breaking my fast."

Well played, Genny.

"Your sister has always owned to quite a vigorous appetite in the morning," Montgomery jested between mouthfuls.

Lucan hid a grin at his brother-in-law's double entendre.

"*Complaining*, darling?" Genny poured her husband's coffee, then added two lumps of sugar while giving him a sensual smile.

Spearing a sausage, Montgomery grinned and winked. "Not at all."

Lucan felt a voyeur, intruding upon their intimate conversation.

She peered around the table. "I would dearly love some marmalade, Tibbs."

"At once, Miss Genevieve." Tibbs had never quite become accustomed to Genny's or Lucan's status as adults. "Young sir, do you require anything from the kitchen while I'm there?"

Searching the neatly scribbled rows for names of ladies he might already know, Lucan glanced up. "No, thank you."

Not unless you can find an acceptable wife in the larder.

Gently bred, well-mannered, above reproach, and from good stock.

The butler pushed his new spectacles to the bridge of his nose and puttered to the door. The apparatuses might well be more of a hazard than the old man's poor eyesight.

A playful glint sparked in Genny's eyes. "Mother and I shall put our heads together and produce more candidates. I shall send them along—"

"No, no." *God, no.* "Send a note around, and I shall come to Chattsworth Park." Lucan scrubbed his hand through his hair while counting the neatly penned names. He glanced up for a moment again. "If the roads are passable, I intend to visit often. I would be remiss in not checking on Mama."

He finished counting.

Eighty-nine?

And they have more?

Glaring at the list, he slumped in his chair.

Holy, bloody hell.

"I can send you updates about her health," Ginny offered, teacup poised at her lips. "So you don't lose a single moment in your pursuit."

"Stubble it, Gen." *Eighty-nine?* He would need

months, not weeks, to do the list justice.

Montgomery released a devilish chuckle, and Lucan barely checked telling his jovial brother-in-law to sod off.

A dish of marmalade in one hand, Tibbs shuffled into the breakfast room, holding his eyeglasses in place with his other. He had reluctantly accepted the eyewear but steadfastly refused false teeth.

Claimed they looked peculiar.

Had the man viewed himself in a looking glass of late?

"The coach is ready, and your bags are aboard, young sir," Tibbs announced, his voice crackling like ancient paper.

"Thank you, Tibbs. Please tell the driver I shall be out momentarily." After folding the list, Lucan tucked it inside his coat and stood.

Genny leaned over and placed her hand on his arm, her earlier bantering demeanor absent. "Lucan, you were generous to promise to marry, but I worry you're sacrificing your happiness for Mama's."

"If it extends her life, it's worth it, I think." He bent and gave her a brief hug, then tweaked her nose. She hated her nose's slight hump.

"Stop that." She swatted at his hand before growing serious once more, concern darkening her eyes to pewter. "Marriage is forever, Lucan. With the right person, it can bring untold joy, but with the wrong one…"

Even when you think you've found the ideal person, they might betray you.

Mother had worshiped Father.

To what end?

His sire's duplicity left a cynical chink in Lucan's heart and a lingering stench more putrid than fish—green and rotting, in the August sun—permanently in his nostrils as well. If Montgomery ever stepped out on his sister, Lucan would kill him.

"You'll have to trust me to make a brilliant match, then, won't you?" He didn't hold hope of that, truth to tell, but Genny needn't know that.

"She's right, you know, Harcourt." Pausing in cutting a bite of ham, Montgomery raised his knife. "Leg shackle yourself to the wrong woman, and you'll endure heartache and misery for the rest of your life. I'd advise you to take your time. I did. And will you look at how I've been blessed?"

The heated look he leveled Genny could've melted butter.

She flushed and busied herself spreading marmalade on her muffin.

Would Lucan ever look at a woman like that?

"Well, only the Little Season is in session, so although the list seems daunting,"—Genny pointed at his coat with her knife tip—"likely you'll find a more manageable portion of ladies present."

Montgomery stood and extended his hand. "We shall stay until Winifred fully recovers, so don't worry yourself in that regard. We'll make sure Jeremy is well-cared for as well."

"Thank you. That relieves my mind greatly." Lucan shook Montgomery's hand, then kissed the cheek Genny angled upward. "I bade Mother and Jeremy farewell last night. I didn't want to wake them this morning. I did speak to James and Arthur earlier, however."

Using the corner of her serviette, Genny dabbed her mouth and nodded. The curls framing her face bounced with the motion. "Jeremy's new assistants have adapted to their duties well. I pray, with them about, he ceases making unsolicited sojourns to Aldecot."

"My thoughts exactly." Since hiring extra hands to monitor the estate, there'd been no more mysterious mishaps. Lucan gave a short bow and then turning toward the door, quipped, "Wish me luck. I'm off to London to find a duchess before Christmastide."

~*~

London, England
A fortnight later

Placing his booted feet atop his London townhouse desk, Lucan tilted his chair back. He perused the list of possible future Duchesses of Harcourt and permitted his upper lip to twist in derision. The eligible ladies populated London faster than rabbits or mice.

True to her word, Genny sent missives, almost daily, reporting Mother's health, Jeremy's activities, the antics of her daughters, and other tittle-tattle she imagined he might find amusing. She also revealed that Renishaw had departed Aldecot Vale, but Genny didn't know where he'd got to.

The fires of Hades, with luck.

For various reasons, Lucan had already crossed twenty names from the bride list, including two who eloped, one who broke into hysterics and then fainted when she'd been introduced, a widow who'd eyed him like a famished tiger, and another who outweighed him by a good five stone and growled when he suggested they might stroll about the veranda.

Truly terrifying, that one.

The four giggling misses scarcely out of the schoolroom wouldn't do.

Three more ladies boasted new betrothals, another had decided all males were toads, and while he strove to act the gentleman and make every woman feel attractive, Miss Blankenship's thick mustache and eyebrows would benefit from a dose of feminine attention. Perhaps she claimed kinship to the Blackhalls.

In any event, Lucan needed to decide which assemblies to put in an appearance at this evening and which young women he'd direct his attention to.

He blew out a long breath and studied the list.

Why, in God's blessed name, had he promised Mother he'd find a wife by Christmas? The task might prove beyond him, and now his honor demanded he keep his word, which meant he might have to settle for a less than ideal candidate.

According to Genny, Mother had already begun preparations for a house party during the holiday, devil it. She should be relaxing and concentrating on getting well, not poring over menus, selecting greeneries, making a guest list, and whatever else went into putting together a lavish Christmas affair.

He considered tightening the purse strings but knew damn well, in the end, she'd find another way to get what she wanted. That trait he'd inherited from her.

Busy pursuing possible brides, Lucan had neglected to retain a mistress. No point now. He'd have to dismiss her in a few weeks. He would be faithful to his wife, which made it even more imperative bedding her wouldn't be objectionable.

A violet-eyed, gold-flecked gaze popped to mind.

Oh, the gypsy lass stirred his blood. Fine, she set it to boiling with want, but one didn't take a gypsy traveller to wife, expressly not a hot-tempered, untamed one. The shock would stop Mother's heart cold, send Genny into an apoplexy, and turn the *ton* on its rear.

He'd rather enjoy the latter, truth be told.

Lucan sighed again and eyed the stack of beribboned parchments atop his desk. Word had circulated on the Marriage Mart thicker and faster than bees to spring blossoms that he sought a wife, and although the official Season hadn't started, invitations and callers inundated him daily.

He focused on the next five women listed.

~*~

Elizabeth Beeton-second daughter of the Dowager Viscountess Beeton. Large dowry, well-educated, a long meg, slightly bucktoothed.

Juliette Maddox-The Marquis of Craythorne's youngest sister. Musically talented, decent dowry, speaks three languages, lisps.

Ursula Amberly-sister to the Duchess of Dunnaby. Bluestocking, bequeathed Rushford Hall, dabbles in writing poetry, one thousand pounds guaranteed annually.

The Honorable Alexandra Atterberry, heiress. (??? Newly arrived in England-no one seems to know much about her other than she's an heiress.)

Margaret Reddington-Vicar Reddington's only child. Intelligent, lovely singing voice, pittance of a dowry, overly fond of confections.

Genny's polite way of saying the chit boasted chubby cheeks and, undoubtedly, chubbier thighs.

The ladies' credentials didn't mean a fig to Lucan. Besides, he didn't know a single one of the chits. They must all be debutantes, which meant they would be young and silly.

And giggly.

God, how he'd come to cringe upon hearing high-pitched female tittering.

Alexandra Atterberry's name drew his gaze once again.

Likely a widow, as she bore a title.

He gave a sideways smile.

No list of glowing attributes for her? Mayhap she didn't have any, other than being female and of marriageable age. Or perhaps, this Atterberry woman was one of the ladies Genny and Mother hadn't met, thus the question marks.

No doubt Mother believed *heiress* a sufficient qualification.

Considering how she'd adored Father and believed in love matches and happily-ever-after, her marked attention to procuring a high-born spouse surprised him. But then, Mother seldom flaunted propriety and appearances. To do so invited the gossipmongers' unwanted attention, and she'd spent a lifetime avoiding the wagchins' censure.

Houston entered the study bearing the post, amongst which peeked several additional invitations. "Where shall I put these, Your Grace? With the others?"

Nodding, Lucan stifled a groan. At least ten more wax-sealed, wife-enticing invites. Too bad the clock hadn't struck noon, so he might indulge in a finger's worth of brandy. Might it be acceptable if he poured a draught directly in his tepid coffee?

"Houston, which do you suggest I attend this evening?" Lucan waved at the stack.

The majordomo's preference might prove diverting.

Houston lifted the invitations and pursed his lips in concentration. After thumbing through them, he displayed three.

"Well, Your Grace, the Eggleston's musical is sure to be attended by several young ladies of quality, as is the *soirée* at the Wrottsley's." He raised one ruby-toned paper adorned with a black ribbon and a monogrammed *R*. "However, Rutledges' annual autumn gala is a Little Season high point. I recommend you put in an appearance at the musical and then finish the evening at the ball."

"Musical and ball, it is then."

Lucan enjoyed musicals as much as getting tossed from his horse.

Naked.

In Hyde Park.

In the dead of winter.

No, he preferred being thrown on his arse, but if he recalled correctly, the Egglestons had four marriageable daughters. Not one of whom sang a note on key. Fighting cats held more talent and harmonized better too. Still, he couldn't afford to ignore a quartet of potential prospects.

The doorknocker echoed.

"Are you at home, Your Grace?" Houston inquired with all the enthusiasm of a funeral dirge.

"Not to females, by God, unless it's my grandaunt." Lowering his feet, Lucan dropped the infernal list on his desk. "I've had quite enough of being ogled like a fancy pastry or a new parasol."

"Most discomfiting, I'm sure." Houston's lips slanted minutely, his version of full-on guffaw, as he left to answer the door.

Lucan rifled through the new post in search of correspondence from Chattsworth. Finding a letter in his mother's tidy script, he settled back into the chair once more.

"Your Grace, Viscount Warrick and the Marquis of Bretheridge have called."

Houston stepped aside as Lucan's friends showed themselves in, still wearing their coats, hats, and gloves. Eyebrows knitted into a single censorious line, Houston pointedly frowned at their attire before sniffing his disapproval and shutting the door.

Lucan hid a grin at his butler's pompous formality.

"Harcourt." Ian, Viscount Warrick strode to the desk, Flynn, Marquis of Bretheridge in his wake. "We've just come from White's. Renishaw, the sot, has placed a bet on the books."

"What concern is that of mine?" Lucan stood and folded the letter. He cocked an eyebrow at the fierce expressions lining his friends' faces. "Renishaw's have always been despots, wastrels, and gamblers."

"Yes, well, the jackanapes has gone beyond the bounds." Bretheridge tossed his hat and gloves atop the desk. "He's bet your *idiot brother*—his words, not mine—will be jailed for trespass by Yuletide."

11

A few hours later, in Grosvenor Square

Alexa attempted to not gape at the woman staring back at her in the floor-length looking glass. No vestige of the Highland Gypsy remained except when she spoke, and her light brogue gave her away.

She would attend her first ball tonight, performing rigid, structured steps vastly different from the free-spirited, creative movements she'd danced since childhood. The notion bathed her in a twofold surge of excitement and dread.

Katrina, exquisite in a gown of ivory lace and Pomona green silk edged in silver braid, grinned at Alexa's reflection.

"You look magnificent, Alexa. Your hair is the most remarkable color, practically midnight black, but when the light hits it so, it shimmers bronze. I'm glad Mama allowed us bolder colors, rather than insipid white or cream for our gowns."

"As am I." Alexa eyed her vibrant gown, the same shade as newly bloomed heather. She yearned for the

Highlands—missed the musical Scottish brogues. Nevertheless, circumstances put her past beyond her reach, and she must forge a new future.

"Lavender is your color." Katrina laughed and grabbed Alexa's hands. "It emphasizes your eyes, and Mama's amethysts are the perfect finishing touch. They match your slippers' beading splendidly."

Alexa lifted her hem, exposing the embroidered shoes enclosing her feet.

Too pretty to wear.

She owed a great deal of her newly acquired wardrobe to a young woman who'd failed to return for the garments she'd ordered.

Delighted upon discovering Alexa and the absent woman wore practically the same size, the modiste had offered the ready-made garments for a pittance when they learned she intended to purchase an entirely new wardrobe, from undergarments to pelisses, muffs, bonnets, and shoes.

Always prudent with funds, Alexa politely ignored her aunt's protests that she should purchase someone else's leavings, and took the entire lot. However, not without a tug of remorse at whatever ill-fortune prevented the other woman from returning for her garments.

The lady's taste had been superb, if a trifle reticent. Alexa preferred bolder colors, but for the price, she would make do.

Katrina's brow knitted as she clasped an emerald and pearl drop earring to her ear.

"You should've been permitted to wear the

Atterberry jewels. I don't believe for a moment Minerva's balderdash about them being locked in a safe at Wedderford Abbey." She crinkled her adorable nose. "No one without a turnip for a brain would. I'll bet Minerva or Shona wear gems tonight. You wait and see."

"Dinna *fash* yourself, dearest," Alexa said, slipping into Scots. "We shall have time to sort everything out while we're here." Alexa half-pivoted to glance at Katrina. "Uncle Hugo has scheduled an appointment with the solicitor, and we'll know precisely where everyone stands after that."

"Yes, well, thank goodness Papa discovered that scheming crow, Minerva, petitioned to have the abeyant peerage terminated in Shona's favor, and did so within days of receiving notice you were alive."

That unpleasant revelation yesterday unnerved Alexa. Her prospects, the hope of helping the travellers and postponing marriage might require reevaluating if she didn't receive the title.

Though, unlike Shona's, Uncle Hugo assured Alexa her parentage remained uncontested. She didn't consider for a moment he'd let that particular remain hidden; Shona's pedigree was no trifling matter. A bastard couldn't be permitted to inherit, or so Uncle insisted.

"It's understandable, Katrina. I've disrupted their entire way of life. I imagine they are quite desperate." And angry. At least Harrison was. The man fairly simmered, bubbling with ire, each time they met.

Alexa couldn't quite reconcile the kind, biddable woman Minerva portrayed herself as at Wedderford

Abbey with the conniving, deceitful wretch who'd pretended to rejoice in Alexa's return, the whole while knowing she'd petitioned to have her stepdaughter disinherited.

What else did she hide?

The entire family seemed a bit off-putting, truth to tell. Harrison *had*, in fact, had the effrontery to suggest he view Alexa's bottom, to which Uncle Hugo had emphatically told him to go bugger himself.

Clearly, Harrison had an agenda; to disprove her identity and claim to the title.

Enough.

Tonight, she'd foray into High Society's evening activities for the first time, and she'd not muck it up. Facing the mirror once more, she rearranged a curl framing her face. Never had she felt half so lovely, yet the thought that gentlemen might find her appealing didn't settle well in her middle. She hadn't sought a man's attention since Rígán's, and he'd been a youth of nineteen when he'd disappeared.

Her chest constricted—more for the loss of her best friend than heartbreak. She'd been terribly fond of Rígán and expected they would marry, yet theirs hadn't been a heated romance, but rather a comfortable camaraderie.

Her right glove crept downward toward her elbow, and she tugged it back into place. How did ladies do anything with their hands constantly in gloves?

So impractical.

What if she needed to use a chamber pot tonight?

Best ask Katrina about that difficulty before they left for the ball.

Aunt and Uncle hadn't mentioned if the Duke of Harcourt would attend the gala. Alexa's pulse gave a queer skip. Imagine their surprise if they discovered precisely how she and the duke had become acquainted.

Yes, his grace risked his life to rescue me, my brother, and my sister from certain violation or death.

Of course, I thanked him properly.

I punched him a good one when he tried to kiss me.

Her stomach quivered, then gurgled. She pressed a hand there. She should've eaten her luncheon, but she'd been too busy practicing her dance steps and reviewing the *ton's* protocols and expectations.

Pray to God she didn't revert to a lifetime of habits and seize a piece of meat with her fingers, talk with her mouth full, or snort when she laughed. She'd never claimed a dainty, musical laugh like Katrina or Aunt Bridget. No, hers sounded like a bleating goat with a head cold.

"I'm fraught with apprehension." She met Katrina's excited gaze in the mirror. "I'm going to commit a gaffe. I know it."

Katrina heaved an exaggerated sigh and wrapped an arm around Alexa's waist. "You'll take London by storm."

Alexa chuckled at her stunning cousin. "You're not exactly street rabble, and I'm sure every gentleman present tonight will wish to dance with you. Me, on the other hand . . ." She pulled a face and stuck out a silk-clad foot. "I'm all heels."

"Flim-flam. You've come so far in two weeks. You have mastered most of the dance steps, and your manners are as pretty as mine." Katrina dimpled. "Papa paid Mr. Beufort handsomely for the little inconvenience he suffered."

In the process of dabbing perfume behind her ears, Alexa shook her head and released an unladylike grunt. "Katrina, I broke the man's toes. He swore in all his years as a dance master, he'd never known anyone as 'maladroit' as me."

"Pooh." Katrina flapped her hand. "He's an old cross bore who likes to use pretentious words. You've practiced with me this entire week and only trod upon my foot twice. My toes are none-the-worse for it."

"Liar." Alexa shook a finger at Katrina. "I saw the bruise atop your foot, cousin."

In the past fortnight, Aunt Bridget and a beehive of others had attempted to transform Alexa from a Highland bumpkin into a lady worthy of a title.

Alexa didn't share her aunt's enthusiasm about presenting her long-lost niece to Society, not only because Alexa's education in comportment had only just begun, but in truth, she had no desire to fit into the *haut ton*. Nonetheless, she wouldn't deny Aunt Bridget her joy, and her aunt's exuberance *was* contagious.

The same couldn't be said for Minerva's and Harrison's eagerness to marry her off. After Shona's remark at Wedderford Abbey, Alexa hadn't minced words. She wasn't in the market for a husband, and when she did decide to pursue marriage, she, and she alone, would select her mate. Even so, their persistence spurred Alexa's impatience and wariness.

They'd soared into Town a mere two days after

Alexa arrived. Thankfully, Minerva hadn't fussed when Alexa insisted on continuing to London with the Needhams rather than moving to her residence on Regent Street where Minerva intended to remain for the Season.

Minerva and Harrison had come around *uninvited* the next day with a slew of suggestions, from practical to outrageous, as to how Alexa might most effectively and efficiently go about acquiring a spouse, post haste. One of their tamer recommendations consisted of hiding in a peer's carriage wearing nothing but her chemise.

One would think them desperate to see her married.

Perhaps they thought she'd reside at her husband's home, and they'd be free to do what they pleased at Wedderford.

The entailment included other properties as well, and Alexa hadn't quite decided how to proceed with her new family or her holdings. Her change in circumstances became a mixed bag of blessings and conundrums. After a visit with Uncle Hugo's solicitor, she'd be in a better position to make decisions.

Difficult at best and humiliating at worst, Alexa didn't envy Minerva and Shona's situation. Nevertheless, that hadn't prevented Minerva from indulging in enthusiastic shopping sprees, which Uncle Hugo politely, but firmly, put an end to. Minerva's generous allowance would have to suffice.

Why Harrison continued to reside at Wedderford Abbey, or tag along wherever her stepmother went, baffled Alexa unless he had no means. He'd been sponging off the barony's generosity for the past two decades. Rather hard to respect an opportunist and wastrel of that caliber, but she didn't know his whole situation either. Perhaps he suffered from a malady of some sort, she conceded with as much grace as she could muster.

Laziness.

She shoved the uncharitable thought aside.

"I'm afraid I shall make a God-awful blunder." Alexa scrutinized her appearance in the mirror one final time.

Katrina gathered her gloves. "You've nothing to worry about. Do as I do and smile. People will understand when they learn of your uncivilized upbringing."

She clapped a hand over her mouth.

"Oh, Alexa. I didn't mean that how it sounded." Laying the gloves aside, Katrina glided to Alexa's side. "I only meant, dear one, you cannot be expected to learn in a fortnight what most members of *le beau monde* have had a lifetime to perfect. And trust me when I tell you, many of that pompous lot are quite barbaric beneath their snooty, outward mien."

"It's fine. I'm not offended." And Alexa wasn't.

Although she'd been in London a short while and attended several intimate functions, she felt as inadequate as a pig draped in chartreuse satin and Brussels lace taking tea in Lady Jersey's parlor. Nonetheless, she intended to learn as much as she could and make the most of the opportunity she'd been afforded. As an heiress, she possessed the power to help the gypsies and other less fortunates.

An hour later, holding Katrina's hand, she entered Lord and Lady Rutledge's glittering ballroom. Several people turned to stare as Uncle Hugo guided the women to empty chairs near parted French windows. As they took their seats, a few guests smiled and inclined their heads while a good number whispered to those nearest them.

By design, Alexa's fascinating tale hadn't remained a family secret. Uncle Hugo and Aunt Bridget had thought it best to let the story out in the open, lest viper-tongued gossips contrive something unpleasant and untrue. However, their romanticized version of her disappearance and life amongst the gypsies didn't include sharing her abduction and imprisonment at the Blackhall's hands.

A stout, older gentleman examined Alexa through his quizzing glass while two dandies openly leered—one wearing a rose and jonquil striped waistcoat, and the other, a neckcloth so stiff and complicatedly tied, he could scarcely move his head.

"The rotund fellow is Mr. Myers, the fop, Lord Craven, and the starchy chap, Sir Howard," Katrina whispered from the side of her mouth while bestowing a brilliant smile on a dark-eyed man with hair slightly longer than fashionable who lounged against a pillar.

You can do this, Alexa. Remember, savoir-faire.

Alexa recited in her mind, again and again, what Aunt Bridget drilled into her.

"A lady must demonstrate *savoir-faire*, Alexa. She must behave correctly and with poise in every situation."

Raising her chin, Alexa smiled at those smiling at

her, unflinchingly met the direct stares of those rudely gawking, and raised an amused brow at the haughty few turning their noses up. She also indulged in a bit of *Name the Lord and Lady*, a child's game she had played growing up. No ill-intent was behind the silly, fabricated names, just nonsensical fun.

A triad of overly perfumed, bejeweled dames sauntered past, taking Alexa's measure as surely as her nose objected to their powerful aromas. Holding her breath and stifling the urge to sneeze, she offered a genial smile and received flat, unblinking stares in return.

No allies there.

She promptly dubbed them *The Three Un-Muses.*

Fixing her smile firmer, she inspected the teeming ballroom, already beastly warm. Alexa inhaled a bracing breath. These people would not intimidate her.

Desperate for the insignificant draft that waving the frilly accessory afforded, she flipped her fan open despite not having concentrated in her studies on how to most effectively use the thing to communicate. Silly her. Here she thought a fan a tool to cool oneself, not to send coded messages.

She had allowed a tiny whimper and slouched onto the salon settee yesterday when Aunt Bridget announced she must also learn the language of parasols and handkerchiefs.

Absurd.

Just talk, for the love of God.

Wasn't that why the Good Lord gifted people with mouths and tongues? Pray she didn't thwack herself on the nose or poke herself in the eye with her fan tonight, though. Or communicate something wholly inappropriate.

A small cluster of distinguished-looking ladies inclined their heads toward her before gliding from the room. Her confidence nudged up a morsel. They'd looked rather important.

Aunt Bridget tapped Alexa's forearm with her closed fan. "Bravo, Alexa. You've won the patroness' initial approval without an introduction."

Alexa's breath caught, and her pulse stuttered. "Is that who they—"

"We shall remedy that oversight before evening's end. Well done. First round to you, dearest. I knew you'd take." Aunt Bridget's giddy whisper and beaming face hardly registered.

A tall, ash-blond man attired in black, except for his pristine cravat, ambled through the French windows accompanied by two laughing gentlemen.

The Duke of Harcourt's languid gaze swept the room, passed by her and her family, then careened back to rivet on her as his eyes widened in disbelief. No sign remained of his injured eye.

A slow, wolfish smile curved his full mouth.

No doubt existed that he'd recognized her.

Look away, Alexa.

Her dratted eyes wouldn't obey. She couldn't blink as he strode purposefully in her direction. What must he think, seeing her here, elegantly attired, and in the company of her well-heeled aunt and uncle?

She permitted a welcoming smile and what she

hoped qualified as a flirtatious flutter of her fan, which, from his astonished expression, confounded him.

Her smile slipped.

Bother.

Perhaps she'd told him to go to the devil or bugger himself with her inept flapping.

His striking companions exchanged amused glances before hieing after the duke. Probably didn't want to miss the sport about to take place.

Heads turned and conversations tapered when people noticed the duke's intent. She'd bet her new fortune *le beau monde* favored him, and that he'd set his attention on her—an unknown—marked her for their regard.

Uncle Hugo scratched his upper lip and murmured beneath his cupped hand. "Alexa, my dear. Do you know the Duke of Harcourt?"

"Stop staring." Katrina nudged her. "People are taking notice."

Alexa still gaped. She'd thought him attractive before, but dressed formally with a predatory glint in his eye—

Her body reacted most peculiarly—hot, shivery, and excited at once.

"Alexa." Katrina toed Alexa's slipper then poked her in the side, using her fan to make her point.

Alexa perched, riveted on the edge of her seat, like a leery bird ready to take flight. Except, where could she escape to? She had the oddest urge to scamper to the curtains and hide behind their protective lengths.

With him.

A sharp pinch to her arm, at last, made her turn and look at her aunt.

"Ouch, that hurt." Alexa rubbed the offended flesh. "Why did you pinch me?"

A glittering false smile on her face, Aunt Bridget conveniently dropped her fan. Bending to retrieve it, she whispered, "A Covent Garden courtesan is less bold. Drop your gaze. He's almost upon us."

No need to ask who *he* was.

At once, Alexa found the parquet flooring's pattern utterly fascinating. Three pairs of glossy black shoes soon obstructed her view. She switched her attention to the even more intriguing toes of her satin slippers.

Silly, this having to pretend demureness.

"Good evening, Mrs. Needham, Miss Needham, Mr. Needham." The duke's voice floated over and around Alexa, churning memories she'd tried to forget. Such as how she could listen to the rumble of his voice forever.

"Your Grace, my lords," Aunt Bridget and Katrina murmured as one, sounding rather like trained circus parrots.

"Alexa." Katrina poked Alexa's elbow with her blasted fan.

Did every *tonnish* woman use the things as miniature swords?

The women stood, then dipped into graceful curtsies. However, Alexa continued to study his grace's polished shoes. She wouldn't want Aunt Bridget working herself into a fuss because Alexa couldn't tear her gaze from a disturbingly handsome duke.

Why did she have to see him right off? Couldn't she have been afforded a night or two— a week—*a month* to practice her newly acquired skills?

Why did it matter? He'd already seen her at her absolute worst and had still tried to steal a kiss.

Savoir-faire, Alexa.

Uncle Hugo swept his hand toward the new arrivals. "Alexandra, may I introduce His Grace, the Duke of Harcourt, the Marquis of Bretheridge, and Viscount Warrick? Your Grace, my lords, this is my niece, Alexandra Atterberry."

"It's a pleasure, Your Grace, my lords." Why, she sounded quite composed. No one present would suspect her heart had sunk to somewhere in the vicinity of her stomach—which tumbled riotously—or that a thousand red ants danced a Scottish jig along her nerves.

"Thank you, Mr. Needham. However, I've had the privilege of previously meeting your niece in Scotland."

The duke's amused silver gaze collided with Alexa's. Heaven forbid he reveal how they'd met. She'd be ruined, through and through.

Lord Warrick sent the duke an amazed look. "*She's the one?*"

Oh, dear. That didn't bode well.

Alexa swallowed and braved examining the ballroom beyond them. *Oh, God.* Nearly everyone present had turned to watch the exchange, and the bolder amongst the crowd sidled closer.

She clenched her fan until the scalloped edges cut into her fingers and clamped her teeth to keep from telling the meddlers to shove off and mind their own business.

"Harcourt, I thought you said the woman you rescued was a gypsy lass?" Lord Bretheridge, his green-eyed gaze baffled, sent Lord Warrick a questioning look before his attention leaped to Alexa.

The viscount shrugged, then scowled at the brazen guests blatantly eavesdropping on their conversation. A half dozen had the grace to blush and, averting their gazes, bustled away. However, one prune-faced man had the audacity to smirk and step closer.

Perhaps the duke had decided to avenge her hitting him after all, and had chosen to do so publicly. He must've known she'd be here. Perhaps, Lord Sethwick had written his grace and told him of her change in circumstances.

No. The Duke of Harcourt hadn't feigned his surprise upon discovering her here. He hadn't known, and nothing he'd done at Dounnich House remotely hinted he possessed a rancorous character. In fact, the opposite might be argued. He'd been contrite and remorseful… thoughtful, in fact.

Uncle Hugo maneuvered until the peers' backs faced the titillated onlookers, but the annoying, prying man slinked to the side in order to see and hear their exchange.

Alexa slid him a surreptitious glance and found him staring at her. His thin lips twitched upward, as did the hair on her nape.

A granary rat claimed better manners. Rather looked like a rodent too, with his narrow face, pointed nose, mousy-brown hair, and close-set, beady eyes. He even wore a gray waistcoat and only lacked whiskers and a tail. She could almost imagine his nose trembling while he cleaned his paws.

Rat man.

"You've met my niece, Your Grace?" Uncle gave Alexa a reassuring smile, although puzzlement lingered in his eyes.

She offered a sympathetic arcing of her mouth in return.

Dear man. He's utterly flummoxed.

"Indeed, I've had the pleasure." The duke didn't sound angry.

Alexa took a deep breath, determinedly affixed a smile to her lips, and lifted her head to meet his gaze straight on.

Do your worst.

I can take it.

I am Scottish and a gypsy.

Well, not gypsy anymore. Her heart gave a sharp pang.

Only warm kindness shone in the duke's eyes, and she relaxed the tiniest bit.

His grace took her hand, then bowed over it. "And a braver, more courageous woman I have yet to meet."

She parted her lips in surprise as a flurry of whispers erupted around them.

Alexa's story might seem romantic to some, but her aunt and uncle had warned her not to breathe a word about her captivity. Surely, the duke, too, knew how disastrous such a revelation would be to her reputation.

Harrison elbowed his way through the throng.

Perfect. Someone else disagreeable to deal with.

One step behind him, both wearing spectacular parure sets, Minerva towed a pale and trembling Shona.

Alexa doubted the shimmering rubies, diamonds, and sapphires were paste, and irritation pricked at their deceit. She couldn't tolerate liars. What else had Minerva lied about?

Shona's parentage?

Most unwise to trust her stepmother.

Every now and again, Shona darted an enamored look at the rat. Apparently, she knew the man well enough to have formed an infatuation. Interesting. *And nauseating.*

"Alexandra was raised as a Scottish Highland traveller. A *gypsy*." Harrison's bold announcement held a gloating note. His eyes shrank to shrewd slits. "Having been abducted, and her true identity recently discovered, she's just returned to her family's bosom."

Now he's done it, the scunner.

Katrina slipped her hand into Alexa's and gave a tiny squeeze.

Alexa forced air into her lungs. *Stay calm.* Mayhap he referred to her first abduction as a child.

Gasps ricocheted around the room, and Aunt Bridget regarded him with the same revulsion she would a headless cockroach scurrying across her dinner plate.

Katrina clenched Alexa's hand tighter.

"Pray tell me, Your Grace, how you came to be acquainted with her?" Harrison presumed to touch Harcourt's arm but dropped his hand when the duke eyed him as if he were plague-ridden and oozing pus from open sores.

Enough of his meddling. Except by marriage, Harrison claimed no kinship to Alexa, and his brazenness set her teeth on edge.

"You assume much, Mr. Peterson. The duke owes you no explanation." She eyed him coolly. "Need I remind you, *again*, I am not *your* concern?"

"I beg your pardon." His terse reply and hardened gaze belied his words.

With family such as he, who needed adversaries?

"Abduction, you say? How very intriguing." Rodent man exchanged a meaningful look with Harrison. "I should like to hear more about your recent…*adventure*."

She sent her uncle a guarded glance.

Brittle smiles painted on their faces, Aunt Bridget and Katrina kept glancing toward the exits.

Excellent notion.

Let's be away.

Now.

Alexa's fingers grew numb in her cousin's viselike clasp.

Eyes glinting, Uncle Hugo smoothed one side of his mustache before answering frostily. "As you've not been introduced to my niece, Renishaw, your question is beyond impertinent."

Several guests murmured their consensus, and a satisfied smile wreathed Aunt Bridget's face.

Renishaw's face grew ruddy, and he narrowed his close-set eyes in vexation. Had he whiskers, they would have twitched spastically as would his hairless tail. He'd probably gnash his pointed, yellow teeth too.

"Quite right, Needham." The look of distaste the duke leveled Lord Renishaw sent a chill clear to Alexandra's shins.

Clearly not friends—not by any exaggeration.

The Duke of Harcourt offered his elbow. "I'll claim that promised dance now, Miss Atterberry."

Lucan itched to reduce Peterson and Renishaw another peg or two, but the gratitude and relief in Alexandra's expression, and the swiftness with which she latched onto his arm, prompted him to remove her from the intrigued bystanders straightaway.

She must be discomfited, indeed, to prefer his company and act upon the fabricated dance promise. They hadn't exactly parted on the most cordial of terms.

He wanted to applaud the frosty setdown she'd given Peterson, but with the ladies present, he'd been forcibly biting his tongue to keep from telling Renishaw to sod off. Or worse.

"Mr. and Mrs. Needham, might I steal your niece away for the next dance?" Lucan wouldn't take no for an answer.

At Mr. Needham's nod of approval, Lucan turned Alexandra toward the dance floor and the bevy of nosy onlookers.

Several gawkers jerked their attention away, stumbling into one another in their haste, and a gentleman spilled his punch down a debutante's flat-as-a-washboard chest.

A sharp reprimand from her mother cut short the girl's strangled screech. Glaring at the hamfisted lord, then at Alexandra, the vexed mama seized her daughter's arm and dragged her from the room.

Alexandra hummed along to the music, oblivious to the misfortune playing out. Either that or she'd mastered masking her reactions. She reminded Lucan of a child on her first outing to a fair or a confectionary. How vastly different this must be from her humble roots.

He studied her goddess-perfect profile.

Did she enjoy dancing too?

Weren't gypsies quite musical?

Roma gypsies, like Lady Warrick, claimed the trait, but Lucan didn't know if the black tinkers possessed the same inclination. Given the penchant most Scots had for celebrating, the travellers might very well be as gifted.

He shot a covert glance over his shoulder.

Peterson and Renishaw slithered to a corner and, heads close together, conversed intently. No good could come of that. Lucan would forgo his coffee for a month to know precisely how the two had become acquainted.

The way those curs leered at Alexandra, as if she were a dockside harlot displaying her wares, had him grinding his teeth. He almost wished one would venture too far and give him an excuse to call them out. Especially since he still fumed about Renishaw's loathsome bet at White's.

Fiend seize it.

He couldn't challenge anyone to a duel, and not because they'd been outlawed, either. After Harvey's death, Lucan vowed to Mother he would never duel, and honorable gentlemen kept their word.

Ought not to make pledges in the first place.

Nonetheless, that wouldn't prevent Lucan from pounding Peterson and Renishaw senseless. Thrice weekly rounds at Jackson's kept him fit and able to lay a bounder out. He knew other ways to control rubbish of their ilk too, and he held no qualms about using those means to teach the boors a well-deserved lesson.

Sidestepping rotund Lady Bellowton, Alexandra accidentally brushed her breast against his arm.

Lucan gritted his teeth to stave off the rush of lust her innocent movement caused.

She looked bloody exquisite tonight—a fairytale vision.

Russet highlights danced among the curls artfully twisted and pinned atop her head, and an intricate amethyst pendant encircled her neck. Her nape beckoned him to rain kisses along its delicate length, then gradually ever lower to her swan-like neck, satin shoulders, and the creamy mounds taunting him above her bodice.

Rather than bow her head in chagrin, she glanced around curious as a kitten, boldly meeting the assembled guests' stares. Few people—no others he readily thought of—traipsed into a ballroom from the wilds of Scotland and endured the *ton's* scrutiny without a blink.

Such lack of artifice proved refreshing.

By God, the transformation in Tasara—Alexandra—from a wild, exotic gypsy to a sophisticated, exquisite lady, graceful and poised, had caught him unprepared and rendered him almost speechless. His genuine and wholly unexpected joy upon seeing her once more astounded him as well.

Reentering the stuffy ballroom, determined to dance with a prospective bride or two despite his friends' admonishments, Lucan feared he hallucinated.

He'd been soundly chastised by Warrick and Bretheridge for his calculated approach to matrimony. Just because they'd found marital bliss didn't mean he could afford the same luxury. He'd made a vow he fully intended to keep, and his time ran short.

Christmas loomed but a few weeks away, and while Mother's health appeared to have calmed for now, Doctor Philpott made it clear as crystal, they had no way of knowing when she would, again, take a turn for the worse.

To divert his friends' harping about his stupidity, Lucan had regaled them with the gypsy wench's rescue, including her soundly clocking him.

Warrick and Bretheridge laughed until tears streamed from their eyes and still chuckled sporadically as they reentered Rutledges' crowded ballroom.

"Good evening. Quite a crush, isn't there?" Alexandra said, smiling at a quartet of debutantes.

Two presented their stiff, unfriendly backs and whispered furiously. The others exchanged a meaningful glance but offered a partial-tilt of heavily rouged lips.

"I should've waited to be introduced, shouldn't I have?" Alexandra's smile dimmed, and her grasp on his arm grew tense. "So many bothersome rules. However do you manage to keep them straight?"

"Never mind that riffraff. Come along." Lucan tucked her arm closer to his side and patted the hand resting atop his forearm as they wended their way through the throng.

"Thank you for asking me to dance." Alexandra gave him a bright smile. "I feared Harrison was about to make an ugly scene. I didn't worry for myself, but for my family. They've done so very much for me. And why rat-man thinks it's and of his concern is beyond me."

Lucan choked back a guffaw. "*Rat man?*"

"Curses. I knew I would commit a *faux pas*." Crimson swept her face, and she hastily peered around to see if anyone else heard her. "Please forgive me. That was a dreadful thing to say. Childhood habit, I'm afraid."

"Actually, that's the most accurate description of Viscount Renishaw I've ever heard." Guiding her past a cluster of young bucks, Lucan grinned. "By God, I like it. Renishaw the Rat, or Ratter Renishaw. Or the Vermin Viscount. Which do you prefer?"

She searched his face, wariness tinging her violet gaze. "None are charitable or kind, Your Grace."

"I assure you, his reputation is well-earned." Lucan's tone hardened, a distinct bite weighted his words. "Believe me, *he* is not a kind man."

"He did seem most intrusive. Thank you for rescuing me. *Again*." Alexandra grinned at him, her eyes flashing with mirth.

He chuckled. "I don't know when I've been taken more by surprise. Am I to presume Sethwick's hunch had merit, Lady Atterberry?"

She inclined her head a fraction, the smooth planes of her face unreadable. "Yes, though I confess, I was as astonished as you, and I'm not a lady yet. There's something to do with an abeyance that needs to be settled before the title is bestowed."

"A matter of formality, I'm sure." Lucan flattened his palm against the small of her back as he steered her along.

They'd reached an opening on the dance floor's periphery.

"Trust me when I tell you"—she made a circular gesture in the air with her forefinger—"this is a trifle much to take in when one is used to eating outdoors with one's fingers, bathing in streams, and sleeping in a tent or wagon."

A vision of her standing in a shallow brook, water dripping from her glorious naked form, and her breasts—nipples puckered and raised to the sky—had him swelling in his breeches.

"And I enjoyed it, truth to tell." Her last words held a challenge, as if she dared him to judge her upbringing or her.

Not a chance.

She intrigued the hell out of him in a way no *properly* raised miss ever would. He would quite like to brave the outdoors with her. Sleep in a tent. Bathe in a stream.

His groin jerked.

Damnation. Much more of this and you'll disgrace yourself.

"Do you miss Scotland? The gypsies?"

Everything she knew, was accustomed to, she'd left behind. That took tremendous courage.

"Yes." Huskiness lowered Alexandra's voice, and her gaze dropped to the floor. "Especially my family—and the heather. The hills were blanketed with the flowers when I left, though they were fading."

Open speculation glinted in several pairs of eyes trained on her. Either she didn't notice or didn't care. What freedom it must be to be able to cock a snook in the *haut ton's* pretentious face. Alexandra wouldn't be caged and tamed by society's dictates, and by God, Lucan couldn't be more pleased.

He bent his neck and murmured, "How much does Peterson know?"

Her guileless gaze swept the crowd before meeting his. "Enough to cause a scandal, but not the entire truth. Not yet, anyway."

It wouldn't take much digging, a few coins greasing a palm or two, and the rest would be uncovered. Lucan expected Peterson would persist until he knew all. Hadn't the Needhams considered the possibility and the ramifications?

A young woman of quality held captive by a band of renegade Scots for hours, let alone days, was ruined beyond redemption, no matter her social standing or familial connections. The gypsies may view things differently, but amongst the *ton's* set, Alexandra was soiled goods.

She needed to be betrothed or married before the ugliness became common knowledge. The sooner, the better. What a fortuitous coincidence he happened to be in the market for a bride and desired speedy nuptials as well.

Scottish, gypsy, *and* a compromised heiress.

What would Mother and Genny make of that?

He could almost hear the clucking and scolding already. But they'd included Alexandra on their blasted list, so they couldn't object overly much. Except they had no idea, she'd been raised as a black tinker or held captive by ruthless killers.

Lucan wanted to rub his hands together in glee. He'd found his bride, and the gypsy waif he had rescued from the Blackhall fortress would soon find herself a duchess. If everything went as he intended—and as a duke, they ordinarily did—he would be wed well before Christmas.

How soon could he call on Mr. Needham and request Alexandra's hand?

He considered that for an extended moment.

Best not rush things. Woo Alexa for two or three weeks first.

Lucan steered her onto the sanded floor. "How is it Peterson knows of your situation at all?"

"He's my stepmother's stepbrother." Her scrunched nose and compressed lips expressed her ill-opinion of the man. "That was her and my half-sister standing behind him. From my understanding, he has resided at Wedderford Abbey since right after my father died."

She lifted to her tiptoes and whispered in his ear, her hot breath caressing the lucky organ. "He gives me the shivers."

Lucan's libidinous desires sprang into a full-on gallop.

She gave *him* the shivers. Delicious, sensual shudders, he longed to further explore. In a tent or stream. He canvassed the room. An alcove or the terrace would do, as well.

"He always leers at my bum and bosoms." She winked innocently as she settled her heels to the floor.

If Jesus stood beside him, Lucan couldn't have prevented himself from assessing those same two luscious attributes. His cock's predictable response would soon have people pointing and snickering if he didn't command some control over his primal urges.

Think of something else.

Miss Blankenship's mustache.

The murderous Blackhalls.

Mother's failing health.

Father's infidelity—

That did it.

Lucan's manhood wilted faster than a water lily tossed onto a Yule log.

No other lady would have mentioned her bum or bosoms to a male acquaintance. That Alexandra did, told him she trusted him. Excellent. Trust between a husband and wife was essential.

Mother trusted Father, and look how well that had ended.

Lucan pelted the thought halfway to next year.

"Did you hear that Isobel Ferguson and the Earl of Ramsbury—he's the man who rescued her—wed?" Why Lucan thought Alexandra want to know, he couldn't say.

"I suspected as much. The way they looked at each other that day, they had to be in love." Alexandra gripped his arm and, eyes glowing, gave a sage nod. "They practically devoured one another with their gazes. I'm overjoyed for them."

Not a jot of envy or insincerity tinged her words.

"They are blissfully happy and honeymooning in Spain, I believe."

She considered him from the corner of her eye. "I'm sorry I hit you." Contriteness giving her husky voice depth, she lifted a shoulder an inch. "I was overwrought and not myself."

"I deserved it, and again, beg your pardon. My behavior was intolerable." Lucan dipped his head nearer hers, as much to breathe in her essence as to speak privately. "I had a devil of a time explaining how an imp your size managed to blacken my daylights."

"A most challenging dilemma, to be sure." Her lips quivered, and laughter cavorted in her heather-colored eyes. "Am I forgiven then?"

"I've forgotten the incident." Too bad his friends hadn't and would continue to taunt him for weeks. *Months.* "Truce?"

She gifted him a beguiling smile. "I'd like that."

The first strains of a waltz sounded. Lucan bowed, and after Alexandra curtsied, he swept her into his arms. "Do you know the waltz?"

It wouldn't matter if she didn't. He possessed superb dancing skills and could easily lead her.

"Yes, I learned the steps, but I must warn you." Lips quivering once more, she peeked at him through thick lashes. "I'm a perfectly horrid dancer."

He pulled her nearer, not enough to be improper, but sufficient to breathe in her perfume. Somewhat musky-spicy, yet soothing too. A lot like her. "Come now, you're too harsh on yourself."

"My dance master said I was his most inept pupil. *Ever*." Her expression resigned, she sighed. "In three and thirty years. I am his worst."

Lucan tried to stifle his chuckle. "A graceful, petite woman like you?"

"Your Grace, I've never been accused of being graceful." Alexandra grinned again, her face lighting up. "He was amiable the first time. When I broke a second toe, less so."

Lucan laughed outright, earning them several inquiring looks, and a few vexed as well. "More than one? What did you do? Stomp the poor fellow's bare feet with your boot heel?"

"I didn't tramp on him deliberately." Her face puckered in concentration, her mouth moved silently as she swayed and counted the steps. And tromped on his foot. Twice.

He hid a wince.

For someone petite, she was not light on her dainty, slippered feet.

"You're not ungraceful." *Altogether.* "You're doing splendidly." *Exaggeration, there, old boy.* "You need practice, that's all." *Lots and lots of it.* He bent his head toward her ear. "I'd be happy to give you lessons."

She gave a little jerk, and he'd lay odds at White's that coldness hadn't caused her to shudder. Had his breath tickled her, perhaps arousing her?

"I'd be grateful." She pursed her plump lips, looking thoughtful. "Is it permitted, though? Would we be breaking some rule?"

Absolutely.

"I shall arrange it with your aunt and uncle." Another inch and Lucan could kiss her ear, but to do so would surely bring immediate censure. Nonetheless, he needed to make clear his intentions to the hawk-eyed fortune-hunters eager to snare an heiress and the husband-hunting damsels hoping to don a duchess title.

He'd made his selection, even if Alexandra didn't know it yet. Moving his thumb up and down the curve of her rib, he inched her closer yet. "I assume it's your aunt and uncle I should speak with and not your stepmother. I shall call tomorrow—"

"Your Grace. I passed my one and twentieth birthday mark while incarcerated at Dounnich House, and I make my own decisions. I would be most grateful for lessons." She missed a step and trod upon his foot again. A throaty groan escaped her. "I'm utterly hopeless. A blind, increasing, three-legged cow has more finesse."

Her groan and his vivid thoughts of how conception occurred nearly undid Lucan.

Wait two or three weeks to marry?

No, blast and damn. Far, far too long. He'd see about a special license tomorrow.

The music ended, and she glanced around as if surprised she'd survived the dance without humiliating herself. She dipped into a curtsy. "Thank you, Your

Grace."

Lucan took her elbow, guiding her to her aunt and uncle while launching a series of dark glowers to deter young swains eager to intercept her before she was safely seated. "Propriety dictates I only dance with you twice. I beg you to honor me with the supper dance. Then I shall have the privilege of dining with you as well."

Surprised delight enlarged her pansy-like eyes.

"That would be wonderful. I would be uncomfortable eating with someone I didn't know." Color swept her high cheeks. "Not that I'm really acquainted with you, Your Grace. I'm comfortable around you, because you already know my secrets, and I don't have to worry that you'll accost me or press your suit."

Uh oh.

"You want to know another secret?" Mischief sparkled in her eyes, completely enchanting him.

God, please.

"I do, indeed." He wanted much more than to know her secret.

What would she do if he kissed her?

Right there in front of everyone?

He'd seal her fate tighter than a bottle of Scotch. She entranced him as no other woman ever had. Nonetheless, instinct told him she'd never forgive him for entrapping her.

"I've acquired freedom and power I never imagined I would have." Alexandra leaned into him and grinned, seemingly completely unaware her breast brushed his arm. "Despite my stepmother's prodding and my aunt's well-meaning designs, I have absolutely no intention of marrying anytime soon."

13

Swallowing her last bite of toast, Alexa patted her mouth with her serviette then scooted her chair back.

Sir Pugsley pawed her slipper.

Little beggar.

She slipped the dog a piece of egg, which he noisily gulped down. Sitting on his haunches, the pug eyed the table.

"No more. You're too fat as it is."

Golden sunlight filtered through the lace curtains, patterning the table and floors like giant, saffron doilies. Her jonquil gingham gown matched her sunny disposition this morning.

She hadn't botched the ball.

That alone called for a celebration, and the day had dawned warm and temperate for October too. "It's such a mild morning, I believe I shall walk to the Temple of the Muses."

The bookstore had caught her attention during several outings, but her dervish of an aunt—bustling Alexa to one fitting or social engagement or another—

insisted they'd no time to stop.

Uncle Hugo peered above his newspaper. "Take Jules and Bindy with you. He's a strapping fellow and can carry your books as well as protect you. She's a chatterbox, but she'll lend propriety since Katrina is abed yet."

"Of course, Uncle." Alexa would take the entire staff wearing nothing but their undergarments if it meant escaping the house this glorious morn.

Mornings had always been her favorite time of day, but she hadn't had a bit of time, let alone an entire morning, to herself since her aunt had descended on Craiglocky like dirt in a dust storm. Accustomed to hours of solitariness, weeks of constant company proved wearing, no matter how much Alexa adored her new family.

A prisoner claimed more freedom.

Nor had she indulged in a rigorous walk either, something she'd done habitually as a traveller. A wonder the *ton's* ladies weren't plump as partridges from lack of physical exertion and the many sweets they nibbled.

"Please return by eleven, dear, won't you?" Aunt Bridget, a crisp invitation in her hand, paused in sorting her correspondence. "From the plethora of bouquets arriving for you and Katrina, I expect a crowd of callers today."

Several gentlemen introduced to her at the ball had presumed to send posies, poems, and sonnets, some so silly, Alexa hadn't been able to finish reading them for fear of bursting out laughing.

Eyes the shade of grape jelly, indeed. Might as well say teeth or skin as white as chalk or hair as black as soot.

Apparently, a fortune paved the way to forgiving an heiress her unorthodox upbringing, at least where the males were concerned.

If she held the title that the Needhams adamantly maintained rightfully belonged to her. It would be interesting to see what happened to her beaux's benevolence if her imprisonment at Dounnich house became known, or if she didn't possess a fortune after all.

The arrival of Viscount Renishaw's enormous bouquet came as a complete surprise, however. Perhaps, he meant to make amends for his boorish behavior last evening. Odd, considering the card accompanying his flowers didn't mention regrets or hint at an apology. Perchance he wished to express his remorse in person.

Jules entered, bearing another armful of blossoms. "More flowers for Miss Needham. Where shall I put them, ma'am?"

Aunt Bridget glanced up from her letter. "Anywhere in the garden salon or the drawing room will do."

The Duke of Harcourt hadn't sent flowers.

No shock there, yet Alexa's heart twinged the tiniest bit. She'd counted him as a friend, an ally, a haven from this unfamiliar world into which she'd been cast.

Not that she considered his impudent request for a kiss at Dounnich House acceptable. Or that the velvety touch of his lips upon hers haunted her still—causing her to yearn for a real kiss from his perfect mouth while wrapped in his sinewy arms.

But at least she knew he'd found *her* attractive and not the fortune attached to her position. He made her feel safe, was easy to talk to, and knew her history before she'd acquired her new station—one she didn't care for, truth to tell.

She didn't want to abide by *le beau monde's* stringent rules, nor did she have the makings of a *tonnish* lady. Frankly, she disliked most of what she'd seen in London thus far and couldn't wait to escape to the Highlands.

Last night, the duke had gone from an engaging, easygoing companion to a brooding, aloof nobleman, and she hadn't a fool's notion why. Mayhap she'd tramped upon his toes one too many times, or her conversation hadn't been witty or flirtatious enough. Batting her eyelashes, bowing her mouth into coy pouts, or giggling like a featherbrained nincompoop, she simply couldn't manage.

Och, well, whit's fur ye'll no' go past ye.

What's meant to happen will happen.

The duke had become contemplative after their first dance. While they dined, she kept catching him staring at her, as if trying to see inside her head and read her thoughts. He'd left shortly after supper ended.

Alexa bussed her aunt's cheek. "I told you not to get your hopes up. I'm not interested in being courted."

Particularly not by a dandy who spends more time preening than a muster of peacocks.

She found vain women difficult enough to stomach,

but strutting coxcombs? Most repugnant. Long ago, she'd learned vanity didn't often follow the path of logic, and people overly concerned with their appearance were often self-centered and unreasonable.

"Tish tosh. Every young woman is interested in being wooed." Aunt Bridget flapped the note she held, and a speculative glint entered her amused gaze. "I wonder if you'd protest as much if a certain handsome duke paid a call or sent posies round?"

Uncle Hugo lowered his paper a fraction. "Rumor has it Harcourt's in the market for a wife."

Alexa sent him a startled glance. His grace hadn't indicated any such thing to her. "Are you sure? He didn't seem particularly attentive to anyone last evening."

That she'd noticed gave her another start.

Uncle Hugo nodded, humor twinkling in the gaze he centered on her. "I know it's crass to mention it, but there's a bet at White's he'll wed by Yuletide. Something to do with his mother's poor health. Don't put much faith in that twaddle myself, but I know there are those who do."

"Indeed?" Teacup to her lips, Aunt Bridget eyed her husband, and he winked at her. She flicked Alexa a speculative look. "The young lady who snares his grace will be most fortunate."

"He's handsome and intelligent. A born leader, well-respected in the House of Lords." Uncle folded the paper, then set it aside. He rested his elbows atop the table, forming his fingertips into a steeple. "Honest too, from what I've gleaned from my business associations with him."

And he's kind, witty, and has the most delicious mouth.

"He dances divinely, plus the man's a Corinthian and top sawyer. Few men seat a horse or drive a team as well as the Duke of Harcourt." Aunt Bridget clasped her hands to her chest theatrically.

Alexa laughed and shook her head. "Cease, you two. I'm not in the market for a husband, and trust me, his grace wouldn't consider a woman who doesn't know which fork to use, let alone one who prefers eating outdoors rather than at a table, as I told him last night."

Eyes bulging, Aunt Bridget gagged on her tea. Coughing and sputtering, she managed, "You…you actually told him *that*?"

Grinning naughtily, Alexa nodded.

Her aunt's eyelashes fluttered closed, and her lips moved silently.

Counting or praying?

She cracked an eye open. "Dare I ask what else you told the duke?"

"That I bathed naked in streams—"

"Oh, dear Lord." Aunt Bridget slouched in her seat, fanning herself with the letter.

"—ate with my fingers and slept in a tent. And liked it too." Alexa shuddered and rubbed her arms. "Not the bathing part. I about froze my—"

"Ahem." Uncle Hugo rustled his newspaper. The tips of his ears had gone crimson as beets. He smoothed both sides of his graying mustache, probably to cover his ruddy cheeks.

Alexa couldn't prevent her tickled smile. She'd never seen Uncle disconcerted before. The man was as stoic as a brick.

Red as one too, at the moment.

An icy creek *did* wreak havoc on one's nether regions and nipples.

Aunt Bridget coughed into her serviette, her shoulders quaking. "What I wouldn't give to have seen the duke's face."

"I oughtn't to have mentioned the bathing." Alexa chuckled in remembrance. "Most unacceptable, to be sure, but the man is self-possessed. He didn't so much as twitch."

"You might be surprised what a man of Harcourt's caliber would find acceptable for his duchess. He's not a shallow man, Alexa, and he's known for his devotion to his family." Uncle Hugo's words contained the faintest hint of censure.

"I meant no disrespect, Uncle." Even though she might very well be named a baroness, she honestly had no aspirations to marry a peer, especially a title as elevated as a duke. The idea quite alarmed her. The expectations and duties of a noblewoman were beyond her knowledge and scope of experience. When she married, it would be to an unassuming man with unpretentious ways.

"Is there anything you have need of while I'm out?" She offered a bright smile by way of apology. He shook his head, so she turned her attention to her aunt. "Aunt Bridget?"

"No, dear. Go along now." Her aunt cracked the

seal on another letter. "Remember, eleven o'clock. You'll need time to change and freshen up."

Tempted to salute, Alexa grinned instead. "I promise. Eleven straight up."

"Oh, Alexa, wait. This is from Craiglocky." Aunt Bridget made a staying motion with her hand as she quickly perused the letter. "Seonaid will be here by Friday, in time for the Lumberton's *soirée*. Oh, that's a grand affair." Beaming, she turned to Uncle Hugo. "Tell her, dear. The *soirée* is always well-attended and promises to be highly entertaining."

Uncle responded with a noncommittal grunt and a rustling of the newspaper he'd buried his nose in once more.

"I shall have the room next to yours prepared, Alexa." Aunt Bridget refolded the letter.

Alexa hugged her. "Thank you. For everything."

Aunt Bridget cupped both sides of Alexa's face and gave her cheeks a little squeeze. "You are welcome, darling."

Five minutes later, Alexa ran down the front stoop, her raspberry hued redingote held a mite too high to be proper. A duchess would never permit her ankle to show or run down the stairs, for that matter.

Followed by the burly footman and cheerful maid, Alexa whistled as she strode along, intent on purchasing several volumes at the bookstore. Duchesses didn't whistle or stride either. They took dainty, mincing steps. She let loose a long, warbling trill, earning her several curious looks and a chuckle from Jules.

If she had time, she planned to inquire about

purchasing a violin and paying a visit to Floris's to select combs for Aunt Bridget, Katrina, and Seonaid. She wasn't sure how far the perfumery lay from the bookstore, however.

Marching past a milliner's, she pulled a face at the bonnets displayed in the window. Some poor peafowl must've sacrificed its entire plumage for the blue atrocity the size of a small skiff. Why would anyone wear something so preposterous? Almost as heinous as the garish puce and pea-green parasol Minerva toted the other day when she called to snoop about Alexa's nuptial plans.

Outside the Temple of the Muses, practically pressing her nose against the windowpane in her excitement, Alexa paused to admire the impressive array of books within. Choosing three or four amongst the mass of volumes could take several wonderful hours.

"I say, Miss Atterberry, is that you?" A lanky gentleman whose name she couldn't recollect hurried her way.

She did recall he'd talked, at length, about various poisonous floras native to England. His detailed descriptions of the consequences of such poisonings quite put her off her food.

His hat slid frontward until it rested on his nose, but he didn't lessen his pace, just held the brim in place as he scurried forward. "Beg your pardon for shouting. Did you receive my flowers? I thought the irises matched your lovely eyes."

Shoving his hat back into place, he sketched a bow, so eager to please, he reminded her of Uncle Hugo's pug. Alexa dipped into a curtsy.

Irises. Irises. Who sent irises?

Ah, Mr. Mortimer, the amateur botanist-biologist. He quite enjoyed dissecting things. Rather revolting. "Yes, Mr. Mortimer. They are lovely and one of my favorite blooms."

"Dare I hope you'll be receiving visitors today?" He beamed broadly, his ears scooting up the sides of his narrow face, as if she'd granted him a duchy.

"I believe Aunt Bridget is expecting a houseful." Alexa's bonnet's ribbon flitted across her lips. She brushed it aside, and as she did so, her attention fell on Viscount Renishaw conversing with a couple of coarsely attired men across the street.

That was all she needed—for him to see her and make a pest of himself. "I must be off. I've errands to complete if I'm to return home on time. I shall see you later."

Mr. Mortimer's face fell. "Ah, yes, but of course." He doffed his hat and bowed again. "I quite look forward to chatting with you."

With a smile and a wave, she escaped into the bookstore's interior, fully aware he watched her bum until the door swung shut. Why were men so fascinated with women's behinds? She'd never once caught a woman ogling a man's posterior.

She grinned.

Well, perhaps not so brazenly.

Alexa dashed to a pillar, and from behind its protection, scanned the street. Mr. Mortimer paused to chat with Viscount Renishaw. Pray God he didn't mention he'd met her. The viscount rubbed her the wrong way. There was something peculiar about the man.

Drawing in a deep breath, she savored the aroma of leather, ink, parchment, and a myriad of other smells she couldn't quite identify, but which delighted her nose. The store hummed with patrons, clerks, and a few children.

Where to start?

Perhaps less congestion occurred in the upper levels. She didn't mind crowds, *per se*, but she coveted this fleeting time by herself and didn't want to run into a new acquaintance and have to waste precious minutes on innocuous small talk.

This was her first excursion into a bookstore, and she quite intended to savor every moment.

"Bindy, you and Jules may wait there for me." Indicating a nearby seat, Alexa grinned and rocked onto her heels in excitement. "I'm afraid I may be awhile. I've never seen this many books."

"Thank you, miss." After sinking onto the bench, Bindy lifted a foot. "I'm afeared I have a blister on my heel."

Contriteness lanced Alexa. The short, portly maid had struggled to keep up. "How thoughtless of me. We shall take a hackney home. Jules, can you procure one for us?"

"Certainly, miss." He sat beside Bindy, exchanging a nod with another liveried footman. "I shall make the arrangements for a hackney and find you in a few minutes to see if you have any books for me to carry."

As if I cannot carry a few volumes myself.

"Give me at least a half an hour, Jules." If only Alexa dared remove her bonnet. The wide brim proved useful in keeping the sun from her face but obstructed her view of anything not directly in front of her. "I don't want to rush."

"I understand, but Mr. Needham was most clear. I am to be watchful and keep you from harm. I even hesitate to step outside to hail a hired carriage. There's riffraff about today." Jules scowled at a young buck examining Alexa with his quizzing glass.

The man pivoted and plowed straight into a post, knocking his hat onto the floor and likely blackening his eye.

A giggle escaped Alexa as she patted her reticule containing her knife. "I'm quite prepared for, shall we say, unwanted company. I was raised as a gypsy, you know."

"*Aye*, I'd like to see that, I would." Jules grinned and folded his arms. "Thirty minutes, then."

Bindy cricked her neck, gawking at the upper shelves. "Blimey, I ain't never seen so many books afore. Almost makes me wish I knew hows to read."

"I cannot promise to hasten." With a hurried wave, Alexa strode to the stairs. She decided against the next gallery she ascended as it too held a good number of customers perusing the laden shelves, or clustered in intimate groups, animatedly conversing.

Fewer patrons frequented the third floor with its shabbier, yet altogether fascinating contents. Piles of books lay stacked, haphazardly, amongst the shelving.

Breath suspended, she tiptoed to an overflowing, dusty shelf of what must've been used books.

So much the better.

Others had enjoyed hours of solace turning the worn pages. Who had the people been, and what were their lives like, that they chose these particular books to pass the time with? Wouldn't it be grand if the pages talked and shared the secrets they'd witnessed? What a marvel that would be.

Reaching for a volume, she paused. Her white gloves were sure to become soiled, and they cost her dearly. Giving a covert glance around, she stripped them off.

Finally, after much indecision, she selected three novels, then searched for something a little less frivolous.

The Mirror of the Graces snagged her attention.

Couldn't hurt to educate herself about proper comportment, and if the contents proved too absurd, she might have a good chuckle at least. Now, where to put her books that didn't boast a thick layer of dust so she might don her gloves again?

A windowsill beckoned, and she maneuvered a path between lopsided book piles to the grungy panes. The street and sidewalks below bustled with mid-morning activities and those eager to enjoy the pleasant day.

Bending, she blew away the worst of the dust which, unfortunately, caused a fit of sneezing. Alexa set the books down, her gloves atop them, before searching her reticule for a kerchief.

"What a surprise to learn *you read, Miss* Atterberry."

14

One hand within her bag, Alexa spun around.

Lord Renishaw leaned against a shelf, his beady-eyed gaze raking her, toe to top. Drat, Mr. Mortimer. The viscount straightened and blocked the aisle, a predatory grin slanting his mouth. Except for an azure and black patterned waistcoat, he wore gray again.

His dual insult didn't escape her.

"Do *you* actually intend to read them, or are they for show? Or for the Needhams, perchance?" He pointed at her books. "I wasn't aware gypsies knew how to read, although, I've heard tell of certain other unusual *skills* they possess."

Repulsive rat.

She'd like to show him precisely what a gypsy knew how to do, the pompous boor. Instead, she gathered her belongings, leaving off her gloves. "I was headed below."

He didn't budge, and the three whispering matrons—in addition to a stoop-shouldered, elderly gentleman and a sophisticated dame on the room's other side—paid them no notice.

Alexa narrowed her eyes upon recognizing The Three Un-Muses who'd given her the cut last night.

No help from their quarter.

She ought to turn round and leave in the other direction, but if she did, she'd no longer be visible to the patrons, and instinct told her the viscount would follow. She didn't want to be caught in a dark corner, alone, with him.

No, better and safer to face him here, even if her knees did quake beneath her skirts. Memories of her treatment with the Blackhalls resurfaced, and familiar dread choked her, strangling her breathing and crushing her pulse.

She recognized the look in Renishaw's eyes. Her abuse, and the harrowing experience at the Scots' hands, had left her with a lingering leeriness of men. Intimidation brought knaves like him perverse enjoyment, and she'd learned early on at Dounnich House to mask her fright. Fear had fed her tormentors' warped sensibilities.

Forcing calm to her features, she inhaled a bracing breath while strategically placing her open reticule atop her book stack. The blade's handle, easily accessible beneath her gloves, bolstered her confidence, and Alexa met Renishaw's gaze square on.

Burying her dagger in him would be as easy as slicing bread. "Please move aside. I wish to pass, my lord."

"Why the rush? We didn't have an opportunity to become better acquainted last evening." His oily gaze sank to her breasts, and he flicked his tongue out to lick his lower lip.

Perhaps viper better described him.

A fat hog sought a butcher's company more eagerly than she desired to further her association with Lord Renishaw. His eyes bespoke a depth of evil equivalent to her abductors. He advanced a few steps, but she stiffened her quaking knees and stood her ground. She wouldn't give him the satisfaction of knowing he jarred her.

"I'd hoped to ask you to take a drive with me in Hyde Park this afternoon. How providential you are here now." His mouth eased into a disturbing smile. "My carriage is outside. I'd be delighted to see you home. I'm sure your uncle would frown upon you trotting about London unescorted."

The man was daft as a drunken troll.

First, he insulted her and then had the effrontery to ask her to take an unchaperoned drive with him?

When chickens sang opera.

In Italian.

And how did he know she hadn't come by carriage?

Mr. Mortimer again?

"My escorts wait below, and I'm not returning home yet. Thank you for your concern and kind offer." She wanted to gag on her last insincere words.

"Well, at least allow me to accompany you to your next destination." He wrapped his hand around her arm, none too gently, and tugged her closer. "Your uncle would like us to become better acquainted. As would I."

I'll bet you would.

"Release me, this instant." She pulled against his

grip. Her heart galloping, Alexa slid her hand beneath her gloves. "Harrison Peterson is not my uncle."

Leering, Renishaw grunted a dismissive sound. "Come now, Alexandra. It seems Fate has favored us with this chance meeting as I should very much like to court you."

Her breakfast fought to make a violent reappearance. Lips pursed in revulsion, she swallowed past the bile burning her throat.

Had it been Renishaw who offered for her hand?

Did poor, smitten Shona know?

Ogling her breasts, he blathered on. "Show me some favor, and I'm sure I can convince Harrison not to press charges against the Scottish gypsies who abducted you."

What?

Bring charges against the tinkers?

She'd see about that. Wait until Alexa saw Harrison Peterson again. His ears would blister and ring for a week when she finished setting him straight, the scheming worm.

"As we haven't been formally introduced, this conversation is wholly inappropriate, my lord. And as such, requesting to court me, equally so."

The viscount sidled nearer and trailed his finger over her cheek. "I would enjoy taming you—"

Alexa now understood what it meant to have one's skin crawl. To avoid his caress, hers practically leaped from her skull and scampered beneath a shelf to cuddle with the dust bunnies.

Jerking her face away, she whisked her blade from

its hiding place. Dagger tip pressed to his manhood, Alexa yanked her arm free of his grasp. "I haven't given you leave to touch me or use my given name."

A greenish-gray pallor suffused his face, and his eyes narrowed to vengeful slits.

"I can unman you before you open your mouth. So, I suggest you keep it sealed and listen to me unless you want me to sever your ballocks quicker than plums nipped from a branch." She didn't dare take her gaze from him to see if anyone took note of their discord.

"What Harrison Peterson wants is of no account to me. I make my own decisions, and I want you to stay away from me. *Very* far away. I'd rather have a rotting corpse court me. Is that clear?"

For emphasis, she gave her knife a jabbing twist.

"Why you little, gypsy bitch." He raised his hand to slap her, and she pressed her blade harder into his groin. He winced, and a white line ringed his mouth. "You wouldn't dare."

She curved her mouth into an exaggerated, sweet smile. "Try me."

"I—" He froze, utter loathing settling upon his features.

A large, firm hand suddenly gripped her elbow.

She jumped and looked behind her, nearly dropping her dagger.

The Duke of Harcourt stood there, jaw rigid and fuming gaze darkened to ebony.

Relief flooded her, and Alexa practically sagged against him.

"Lady Atterberry has made her position abundantly

clear, Renishaw. Dare to touch her again, and I'll run you through."

Jules came tearing around the shelving's other end. His troubled gaze shifted between her and the viscount. "Are you in need of assistance, miss?"

Two heroes to her rescue.

Hands fisted, Jules and the duke looked ready to throttle Renishaw, which she wouldn't mind in the least. It might teach the beef-wit some manners.

The viscount abruptly developed the good sense to retreat a few paces, and the duke bent his neck and whispered in her ear. "Smile and subtly put the knife away. We've drawn unwanted attention."

Forcing a grimly congenial smile, Alexa hid the blade in her skirts as she deftly lowered her reticule and tried to ignore the delicious frisson his warm breath caused.

The duke's long fingers closed atop hers, and in an instant, he slid the knife from her palm and then dropped the dagger into her bag. Her skin tingled where he'd touched her.

The line of Lord Renishaw's mouth flattened further. "A little premature, calling her Lady Atterberry, Harcourt. Surely, you're aware both daughters inherit until the Committee of Privileges settles in favor of one. Usually, the one who petitions, which isn't always the heir presumptive."

The chinwags' full attention fell on them. Their eyes buggy and ears flapping like giant windmills, the intrigued threesome sidled closer.

Alexa clenched her teeth against an oath.

"This is hardly the place for such a discussion, and the subject is none of *your* affair." Reassurance in his eyes, the duke gave Alexa a closed-lip smile as he turned her to leave, effectively dismissing the viscount. "Are you ready to make your purchases?"

"Yes, quite." Clasping her bag and gloves, she passed her books to the footman. "Thank you, Jules."

Broad-shouldered and thick-chested, Jules boasted a good eight inches on the scrawnier viscount. A man with more sense would have heeded the glowering footman.

Renishaw stomped forward a couple of paces.

Idiot.

"A petition to have the abeyant peerage terminated in Shona's favor was submitted within days of receiving word this"—he jabbed a finger at Alexa—"interloper lived."

"I'm quite aware of that particular, Lord Renishaw." She would eat worms before she revealed Shona's bastardy to these lickspittles. She scrutinized him from beneath her lashes.

Why the facade of wanting to court me and then this hostile about-face?

Is the man dimwitted?

"Interloper?" A dame gasped dramatically, then raised her voice. "She's not the Atterberry heiress? She's a... *fraud?*"

Rather than sounding surprised, the woman's shrill voice rang with glee.

Other patrons turned to peer in their direction.

Alexa hid her dismay.

This didn't portend well.

"I suspected something wasn't right the moment I laid eyes on her," another matron scoffed, raising her humped nose skyward. "That hair and accent give her common breeding away."

Better they think that, no matter how inaccurate, than know of Shona's illegitimacy.

"Those Needhams have always been upstarts—mushrooms—trying to shove their way into Polite Society." The third woman sniffed disdainfully and pursed her lips as if she'd tasted something foul. "They smell of the *shop*."

She spat the last word as if ridding her tongue of excrement.

Alexa refused to look in the dames' direction. Their opinions meant nothing, the irksome cackling of eggless, old hens, but that they dare speak of her aunt and uncle…

Oh, she longed to give them a piece of her mind, the *seanchas ban-draoidh,* gossiping witches. If it wouldn't bring more censure to her family, she'd speak her piece and be done with the biddies, once and for all.

"Who do you think the committee will support? The daughter who's lived a respectable life as a peeress for years, or one raised in the wilds of Scotland with the scruples of a gypsy?" A gloating smile wreathed the viscount's face as he sliced the gawking women a sideways glance. "Tell me, exactly how long did those rogue Scots hold you captive, *unchaperoned,* Miss Atterberry?"

~*~

Hell.

"That's outside the bounds, Renishaw. Hold your filthy tongue." Lucan surged forward reflexively before checking himself. Self-control wrestled with revenge, each intent on pummeling the other. One thing kept Lucan from laying Renishaw flat, then and there—Alexandra's turbulent violet eyes and the alarm flitting across her face before she schooled her features into a composed mask.

The three ogling bystanders played a part in his restraint as well. Each one a vicious she-cat, today they bared their pointed teeth and freshly sharpened claws.

"I cannot wait to see how you explain that savory abduction tidbit." Laughing snidely, Renishaw sketched a mocking bow and took his leave, having wreaked the havoc he intended.

As soon as he'd deposited Alexandra at home, Lucan would direct Darley to investigate the connection between Peterson and Renishaw. His man of business generally proved quite adept at unearthing unpleasant scraps people preferred to remain concealed.

Hound's teeth.

Darley hadn't yet returned from checking on Lucan's silk mill in Derbyshire. Well then, he'd arrange a meeting at White's with Bretheridge and Warrick and see what they knew. Besides, Lucan wanted to view the bet Renishaw had placed.

Had the cur even attempted to couch the terms to protect Jeremy's identity?

Perhaps Lucan could persuade someone to blacken out the bet. Not bloody likely, but worth a try. He turned to the footman. "Have Miss Atterberry's books charged to my account and have my carriage brought around to the store's front. You and Bindy wait inside the vehicle, please."

Earlier, he'd recognized Jules as a Needham servant, and Lucan had hoped to find Alexandra within the bookstore. It never occurred to him to question whether she could read or write.

Happening upon her applying a knife to Renishaw's balls came as a delightful shock. Lucan fought an internal battle whether to step in or let her finish the job, except the notorious tattlemongers—the Hinton sisters—had caught wind something was afoot.

Those busybodies possessed noses more superior for detecting potentially scandal-worthy morsels than hounds tracking a fresh fox trail. Better them than Lady Clutterbuck, however. That raucous crow had a penchant for viciousness that did Satan proud.

Then, Renishaw dared to raise his hand to Alexandra, and in public too. The bloody sot knew no bounds. If slaying the bastard on the spot were permissible, Lucan would have done, with relish. His blood boiled, and reason flew in the face of rage when he'd threatened to run the cur through—his vow to Mother be damned.

Some things took precedence over honor and promises, no matter how well-intended.

"Splendid morning, isn't it, ladies?" Doffing his hat, he elevated a questioning brow at the gaping, stocky threesome and flashed his most disarming smile. "Has your excursion been successful?"

Lucan peered expressly at their empty hands. He didn't refer to their reading choices, but the rumor mill fodder they fervently gathered wherever they descended like harpies from hell.

Huffing their displeasure, they scurried from the gallery, whispering furiously the whole while. By evening, all London would know an embellished version of what had transpired.

Probably some outrageousness along the lines of Alexandra being the bastard daughter of a diseased Whitechapel doxie, as well Alexandra willingly sharing her favors with the Scottish barbarians who abducted her.

After dancing nude as a nymph.

On a tabletop.

In a brothel.

Oh, and foxed-to-the-gills, Renishaw and Lucan had engaged in a drunken public display of fisticuffs. In their shirt sleeves and stockings, no less.

A few moments later, Lucan handed an admirably poised Alexandra into his carriage. Seemingly unaffected, his petite gypsy possessed a great deal of gumption, yet he couldn't help but wonder what went on inside her pretty head.

She hesitated and then slid onto the unoccupied seat where sprigs of heather lay wrapped in paper and tied with a wide purple ribbon. Upon spying the flowers, her gaze swerved to him, and a sweet smile curved her kissable lips. Her unpretentiousness endeared her to him all the more.

Too bad, he had instructed the servants to ride with

them. He might've enticed a kiss of gratitude from her if they'd been alone. Now, however, he would do well to not erupt into a cold sweat as he endured their four bodies crammed into the coach and knocked knees with Jules.

What possessed him to invite the footman and maid?

Ah, blasted propriety.

He sucked in a labored breath and eyed the window. Wouldn't look respectable, he supposed, poking his head out the window during the short jaunt to the Needhams' as he had the last leg from Scotland.

After giving the driver directions, Lucan lifted the bouquet and settled into the remaining seat. Fully aware of Jules's and the maid's curious gazes, he handed the spray to Alexandra. "I had a devil of a time finding heather in London, I'll tell you."

Last night, she had mentioned she missed the Highland's heather, so this morning, he and three footmen turned London inside-out searching for the stuff. He'd found the elusive plant at a perfumery and spent a tidy sum convincing the alchemist to depart with the sprigs.

"Thank you." She pressed her face to the blossoms and inhaled. A shadow darkened the contours of her face for a fleeting instant. "They smell of Scotland."

"The color matches yer eyes." The perky maid grinned, oblivious to what transpired in the bookstore. She giggled. "That's what Lord Mortimer said too. The flowers he sent matched yer eyes, just like the duke's do."

"Mortimer sent flowers?"

Surprise launched Lucan's eyebrows high onto his forehead. "Not like the chap at all. He prefers dissecting botanical specimens." Momentarily taken aback, Lucan folded his arms and relaxed against the seat. That others vied for Alexandra's hand didn't sit well. He'd not made his intentions clear enough last night, it would seem. "I suppose hothouse treasures and romantic odes have inundated the Needham household today."

"Yes, though Katrina received more than I, and truthfully, some prose was a bit off-putting." She laid the bouquet in her lap and raised her fine eyebrows. Pointing to her eyes, she fluttered her lashes coyly. "Grape jelly."

Lucan and the servants laughed before he nodded at the footman. "I meant to tell you, Jules. That was well done of you in the bookstore."

"I regret I did not arrive sooner." The footman slanted a guarded glance to Bindy.

Alexandra sniffed the heather once more. "Do not blame yourself. I told you to give me time to shop."

"Did somethin' happen?" Confusion settled over Bindy's round face, and she wrinkled her bud of a nose. "I should've stayed at yer side, miss. I'm sorry. Me blister wasn't bad—"

"Never think it." Alexandra waved her apology aside and shook her head. A raven tendril slipped from beneath the bonnet's confines and teased her cheek.

Envy seared Lucan that the wisp was granted the pleasure denied him.

"I found some delightful books." Alexandra patted

the tomes. "And the duke and Jules happened upon me as I prepared to make my purchases."

The carriage jerked to a halt before a stately, yet tasteful house. No one peered from behind curtains to see who'd arrived.

He touched her arm. "Might I have a word with you?"

Alexandra cocked her head, again reminding him of an inquisitive kitten.

What he wouldn't give to have her beneath him, purring from his touch. He crossed his legs to hide the embarrassing bulge his stray thoughts produced.

"Certainly. Jules, please tell my aunt I shall be in momentarily." She passed the heather to her maid. "Put these in a vase in my chamber right away, will you? I shouldn't want them to dry out yet. Nip a little off the bottoms first. They'll stay fresher longer."

Jules made quick work of exiting the conveyance and then handing Bindy down. "Shall I leave the door open, miss?"

Commendable chap, taking his chaperonage so seriously.

"I'd prefer it closed." A blatant lie, given Lucan's dislike of enclosed spaces, but he required a private word with Alexandra. He shot a glance at the uncovered windows. "We are clearly visible from the street, and we shall be but a moment. My outrider will stand beyond the door."

Jules shifted his attention to Alexandra. "Miss Atterberry?"

His willingness to defy a duke to protect his

mistress raised Lucan's estimation of the chap further. Might be the perfect fellow to take old Tibbs's place at Chattsworth.

"It's fine," she said. "We're as visible as a sandpiper's white rump."

Lucan bit the inside of his cheek.

White rump, indeed.

She turned to Lucan expectantly as the door latch clicked home. "We must be swift, however. I promised my aunt to complete my errands by eleven."

He flicked his watch open. "We've fifteen minutes."

Leaning frontward, he searched the landscape as he pocketed his timepiece. His back to the carriage, an outrider stood as sentinel. Lucan gathered Alexandra's hand in his, marveling at the fineness of her bones.

"Your Grace?"

She hadn't donned her gloves, and her fingers, browned from the sun and in places slightly work-roughened, curled into his grasp. She didn't attempt to pull away, but something more than guileless curiosity glinted in her lash-shadowed eyes. Her focus dropped to her hand clasped in his.

He gave her fingers a little squeeze and rubbed his gloved thumb across her palm. Did she tremble? "Alexandra, please forgive me for the abruptness and the inadequate location, but given today's unfortunate events, I think it best we marry without delay."

15

A tiny burble of laughter escaped Alexa as she withdrew her hand from the Duke of Harcourt's. To hide her discomfit, she laid her gloves atop one another, her lips bowed in amusement.

Not a man to mince words, was he?

Not a proposal really, just an announcement.

"*Marry*. Without delay? How about tomorrow?"

He opened his mouth, but she soldiered onward before he could speak.

"Heavens, why wait *that* long? This afternoon should suffice. I shall send a footman round to collect Uncle Hugo from the bank, and he can purchase a special license on his way home." Chuckling again, she tucked her gloves into her reticule. "My, but you do have an irregular sense of humor, Your Grace."

A proposal from him, even in jest, had never crossed her mind. Perhaps, he sought to put her at ease about the disagreeableness with Renishaw, which oddly enough, the duke's casual quip had accomplished.

She almost believed he felt compassion for her, cared about her honor, and what would happen to her when the disgrace of her captivity, looming like a storm-laden cloud, erupted and wreaked a tempest's chaos.

Alexa couldn't think of another man whose wit she enjoyed more. Or whose company she took such pleasure in. The duke felt like an old, familiar friend—easy to talk and listen to, and she acted herself around him, as she had with Rígán.

However, her gypsy beau—God rest his soul, for she long-since abandoned hope he still lived—hadn't caused her to obsess about his lips or set every pore to tingling with awareness.

Or make her wish—in the secret, most remote region of her mind—for something which couldn't be, something she daren't give a name to, so outlandish and improbable the fantasy.

Yes, the Duke of Harcourt was too attractive for her wellbeing—mind *and* body.

"We two, marry," Alexa muttered, grinning and pointing her attention to the carriage ceiling, her forefinger to her chin. "Now, wouldn't that be something to set the tongues flapping till next Season."

She could no more do a duchess title justice than the devil could encourage sinners to repent. True, she found Harcourt dashing and deucedly attractive, and if he weren't a duke, she might've considered his address.

Someday.

A union between them would be a complete disaster. A wholly, calamitous mismatch. They didn't want the same things from life.

She preferred an unobtrusive, modest existence.

Accustomed to position and privilege, as well as the

attention and whirlwind of activity his status mandated, he'd become resentful and embarrassed as she repeatedly bungled being a duchess. A lifetime of humiliation and an embittered husband did not make for a tolerable marriage, much less a happy one.

"*That* would give the tattlemongers something to bandy about. Preposterous." She formed a small *moue* with her mouth while she considered him from beneath the fan of her lashes. "However, Your Grace, I didn't take you for the type to make a May game of someone."

Astonishment registered on the duke's face, his smoky eyes widening in incredulity. "I suppose it's hard to believe, and I've quite blundered the suggestion. But I assure you, Alexandra—"

"Alexa, please. If you insist on addressing me by my given name. Although I'm sure, it's most improper."

Wasn't it?

Another bothersome rule to keep track of.

"Very well, Alexa. I am perfectly serious. I'm obligated to acquire a wife by Christmastide, and given Renishaw's ill-timed disclosure about your abduction, and the Hinton sisters' penchant for rumormongering, your reputation will be in tatters by week's end."

The outrider tossed a peek over his shoulder before facing frontward again.

Impatient?

Or had he heard part of their conversation?

Unfortunate if he had. Even the best of servants talked. She'd lay odds ten-to-one Jules and Bindy wasted no time warming the ears of anyone who would listen of Alexa's bookstore escapade.

"That horrid viscount and those spiteful tabbies can say what they please." Alexa shrugged, a spark of defiance causing her to narrow her eyes. "I wasn't unchaperoned, as you well know. Lala and György never left my sight. Not for a second."

"Be that as it may, I hardly think two young children constitute proper chaperonage. At least not in the *ton's* eyes. No one will believe nothing occurred, Kitten." The duke offered a gentle smile to temper his words.

Kitten? He called me Kitten?

He touched her knee, and a jolt spiraled to her hip, its disturbing warmth spreading outward. "Wasn't that why your aunt and uncle wanted the Blackhall business kept a secret?"

"Yes, but I have nothing to be ashamed of. I'll not hang my head, or cower, or hide in disgrace because barb-tongued busybodies spread false tales." Alexa jutted her chin defiantly. "And making a match to stop the tongues of chinwags spewing malicious claptrap, I shan't do either. I have a fortune at my disposal and have no need for a husband, *ever*, Your Grace."

Despite her bravado, a hint of uncertainty did gnaw. If Renishaw spoke the truth, she mightn't have a fortune at all. Her circumstance would change dramatically, for the worse, leaving her with few alternatives.

She needed to seek Uncle Hugo's guidance at once.

"Please, call me Lucan, or if that's too familiar, Harcourt." The duke folded his arms and scrutinized her. "You should know, I still intend to present my suit to Needham, and I'm confident he'll accept."

"Aren't you listening to me?" Twisting on the seat, she slapped her palm against her knee. Better that, than clobber him again. "I've no intention of marrying a stranger by Yuletide, especially a duke. I'd have to be mad or desperate, and I assure you, I am neither."

The outrider turned to look again, this time boldly staring into the carriage.

Brazen fellow.

She bobbed her head in the servant's direction. "Are all your retainers so forward?"

The duke cast his servant a contemplative glance and rubbed the bridge of his nose. "No. Warner was hired while I was in Scotland. It appears he's in need of some further instruction regarding his position."

Alexa needed to end this conversation and then prepare for the expected callers, as well as send word to Uncle Hugo that she must speak with him at once.

As well as brace myself for the repercussions of Renishaw's malicious chatter.

Just how had he learned of her time with the Blackhalls?

Bah, she hadn't spare minutes to ponder that disagreeableness.

Alexa lowered her voice, for once grateful the obnoxious bonnet hid most of her face. "My uncle can accept on my behalf until his hair falls out, but I am of age. I alone shall make the decisions that affect me for the rest of my life."

"Your intrepidness is admirable, Alexa."

In a silent challenge, she lifted her gaze to Lucan's. "I don't have a single doubt you can list dozens of eligible young women who'd be beyond thrilled to become your wife. Ask one of them to be the next Duchess of Harcourt. I don't know a thimble's worth about being a duchess. And, truthfully, I don't want to learn the poppycock the position requires."

The duke closed his eyes and chuckled, a delicious, melodious rumble caressing her senses and giving her the strangest urge to lay her head against his chest and listen to the vibration. A man's laugh shouldn't have such power.

"Actually, I do have a list—a frighteningly long, rather terrifying one, truth to tell. My mother and sister contrived it to assist me in my search." His smile turned charmingly sheepish, and her stomach toppled over. "However, the women listed—except for you—excite me as much as a leech bleeding me or the barber pulling a tooth."

The list included her?

His silver-gray gaze probed hers, besetting her with a fluttery sensation in her middle again. "It's *you* I want."

"And I'm sure you always get what you want, Your Grace."

The shrewishness of Alexa's tone scraped her nerves raw—not typical at all. But, by thunder, when he'd revealed he had a list with her name, her hackles rose, sharp and taut. "Are the ladies' attributes cataloged as well? Does the list contain a hierarchy noting which damsels make the best candidates for a duchess?"

Who did that?

Compiled a registry of potential wives, as if going

to market to buy a turnip or parsnip or a...*potato*? Although to be fair, the Little Season and the Season had always been a buyers' delight.

"Yes, to the attributes, but no, to the hierarchy." Laughter glinted in his eyes and shaded his words.

Alexa pinned him with her haughtiest look.

A duchess would know how to do so with practiced perfection.

He brazenly grinned in return.

What audacity.

Though spared the expectations and unpleasantness of Polite Society thus far, she shouldn't be astounded at the absurd activities of the *ton's* denizens. Nevertheless, she wasn't obligated to buy into the insanity, and neither had the Needhams. Not fully.

Alexa squared her shoulders and gathered her books, gaping askance at the servant half-turned in an attempt to eavesdrop on their conversation, blatant as a zebra's stripes. She coolly returned his perusal until he angled away once more.

"I don't always get what I want, Alexa, but in this, I must remain adamant." His eyes crinkling at the corners in displeasure, Lucan partially lowered the blind when the outrider dared peek at the carriage again. "Insufferable. Better change his ways, or I'm dismissing him without reference. I cannot tolerate meddlers."

"To prevent more scandal landing at my aunt and uncle's doorstep or ruining Katrina's chances of a good match, I've reconciled myself to leaving London." Alexa jerked her hand, indicating the neat row of houses lining the street. "I'm a person of humble beginnings and modest desires, and I never wanted this life to begin with."

When everything was said and done, she'd gained one family and lost another, traded a contented lifestyle for one completely foreign.

"Why are you in London, then?" He idly traced a path along his firm thigh, drawing her gaze to a portion of his anatomy she shouldn't ever notice.

Were all men as generous *there*?

For God's sake, Alexa, pry your gawking eyeballs from his loins.

And she'd fussed about men ogling her bum.

She dragged her errant gaze upward, scanning his lean form along the way, to find his attention fixed on her bosoms. What a salacious pair they made.

His gaze gravitated to her face. "I am heartily glad you are here, but I'm curious. Why did you agree to leave Scotland?"

Growing pensive, she fingered her beaded reticule.

"For everyone's sake, I was determined to make the best of what fate thrust upon me." She had little choice, but that was neither his concern nor business. "Now, it seems my tutelage and the efforts of my aunt have all been for naught. I'd best prepare myself to have everything come crashing down. That's easier handled more tactfully away from Town."

"Where will you go, and how will you live? Until the Committee of Privileges settles in your favor, you don't have the authority to do what you will with funds or properties, and I cannot see you living with your stepmother when Peterson resides there as well."

Lucan's nostrils flared, and he clenched his thigh. "You shouldn't trust the man. Not one iota."

"Rest assured, I do not. He makes my skin crawl."

Alexa hadn't trusted Harrison from the moment she met him. If Renishaw personified a rat, Harrison embodied a snake.

The duke uncrossed his preposterously long legs and shifted to look at her more fully. "Do you intend to return to the Highland travellers or Craiglocky?"

Sighing, Alexa sagged against the squabs, feeling more lost and alone than when Father abandoned her. "No, I cannot rejoin the gypsies. For reasons no one has explained, I've essentially been exiled."

The park-like setting visible through the far window in no way compared to the Highland moors' and crags' wild beauty. How long before she ceased yearning for their familiar sight? "I believe there's more to my childhood disappearance than I've been told."

She returned her attention to the commanding man, lounging wholly at ease, opposite her. "As for Craiglocky, I'm confident Laird McTavish would welcome me, but I'd be worse than a poor relation, living off his charity. I may have been raised as a gypsy, but I do have my pride if naught else."

Harcourt's molded lips bent the merest bit. "I imagine it's a mite hard to stomach, the forthcoming judgment and censure, and the choices you are being forced to make."

Alexa released a loud sound, somewhere between a snort and a laugh.

Oh, that's duchess-like.

Well, good.

Let the duke see just how unrefined and inadequate she was. "It would be if I cared a fig for what those pompous nitwits think. But even if I did, I wouldn't seek the pleasures of your arms and bed solely to keep their tongues from wagging."

16

*G*ood God.
Why did I say that?

Alexa could've bitten her errant tongue in half for betraying her.

Lucan's dark eyebrows swooped to his hairline, his mouth sliding into a devilishly sensual smile. "Oh? I confess to being curious. Why else would you seek the pleasures of my bed?"

Everything, from her breasts to her nether regions, contracted with a strange heat. "What I mean to say is, *no one* should be obliged to marry."

"How disappointing. I thought perhaps you'd been fantasizing about bedding me." He gave a wicked wink.

The carriage's interior had become suffocating, and Alexa no doubt glowed as red as hot coals from warmth and chagrin. She shifted, uncomfortably aware of the dampness beneath her arms. A fan would be lovely, but she hadn't thought she'd need one.

For a walk.

In the morning.

In October.

Stop your mental babbling and change the subject.

"Why do you have to wed by Christmas?"

"My mother's health is frail, her heart extremely weak." Real concern and affection tinged his deep voice. "She may not have long to live, and she begged me to procure a bride by the holiday." He shrugged. "I could not refuse her."

A gallant, if somewhat misplaced sense of honor—one which resulted in a lifetime of heartache if he rushed in making his choice. The matter was none of her affair, however. "I'm sorry to hear it. I wish you luck in your pursuit of a wife, and"—she braved looking straight into his unfathomable eyes—"I hope we might still be friends."

Alexa forced a congenial smile, not pleased at the notion he'd be wed in a few weeks. Stupid, that. She didn't want to marry Lucan, so why did the knowledge he'd soon wed another set her teeth on edge?

In truth, she scarcely knew the man.

"Most definitely, we shall remain the closet of friends, Alexa." The way he uttered her name, a verbal caress, tantalizing and poignant, caused another wave of dampness in the most humiliating of places—between her legs.

Only he had the disturbing ability to turn her into a soggy wretch.

His expression amused but determined, the duke raised her hand to his mouth, and unblinkingly meeting her gaze, brushed his lips across her knuckles. "You see, I'm not willing to take no for an answer just yet, and you readily admit you have few alternatives but to marry."

Her stomach tumbled end-over-end, and she pressed her other hand to her cavorting middle. The ruddy man didn't know when to concede defeat, did he?

"Bah, you're hopeless. I am not marrying you, Your Grace. Please do let the matter go."

Lucan winked and released her. "Well then, if you refuse to discuss marriage, *at present*, perhaps I may persuade you to allow me to escort you to the theater tomorrow?"

He settled in his seat once more. Surely, he realized the longer they remained in the carriage, the more risqué it appeared.

"I'm not sure…" Alexa must go inside.

"The Needhams do plan on attending the theater. One of my footmen heard it from Wickershams' footman. He was told by his cousin, the Potteridges' maid—she is to marry the Flavelles' driver…" He scratched his chin and scrunched his nose. "Or was it the Flavelles' maid who is the cousin to Wickershams' footman, who told—"

"Yes, yes. Do stop prattling." Alexa couldn't restrain her giggle. Absurd man. "I shall go with you if only to make you hush your litany of drivel. Though how you're to pursue eligible misses with me on your arm remains to be seen."

Soberness replaced Lucan's jovial countenance. "Alexa, I shan't have you battered by idle tongues. My position affords me power and influence. Few will dare whisper of today's occurrence in my presence. I have persuasive friends who, at my behest, will not hesitate to rally round you as well."

He meant to protect her?

To champion her?

Warmth blossomed in the vicinity of her heart.

He sent a contemplative glance to the street. "The sooner you foray into the viper's nest, the quicker the claptrap can be quashed."

Appreciation misted her eyes and formed a lump in her throat. "Thank you. I fretted about the evening, but it's my first venture to the theater, and I'm eagerly anticipating the performance."

"It's settled then. You and the Needhams shall sit in my box." Once again, humor lit his unusual eyes as his mouth made its familiar upward curve.

"I must be off. Thank you again." Alexa scooted across the seat, prepared to open the door, but the outrider did so before she touched the handle. Almost as if he'd been listening. At his impudence, she contrived her severest look and hopped from the conveyance.

Lucan laughed. "Ought to call you a rabbit or a kangaroo."

What the devil was a kangaroo?

Must be something that hopped or jumped about.

Botheration.

Ladies—*duchesses*—did not spring from carriages like frogs.

"I would have helped you alight, miss." The outrider dropped his impertinent gaze as another carriage lurched to a stop behind theirs.

She turned to the interior as much to thank Lucan as to get one more glimpse of him. Her craving for his presence surpassed an opium abuser's need for their pills or laudanum. "Thank you for the heather. It means a great deal to me and reminds me of home. Will you…?"

Alexa glanced away, unsure of a sudden.

Asking him to call today was outside the bounds. She'd refused his proposal, twice in less than fifteen minutes, but he *was* taking her to the theater tomorrow evening.

Upon spying Minerva—striking in an obviously new burgundy and black striped traveling costume—and her usual entourage assembled on the sidewalk, Alexa groaned inwardly.

What now?

Harrison wore his habitual gloating expression, and Shona sported red-rimmed eyes, blotchy cheeks, and an ill-fitting saffron gown that added to the sallowness of her woebegone countenance and made her appear an overripe mango.

"I shall call this afternoon, Alexa, rest assured. I have some important business to attend to first." The duke inclined his head and pulled the door shut, an enigmatic smile teasing his lips. His gaze skimmed the new arrivals, narrowing for a flash before he thumped the ceiling. "Until tonight."

He winked and gave a jaunty wave as the carriage lurched ahead.

Lucan's cocksureness ought to irritate her, but Alexa enjoyed crossing words with him, and the man seemed a jovial sort. And handsome. Too blasted handsome for his own good.

And mine.

Knowing full well she'd have to endure a strained conversation with her stepmother once inside, Alexa closed her eyes for an instant and silently prayed for a miraculous reprieve.

Seonaid's early arrival. Or the tinkers' unannounced visit. Or an angel descending from heaven and requesting shortbread and black tea.

Perusing the street, she lifted her skirt and stepped onto the first riser.

"Young lady, a moment, if you please." Minerva stalked to the stoop, leaving Harrison and Shona beside the carriage.

Confound it.

Grateful no passersby were near enough to overhear, Alexa pushed the hair which escaped her bonnet earlier behind her ear. "Is something amiss, Minerva?"

"I've tried to be gracious. I truly have." Minerva's breasts rose and fell in her agitation, and tears swam in her tawny eyes. She cast her angry gaze to the pavement, her voice quivering. "And Lord knows, I've prayed for strength and patience, tried to be understanding, although you've thoroughly disrupted our lives."

A foursome strolled along the street's opposite side, and a finely dressed woman holding the hands of two young girls propelled them along the sidewalk a scant distance beyond Minerva's carriage. Two dandies on horseback approached as well.

Lord Craven and Sir Howard from last night.

Perfectly wonderful.

"Why don't you come inside where we can discuss whatever has you upset in privacy?" Alexa ascended another two stairs. She didn't need more disreputable talk floating about regarding her.

Harrison indolently crossed his ankles and leaned against the carriage, while Shona continued to splutter noisily into a kerchief and tossed Alexa accusing peeps between snuffles.

Alexa scowled at the shut door.

Where was the butler, for pity's sake?

Or a footman?

Even a maid, for the love of God? Surely, someone had noticed the duke leaving and Minerva arriving.

Still fuming, Minerva followed Alexa, apparently—and most regrettably—oblivious to their potential audience.

"It's not enough you reappear and jeopardize Shona's inheritance, but now you have the gall...the...the audacity, to attempt to steal her best hope for a brilliant match?" Her eyes mere slits, Minerva jabbed her parasol's tip in Alexa's direction. "She and Lord Renishaw are practically betrothed. I have anticipated an offer for her hand any day."

"Pardon?" Alexa's jaw slackened, and the queerest urge to giggle gripped her. Shona and Renishaw? No. That wouldn't do at all. "I did no such thing. That's utterly absurd."

Renishaw, God rot the libelous rat.

The couples across the street slowed their steps, and the men riding exchanged, superior amused glances.

Alexa trotted up the last pair of steps, anxious to get off the street. Lips pressed into a taut semblance of a smile, she rapped the knocker. Hard. "Let's go inside, shall we?"

Sending a furtive glance to the lane, she clapped the knocker again. And again.

God's toenails.

Open the blasted door.

The door flung open as the horsemen, the couples, and the nursemaid towing the girls simultaneously reached the Needhams' house, their enthralled attention trained on the stoop.

"Alexandra Atterberry, I have just learned…" In a complete dither, Minerva made no attempt to temper her strident voice rising to the sky. "*You* tried to publicly seduce Lord Renishaw."

Lucan handed his cane and hat to Houston. "Send for Darley at once, please."

"He's waiting for you in the study, sir." Houston shut the door. "I took the liberty of offering him a glass of sherry. Shall I tell Cook to expect him for luncheon?"

"He's waiting? But why?" Lucan dragged off his gloves, then dropped them in the butler's extended hand. "Rather early for spirits, isn't it? Is something amiss?"

Much like a bee buzzing about in its compulsive search of nectar, Darley seldom remained idle for more than a few moments. That he perched in Lucan's study with a drink in hand suggested his news from Derbyshire mightn't be pleasant.

"I'm sure I wouldn't know, Your Grace." Houston raised his chin. "Mr. Darley is not in the habit of confiding in me."

Lucan cocked a brow. "Houston, don't feed me that gammon. A fly doesn't fart in this house without your knowledge. Now cut line."

"That may be true, but your man of business is tediously closed-mouth. He refused me a hint. Not even the tiniest one." Houston pursed his lips and disdainfully thrust his chin. "However, given the noticeable tenseness about his person when he arrived, I deduced a glass of sherry might be beneficial." His chin edged higher. "I trust I did not overstep the bounds."

He knew good and well he hadn't.

"Not at all, Houston. You're to be commended for your efficiency."

Houston's nose lowered a forgiving degree. "Shall I see to luncheon now?"

Lucan waved him off. "No need. I'm meeting Bretheridge at White's, but I would appreciate fresh coffee, and please let Smythe know I am staying in this evening."

"Very well, sir." Houston turned on his heel, and nose pointed ceiling-ward once more, trod the passageway's length.

Clearly, everything was not well.

A piqued majordomo proved almost as unpleasant as a peevish woman, the blessed difference being that the butler spared Lucan his histrionics and weeping. Pouting, however, Houston had perfected. He took his position seriously and considered himself slighted if he wasn't privy to the intricacies of every aspect of Lucan's life. He proved worse than Smythe, in that regard.

Lucan strode to the study, curiosity grappling with trepidation. A table clock declared the hour half-past eleven.

He'd arranged to meet Bretheridge at one o'clock, first intending to scratch out Renishaw's wager on White's betting-book—hadn't been done before, but he'd give it a go, nonetheless—and then set Bretheridge to rallying their friends to Alexa's defense. Hell, he might confide he intended to marry the fascinating gypsy-turned-lady. *If* he could persuade her to come round in the next few weeks. Damn too few weeks, at that.

Mayhap Bretheridge would have an idea or two to aid Lucan in his quest. After all, Bretheridge's lady's affections had been hard-won too.

Darley, his glass full, and his squat body propped against the sill, gazed out the window but turned upon Lucan's entry. His grim countenance below grizzled eyebrows sent Lucan's stomach lurching.

He paused at the threshold. "What has happened?"

"Fire at the mill. Two men killed. Several more injured. Mill's a total loss." A typical, succinct report from Darley. Not a chap to waste words. he squared his bulldog shoulders and gave a confident nod. "Arson."

"Bloody hell." Lucan hurried directly to his desk. "The mill is the livelihood for more than a hundred men. Any idea who started the blaze?"

"No." Darley set his glass aside before jamming a thumb inside his waistcoat. "During the chaos, a night watchman saw men running from the loading docks. He cannot be positive they weren't workers, though."

Given the irregular events at Chattsworth, a fire at Lucan's mill seemed too deuced coincidental. Still, Renishaw had polluted London with his presence since Lucan arrived, and to his knowledge, hadn't left.

He'd hired it done, then.

Easy enough to do if you had sufficient blunt.

Renishaw seldom bragged deep pockets, however.

Lucan pressed a finger to his left eyebrow to appease the niggling ache behind his eye. It often occurred when he hadn't consumed his morning coffee, and he'd no one to blame but himself. He'd skipped his usual pot in his eagerness to acquire heather for Alexa. What had come over him—gadding about in search of purple posies before his morning libation?

Heather. Not posies.

He couldn't be smitten already. Could he?

Her flippant remark at the ball about not marrying had ruined his ability to sleep. He'd sat in his study nursing a Scotch and plotting ways to change her mind until two in the morning. Her declaration drove his fretful ruminations to Scotland's remote Highland crags and over their hostile cliffs into the wildly churning seas below.

After flopping around in his bed for hours, his mind refusing slumber's seduction, he'd risen at six.

Today, of all days, he depended upon the strong beverage. He pressed his finger harder against another twinge. "The fire started at night?"

"Yes." Darley nodded. "Around one."

Where was Houston with the brew anyway? "Why the dead and injured then?"

"Loyalty." Darley grimaced. "Risked their lives trying to save the factory."

Lucan's gut twisted again. "The men killed. Had they families? How many workers are injured?" Compiling a mental list of the most urgent matters to address, he removed a piece of foolscap from a drawer.

He paused, quill in the air. "Are they getting medical treatment?"

"Yes, they had families, Your Grace." Darley withdrew a crumpled paper from his coat pocket. He held it up. "I took the liberty of retaining a doctor. Once he learned I was in your employ, and you would pay his fees, he was anxious to be of service. His information is here."

He slid the note across the desk.

"That was well done of you." And the most words Lucan had heard the man use at any one time. Ever. He jerked his head toward a chair. "Have a seat. I need the particulars."

Forty-five minutes later, he handed Darley a short stack of missives. Relaxing into his chair, Lucan released a gusty sigh and rubbed his nape.

The destruction of a profitable business meant nothing compared to the loss of two loyal employees and the hardship the others would endure without a means of employment. Rebuilding the factory was paramount. The construction would provide jobs in the interim.

Lucan pointed at the sealed letters in Darley's grasp. "Those give you the authority to do whatever needs to be done to provide for the widows and assure the others get treatment and anything else they require. You'll need to see to the factory's rebuilding at once, as well."

"Yes, Your Grace." Darley nodded and tucked the papers inside his coat. "Anything else?"

"No, not that I can think of at the moment. Send me

an address where I can reach you as soon as you're settled. I'm sure I shall remember a detail or two I've forgotten." Tipping forward, Lucan tapped his fingertips atop his desk. "I regret I cannot make the journey myself, but there are matters here and at Chattsworth which require my immediate attention."

Namely, setting someone to follow Renishaw and Peterson, wooing Alexa, and assuring Jeremy remained safely ensconced on Chattsworth lands. A word in the ear of an acquaintance on the Committee of Privileges mightn't be beyond his scope either.

"Please extend my condolences to the widows." He took a swallow of barely tepid coffee Houston had deemed to serve fifteen minutes ago. The butler's means of retribution.

"Of course. I shall likely be gone two weeks or more." Darley's untamed muttonchops wiggled when he spoke, emphasizing the lines bracketing his mouth.

"Longer, because as soon as you have things in hand in Derbyshire, I need you to search for a Highland traveller named Balcomb Faas and persuade him to venture to London. Tell him Tasara's in danger, and that I have requested he come and bring his family. Start looking in Inverness, and use your utmost discretion."

"Are you certain you won't have need of my services here?" Darley's way of asking what urgency prevented Lucan from overseeing the situation in Derbyshire.

Violet eyes and a mischievous smile, accented by an enticing mole, flashed to mind.

"Well," Lucan grinned, "can you recommend a

couple of reliable chaps to tail a pair of disreputable culls?"

Pulling his earlobe, Darley chuckled and gave Lucan a speculative look. "I may know a fellow or two."

"What about one to unobtrusively follow a woman?"

18

For the umpteenth time, Alexa glanced at the salon's mantel clock nestled between two fresh bouquets, gifts from Katrina's and Alexa's admirers. More than a dozen colorful arrangements sat upon various surfaces, their heady aroma scenting the air and creating a false impression of spring.

The Duke of Harcourt's heather, however, perfumed her bedchamber for her private enjoyment. The humble sprigs meant more than the most ostentatious bouquet. He'd gone out of his way to please her, and her heart gave a happy skip.

Upon entering the salon, Shona's gaze had circulated the room, her eyes widening a bit more with each newly discovered floral spray. Yearning tinged her doe-like expression and turned down her pert mouth, now occupied with chewing yet another biscuit.

Alexa examined the clock again. Only two minutes had passed. How much longer until Uncle Hugo arrived?

Immediately upon finding an overwrought Minerva sullying their doorstep, Shona dabbing her eyes with a soggy kerchief, and Harrison blathering on about

Alexa's indecorous behavior, Aunt Bridget had herded them inside as she instructed a footman to hustle to the bank and request Uncle come home immediately.

At her aunt's insistence—and to spare Alexa their uninvited guests' histrionics—she'd been bustled upstairs.

With Katrina's expert assistance, Alexa swiftly changed into a new confection in shades of pale moss and sky blue, overlaid in gossamer-fine lace.

Her cousin wrapped a ribbon across Alexa's crown and tied it at the nape. Alexa added a delicate peridot pendant and matching drop earrings before tucking her feet into beaded sage-green kid leather slippers and dabbing perfume behind her ears.

Ready for the bevy of expected beaux and snoops anticipating tasty crumbs of gossip to gobble or sprinkle about, Alexa considered offering them quills and foolscap to take notes so they didn't miss a single succulent detail.

Why not invite the gossip rags to tea as well?

Impatience gnawing, she tapped her toes, her attention creeping to the timepiece yet again. A clock's hands had never moved so blasted sluggishly before.

Yes. They had.

Getting the trio—now seated side-by-side on the settee munching ginger biscuits and sipping tea—into the house and away from the enthralled audience outside had seemed interminable.

Hibernating snails moved faster.

Excruciating, that.

Alexa had thought herself immune to the

unwelcome attention, but the pointing and whispering… Fiery little darts had stabbed her with every shrewd glance and calculating word from the audience on the street. She seemed a veritable magnet for attracting gossip and generating *on dit*.

Would Uncle arrive before the callers did?

God, she hoped so.

He'd deter brazen guests' probing questions.

She shifted to better see the door and to present her profile to Harrison, the smug lout. She didn't need the second sight to know this bumblebroth involved him somehow.

Seduce Renishaw, indeed. What utter drivel. A drunken sailor, after a bathless, six-month stint at sea, held more appeal.

The drawing room stood visitor ready, and Katrina and Alexa would act as hostesses while Aunt Bridget kept Alexa's family sequestered in the salon—by lock and key and sat upon by burly footmen if necessary. Unless the situation escalated, in which case, no one would be at home—as if that wouldn't add a hearty helping of scandal to the already bubbling caldron.

"More tea, Minerva?" Aunt Bridget held the teapot, poised to refill Minerva's cup.

"No, I think not." Minerva set her saucer aside, frowning when Shona snatched three more biscuits.

Sending her mother a guilty half-smile, she dropped one, and Sir Pugsley nabbed the treat. Plopping his rotund body beneath the table, he crunched happily.

Minerva brushed crumbs from her lap before scooting the pastry plate beyond Shona's reach. "We've stalled quite long enough, Bridget, and this matter cannot be ignored."

"Hugo should be home shortly. I do believe it best to wait for his counsel." Aunt Bridget lowered the teapot, her brow knitted, either in anxiousness or irritation.

"His advice is not needed or warranted to address Alexandra's fast behavior or the black marks her conduct has caused both our families' honor." Harrison crossed his legs and lounged against the settee's chintz back. Popping a last morsel of shortbread into his mouth, he chewed while speaking. "Viscount Renishaw felt it his duty to report her untoward conduct—"

"Mr. Peterson, *our* family," Aunt Bridget, her spine ramrod stiff and eyes wrathful slits, gestured to Alexa and Katrina, "has *not* been besmirched, and Renishaw's reputation as a scurrilous, untrustworthy bounder reaches far beyond this fabricated tryst." She stabbed with her fiery gaze. "You would do well to avoid his company, lest people assume *your* character is lacking as well."

"Well said, Auntie." Alexa applauded, and when Minerva's and Shona's mouths sagged in disbelief, and Harrison choked on his biscuit and coughed, she clapped louder. Mayhap he'd strangle on a crumb.

One could hope, couldn't one?

"Why, I never, in all my days—" One hand pressed to her heaving chest, Minerva fanned herself with the other, appearing ready to swoon.

Such overdone theatrics.

"*Wheesht*, Minerva." This past half hour, Alexa had

shown great restraint, listening to her stepmother's snipes, Harrison's uncouth double entendres, and Shona's self-pitying whining.

To quiet the sharp retorts begging release, Alexa had bitten her tongue so many times, tea could now leak through the misused appendage like a sieve.

"Renishaw is a liar. He asked to court me." She jabbed a finger toward Harrison. "At *your* urging, he claimed."

Her eyes pooling with tears, Shona clutched his arm. "Uncle Harrison, is that true? When you knew he was about to offer for me?"

"Calm yourself, my dear." He clasped her hand and caressed the plump flesh with his thumb. "You know I always have your best interests at heart."

Something unnatural in his voice sent Alexa's flesh creeping. She veered a glance to her aunt, who'd paused midway with a serviette to her mouth.

Repugnance skittered across Aunt Bridget's face. She'd heard the inflection too. Her keen gaze roved Harrison and Shona before settling on a wan and wilting Minerva.

Face pinched, and lips rigid, Minerva said, "That doesn't explain you attempting to seduce him."

"*Och.*" Alexa threw her hands in the air. "Minerva, the viscount suggested—most vilely and inaccurately— that since I'd shared my *favors* with others, I should do so with him as well."

"That cannot be! Lord Renishaw's a gentleman. He wouldn't." Shona's strangled cry earned a fleeting glance from the others.

At least she'd stopped stuffing sweets in her mouth.

"It's your word against his, Alexandra." A triumphant smile pleated the bags beneath Harrison's eyes.

Alexa jumped to her feet. Enough of the niceties. A duchess would've sat with decorum and self-control while verbally, and in the most moderate of cultured tones, rendered him a eunuch.

She preferred her knife and caustic words.

Once a gypsy, always a gypsy.

"Yes, *he* would, Shona. The man's an unconscionable pig. He cornered me in the bookstore and raised his hand to strike me when I refused his advances. However, my dagger threatening his... er..." She slanted her aunt a penitent look. "Male parts, and the arrival of Jules and the Duke of Harcourt, stopped him."

"So Jules already informed me." The angles of her face taut, Aunt Bridget gave a terse nod.

"I expected he would." Alexa had nothing to hide. She'd been set upon and defended herself with the means available.

Aunt Bridget's countenance relaxed a fraction, and her lips quivered. "I would have liked to have seen that, truth to tell."

"Well." Minerva huffed. "I'm sure I know from where she inherits her uncouth behavior."

Dabbing the corner of her eye, Shona, rabbit-like, nibbled a Shrewsbury cookie.

Alexa paced before the unlit fireplace.

"I'm aware my reappearance has disrupted your

lives, and you fear for your futures." She eyed the clock, then the threesome sitting stiffly, but—blessedly—quiet. "However, as the Scots say, 'Whit's fur ye'll no go by ye.' The seed's been sown. I *am* Alexandra Atterberry. The proof is irrefutable, although you, Harrison"—she impaled him with her gaze—"have tried to raise doubts in the minds of others."

Having recovered from his coughing fit, he jeered. "Are you aware, Alexandra, daughters inherit equally until the Committee of Privileges settles in favor of one or the other?"

"Yes. I know. Are *you* aware, I haven't received *my* portion of my father's inheritance? Not so much as a shilling?" Alexa canted her head, quite enjoying herself.

Harrison's mouth twisted further, increasingly resembling a hen's back end as his countenance grew sourer and sourer.

"Oh, and Harrison?"

"What?" he snapped, shooting her a venomous scowl and slouching into the settee, abandoned any pretense of civility.

Shona busied herself disposing of a ladyfinger with the alacrity of a starving street urchin.

Goodness, she appeared famished.

Alexa prepared to deliver Harrison a carefully calculated blow. As surely as the sun rose each day, he had padded his pockets with her funds and Shona's too. Uncle Hugo had found evidence of forged documents and signatures.

Maggots possessed more integrity. They, at least, feasted upon the dead while Harrison sucked his livelihood from the living. His relatives, to boot.

Flashing him a bright smile despite his surliness, Alexa readied her verbal sword. "My solicitor will remedy the oversight, and at my behest, he'll want a detailed accounting of my funds—from the time I went missing until today."

First blood to me.

"I'm confident you've kept meticulous records. After all, as Minerva's man of business, and I'm sure Shona's too, such a failure to account for the monies might lead to worrisome speculation and cause for investigation." *And a deft twist of the blade.* "By the authorities."

19

Lips slightly curved, Alexa fixed Harrison with a disdainful stare. No more pretending affability.

He blinked, seemingly taken aback for an instant but recovered his bluster with the swiftness of a practiced charlatan. "Rightfully, the title should be awarded to the daughter who's been raised as a lady of quality. The one who expected to inherit and who knows how to behave in a manner worthy of the title."

Ah, now he came to the truth of it.

He might as well add, to assure *his* continued life of leisure and comfort.

This seemed far more about Harrison's position than Shona's. As her maternal step-uncle, and Minerva's obvious confidant and man of business, he'd enjoyed an elevated status these many years. If the committee granted Alexa the title, his status sank to a poor relation of her stepmother.

Alexa studied him from beneath her lashes. He stood to lose a great deal—the most, in the end, of everyone.

"The committee will make their decision based on

all the facts at their disposal, Mr. Peterson. Are *you* aware, collusion is cause for denial of a petition?" Sparks flew from Aunt Bridget's eyes, which had shimmered with humor moments before.

His nostrils flared.

Ire or trepidation?

Did Aunt Bridget worry the committee wouldn't settle in Alexa's favor?

Shona, her eyes wide as a terrified mouse, stuffed another Shrewsbury tart in her mouth. Whole. Chubby cheeks full, she resembled a frightened squirrel with a store of acorns.

Uncle Hugo marched into the room, followed by a somber-faced gentleman Alexa didn't recognize.

She examined the clock again.

Callers would arrive soon.

Uncle Hugo's genial smile warred with the stern glint in his eyes. "Katrina, why don't you take Miss Atterberry for a stroll in the garden? You shan't have many more days to enjoy the outdoors or the sun. Months of drizzle and gloom shall be upon us soon."

"Certainly, Papa." Katrina's intelligent gaze darted between Shona and her father. "Shona, shall we?"

"No, she should be present." Minerva sliced Harrison an uneasy glance and fidgeted with her serviette. "After all, this concerns her future too."

Aunt Bridget cleared her throat and exchanged a speaking look with Uncle. "True, but mightn't it be wise to spare her the, ah, delicacy of the situation?"

"Go along, Shona dear." Cheeks glowing, Minerva flapped the ill-used finger cloth. "This won't take long in any event. We're expected at Dorthea Hinton's shortly, in any event."

Why would Minerva subject herself to that harridan's company?

Uncle Hugo waited until the door closed behind Katrina and Shona before introducing the gentleman. He gestured to Mr. Ponsby. "Alexandra, Lady Atterberry, please allow me to introduce Mr. Ponsby, our solicitor. Mr. Ponsby, my niece, Alexandra Atterberry, Minerva, the Dowager Lady Atterberry, and Harrison Peterson, Lady Atterberry's stepbrother. You are already acquainted with my wife."

Minerva, once again pale as chalk, attempted to school her features, but alarm shadowed her eyes.

Harrison's skin acquired a sickly parlor, a shade lighter than his chartreuse waistcoat. Or perhaps, his overindulging in spirits contributed to his greenish tint.

"A pleasure." Mr. Ponsby bowed briefly.

Both his mien and his tone suggested otherwise.

"Do have a seat, Ponsby. Tea? Refreshments?" Uncle Hugo sat beside his wife. "Alexa, you should sit as well."

"No refreshment or tea, thank you." Ponsby settled into a chair, then rustled around in the unremarkable leather satchel he brought.

Alexa chose an armchair the greatest distance from Harrison. She snapped her fingers, and Sir Pugsley jumped into her lap. Licking a crumb from his droopy chops, he turned around twice and, with a loud sigh, settled his chubby form.

"What are you about, Needham? Why a solicitor?"

Like a cranky rooster, Harrison puffed out his chest, the lines of his face folding into a belligerent glower. "We came to address Alexandra's indecorous behavior at the Temple of the Muses today."

Uncle Hugo directed his astute gaze to Harrison, and for the first time, Alexa recognized the shrewd businessman who'd amassed a banking fortune. An intelligent person didn't trifle with or cross Uncle.

"Within fifteen minutes of Alexa's departure from the bookstore, Sir Baldwin visited my office, and Lady Middleton sent a note around," her uncle remarked in a controlled voice. "Each expressed concern Renishaw had attempted to accost my niece."

Sweating profusely now, Harrison's bravado wilted a fraction, and Minerva looked positively deathly.

"If not for the Duke of Harcourt's intervention, and the timely arrival of our footman, they are positive Renishaw would've harmed her." He turned to his wife. "I invited both to tea today, my dear. I'm sorry I didn't give you advance notice."

Uncle gave her a conspiratorial wink, and Aunt Bridget blushed prettily. "It's of no consequence, Hugo. I expect quite a number of guests already."

"As for Mr. Ponsby's presence, why don't I let him tell you why he is here?" Uncle waved his hand at the papers the solicitor held. "Tell us what you have there."

One by one, Mr. Ponsby regarded those assembled. After setting his satchel beside his chair, he tilted the folded pages drawing everyone's attention. "This is a copy of Steafan Atterberry's last will and testament as well as several correspondences he sent me. I was his solicitor too."

Confusion danced across Minerva's face, and her gaze flitted to each person before returning to Mr. Ponsby. "But…but Steafan's lawyer's name was Russell, and I received a copy of my husband's will. Everything seemed quite straightforward when Mr. Russell read it to me. As an entailed estate, the holdings and monies were bequeathed to his heir, who—due to the abeyance—hasn't been determined."

Alexa folded her hands to calm the rush of nervous anticipation and unwarranted sympathy for Minerva. Had Harrison manipulated her, used her as a pawn, or was she a master-deceiver playing a well-rehearsed role?

Uncle's warning for Alexa to take care who she trusted was wise.

Mr. Ponsby nodded while extracting a pair of pince-nez from his coat pocket.

"Yes, Russell and Ponsby. We've offices in Edinburgh, Glasgow, Manchester, and London, though due to ill-health, Mr. Russell no longer is active with the firm." He met everyone's gazes in turn, lingering longest on Harrison. "Let me be perfectly clear. The elder Miss Atterberry is alive, and therefore, there is no question she is Steafan Atterberry's heir. Only the title and entailment remain to be bestowed."

"Shit." Like a sullen toddler, Harrison flopped angrily against his chair, his leg jarring the tea table and rattling the tray's contents.

Shouldn't be surprised if he doesn't stuff his thumb in his mouth or heave himself onto the floor and caterwaul like a wee bairn.

"I beg your pardon, Mr. Peterson. Refrain from such uncouth expletives in my home, if you please." The way Aunt Bridget fisted her spoon suggested she'd like to rap him atop his head.

"I don't understand." Minerva drooped further, her expression resembling a bewildered child's. "How can Alexa inherit after his estate has already been bequeathed to Shona? You cannot simply take *everything* back. Not after this many years."

That was delivered on a high-pitched whine.

Ah, Minerva thought her position and Shona's secure.

In fairness, who wouldn't have after so much time?

The solicitor's features and voice softened a trifle. "Because, my lady, the estate wasn't bestowed upon Shona. Lord Atterberry left everything, except Shona's trust and annual allowance, to Alexandra. As for the monies in Alexandra's trust, they would've eventually been transferred to Shona if her sister hadn't returned."

Alexa was glad her father had provided for Shona.

Mr. Ponsby directed his attention to Alexa. "Except for your annual allowance, you cannot access your monies until you are five and twenty. I suspect your father worried about fortune hunters. He had another stipulation as well."

Steafan Atterberry might've left this world earlier than he'd anticipated, but he'd guaranteed his wishes were honored, nevertheless. Her father had possessed keen intelligence and foresight.

"And the stipulation is?"

Please, God, not that I have to live at Wedderford

Abbey with Minerva.

Residing underneath the same roof as her stepmother would test her fortitude, but to endure Harrison's continual, obnoxious presence…?

She thought she might be ill.

No. That notion didn't bear contemplating.

The solicitor flipped past a couple of pages. "In order to receive the full inheritance, you must marry a Scot."

Struck dumb, Alexa blinked.

Well, that put a chink in her well-laid scheme. Not the marrying-a-Scotsman bit since, at present, she hadn't any plans to marry, but having to wait until she was five and twenty? Wait four years to put her plan into action?

Impossible.

How much was her annual portion?

"Will I have access to the accumulated allowances to this point?" she asked, quite proud of how composed she sounded.

"Indeed. I can arrange to have the monies transferred from the trust account to your bank. It just requires a note with my signature. Do you have an account at Mr. Needham's institution?"

Harrison's complexion developed a grayish-green hue, and moisture beaded his upper lip.

"I can open one for her tomorrow." Uncle Hugo scratched his eyebrow while turning a bland stare to Harrison.

Minerva fidgeted with her serviette, mercilessly twisting the square. "Yes, but I thought—When Alexandra disappeared—It's been many years, and as

I'm certain you can imagine, we've had countless expenses..." She drew in a tremulous breath. "Does Shona have to marry a Scot as well? How could I have missed such a critical detail?"

Dashes her hopes of a match with the Rat, if that's the case.

Tears trickled parallel paths over Minerva's cheeks, her misery either authentic or she missed her calling as an actress.

"No, she does not, unless she holds the title prior to marrying." Mr. Ponsby cleared his throat and rattled the creased documents he held. "This is an amended portion of the will and was not to be revealed until such time Alexandra Atterberry was present to hear the reading. It clearly states who Steafan Atterberry also preferred to inherit his title."

A vulgar noise sounded from Harrison's direction.

Alexa rubbed her forehead and gave an imprecise shake of her head. "Until I was present? My father couldn't have known of my disappear—"

"But, what of Shona's birthright?" Minerva blurted, then swallowed and slid Harrison a beseeching glance. "You promised." Her voice sounding as if she'd gargled hot coals, she railed against him. "You said requesting the abeyant peerage's termination protected Shona's holdings—her position and inheritance."

So, the petition hullabaloo was that snake's doing. Minerva put far too much trust in her stepbrother. Equally disturbing was her singular focus on Shona's patrimony.

Harrison's mouth worked for a moment before he

clamped his lips and, for once, remained silent. However, his fingers drumming on his thigh, and the muscle twitching along his flaccid jawline revealed his agitation.

Aunt Bridget tossed her serviette atop the table, rattling the empty cups. "Leave off, will you, Minerva? Enough of your flim-flam. You cannot mean to pass Shona off as Steafan's child. That fabrication might've served you at Wedderford Abbey, but it won't here. You know full well, only a legitimate child may inherit."

Minerva jerked, and her lips quivered. She wadded the cloth tighter.

The laundress would never iron the wrinkles out.

"Shona *is* Steafan's. He…" She peeked at them through tear-spiked lashes. "We had an affair. I'm not proud of the liaison, but I'd met him in Edinburgh years before and had fallen in love. Harrison stayed with me occasionally, he knew—"

Aunt Bridget released a snort worthy of an enraged stallion as she removed the tongs from the sugar bowl and replaced the lid.

Unwise move, that, using Harrison to corroborate the tale. Minerva would've been better served to claim the devil as her witness. Had Harrison, the parasite, always relied upon his stepsister for his keep?

They boasted an unusually close relationship for stepsiblings.

"Poppycock? Balderdash and twaddle, I say! Steafan did no such thing. Pure rubbish, I tell you. He adored my sister and wouldn't have strayed. Never." Aunt Bridget shook her hand back and forth vehemently, almost poking Uncle Hugo in the eye with the tongs.

Alexa hadn't ever witnessed her aunt so incensed. That side of the family must be where Alexa came by her fiery temperament.

Uncle Hugo ducked, seizing his wife's flailing hand. He gently set the tongs aside but kept her fingers wrapped in his.

"Steafan didn't venture anywhere near Edinburgh during the time of Shona's conception,"" he said matter-of-factly. My sister-in-law had just died, and the man was a complete wreck."

Minerva shook her head and daintily patted the corner of one eye. "It happened afterward, not while Lyette lived. Steafan was an honorable man. He'd never have been unfaithful. But, in time, he became lonely, as did I. He visited me several times before we married."

A fresh flurry of tears flooded her eyes and spilled onto her gaunt cheeks.

"Hugo and I paid an extended visit to Wedderford after my sister passed, and we can attest to Steafan's whereabouts. Until he brought you home, he hadn't had an absence longer than an hour or two." Visibly shaken, Aunt Bridget leaned into Uncle Hugo's comforting embrace.

Reliving this must be awful for them. Strangely, Alexa remained detached, rather like a spectator watching a parody, a fabricated story, not someone's reality.

Certainly, not *her* reality.

Minerva sniffled noisily before blowing her nose. "Steafan didn't have to go to Edinburgh. I lived in a cottage outside the village."

After her whispered words, silence hung dense and heavy as wintertime fog clinging to the River Thames.

She's telling the truth, at least about the cottage.

Alexa pointed to Mr. Ponsby. "I assume there's proof, one way or the other, as well as instructions in the event I didn't return amongst those papers?"

How could she sound so collected and composed?

The future she hoped to build might well tumble bosom over bum in the next few moments, and Alexa hadn't a past to return to. In an instant, she could find herself a rudderless ship sailing a sea to nowhere with limited means.

No position.

No place to live…

"I was declared dead. How could my father have antici—"

"I demand to know why these documents are being produced now," Harrison bit out. "It's been *eighteen* years, for God's sake. How long was this farce to carry on? This cannot be legal. I shall challenge it in court."

His face gone crimson, he leaped to his feet, crashing into the table while shaking his fist.

Enough.

Tamping down her fury, Alexa cocked her head and stroked Sir Pugsley. "It's none of your affair, you intrusive *trow*. That's Scots for a troll, in the event you weren't aware. Sit down, and be quiet. This does not concern you, and if you interrupt Mr. Ponsby again, I shall ask Uncle to have you removed from the house."

Chew on that, you blasted rotter.

Harrison turned impossibly rosier, his eyes bulging as he emitted strange, inarticulate sounds. A full-on tantrum didn't seem a farfetched notion at all.

Aunt Bridget snickered—*actually snickered*—and Uncle Hugo's eyebrows and lips jerked spasmodically as if he, too, longed to laugh.

"Come now, Peterson. Give over." Uncle gestured toward Alexa. "With Alexandra's return, and her identify verified, her death in absentia has been rebutted. I'm sure you're aware it's not uncommon for wills to specify terms which are honored years postmortem."

"Still doesn't explain why he"—Harrison speared a finger at the solicitor—"has new documents. How do we know they aren't forged claptrap and dribble?"

He tried to grab the papers from the table, but Mr. Ponsby seized them and eyed Harrison icily.

"I assure you, they *are* authentic, Mr. Peterson. Their presentation at this time is warranted because Lord Atterberry had feared for his life and his firstborn's. He took measures to make sure she"—he rolled his head toward Alexa—"would be safe, in the event anything happened."

The color left Harrison's face as quickly as it appeared, and Alexa didn't doubt she'd blanched white as virgin snow too.

God above.

Her father had feared for their lives.

Why?

What could have happened to make him think such a thing?

Did the solicitor know?

Should she be concerned about her safety still?

"*Fear*? For his life?" Her hand pressed to her throat, Aunt Bridget went as gray as Sir Pugsley's aged muzzle. She gave Uncle Hugo a frantic look, but he didn't notice.

Head inclined the merest amount, he scrutinized Harrison as one would a convicted felon dangling from the gibbet.

"That's ridiculous and bloody impossible to substantiate." Harrison slammed his fist on the settee's back. "And you damned well know it."

"That's outside of enough, Peterson. My wife already asked you to hold your vulgar tongue." Uncle Hugo patted Aunt Bridget's shoulder while pinning Harrison with a deadly glare.

"We assumed—in fact, we were told by the both of you"—Uncle Hugo extended his forefinger and wiggled it back and forth between Harrison and Minerva—"Steafan's death was accidental. Unfortunately, no one requested an inquest. Who, besides Alexandra, benefited the most from his demise?"

Minerva's confounded gaze fluttered from person to person once more, and she touched her fingertips to her throat. "I cannot think you mean to imply *I* had anything to do with my late husband's death."

Perhaps not you, but the viper beside you could have.

What had started as a wonderful day had turned into a wretched nightmare Alexa couldn't rouse from. She curled her toes in her slippers and clenched the chair's arms. "Those other papers. What do they say? What would've happened if I didn't return?"

Lifting his focus from the documents he'd been thumbing through, Mr. Ponsby considered her above the lenses perched atop his nose. "These are sworn and witnessed letters from your father, which specify if, after twenty years, you hadn't been found, Miss Shona would inherit. They also clearly state Shona is his offspring. The dowager carried Shona when Lord Atterberry married her."

"No. It cannot be true." Aunt Bridget gasped and slapped her hand to her mouth, her eyes swimming in tears.

Minerva moaned and, hands covering her face, collapsed onto the settee's arm, weeping. "I told you. I wasn't lying."

A groggy haze blanketed Alexa.

Did this change everything?

How could it not?

She blinked and shook her head, relieved for Shona. Some good had come of today's upheaval.

Ponsby produced two letters. "These have not been opened yet. My directions are to read this one." He lifted the first at the corner. "The other is to be given to Miss Atterberry. Do you read, or shall I read it for you?"

Stark humiliation rent Alexa. Another reason to refuse the duke's offer. Society would always assume her an ignorant illiterate, beneath his touch. And theirs.

Fired by the defiance winding through her, she lifted her chin. "I can read."

"Very well." He laid her letter on the tea table beside the silver tea service before adjusting his pince-nez. "A word of advice. Until a ruling has occurred as to which daughter is awarded the title, no one should be addressed as Lady Atterberry."

Harrison straightened and addressed the solicitor. "Doesn't the committee tend to grant in the petitioning party's favor?"

Alexa longed to slap the crafty expression from Harrison's face.

"Often, but not always." Ponsby peered down his nose, which twitched as if detecting ripe offal. "They consider the particulars, and if an objection is raised or a second party challenges the petition, they can be convinced to make another ruling."

"Harrison, as my niece said but moments ago, stubble it. One more word and I shall have you forcefully removed." Uncle Hugo's carefully enunciated words revealed how near to losing his temper he'd become.

Ponsby rattled the folded paper. "I shall read this and learn what Lord Atterberry thought so important, he insisted it be kept secret."

Breaking the letter's seal, momentary surprise skittered across Mr. Ponsby's face when a second sealed missive slipped from the first's folds. Other than her father's instructions written on the front, the first page was blank. He must've worried someone would try to decipher the contents. Every person in the room remained captivated by the second note.

Breaking the seal with his thumb, Mr. Ponsby read the letter, his face indecipherable. The solicitor directed his gaze at Alexa, and sympathy tempered his stern features.

She battled the urge to cover her ears with her hands like an intractable child. Whatever he meant to say, she didn't want to hear it. Instead, she spread her fingers through the coarse fur at Sir Pugsley's nape.

The dog groaned and wiggled in bliss.

Savoir-faire, Alexa.

"Please, what does it say?" She ran her tongue across her unexpectedly dry lips.

Mr. Ponsby removed his lenses and drew a deep breath. "Your father arranged and paid for someone to hide you until such time you were old enough to protect yourself, and it became safe for you to return and claim your inheritance and title."

A mélange of gasps and rude noises met his announcement.

Did Alexa cry out?

Someone had.

From the grave, Steafan Atterberry had thoroughly flummoxed the lot of them.

"We can but speculate who he sent you to—why you weren't returned earlier." Mr. Ponsby droned on, "And the reason he didn't send you to the Needhams. Those details he didn't reveal."

Steafan sent her to live with the travellers? A wave of dizziness swept Alexa, and sheer determination prevented her from bursting into tears.

Betrayed.

Holding herself stiffly to maintain a rigid grip on her self-control, she looked to her uncle. "Did you know? That I'd been hidden amongst the gypsies?"

20

S canning White's for familiar faces, Lucan's scrutiny skipped across the table where he'd sat with Yancy before they toddled off to Scotland a few short weeks ago. At that very same spot Lucan had questioned whether he'd ever marry.

He gave a minute, self-castigating shake of his head.

Now, look at me.

Doggedly pursuing a tantalizing, mystifying temptress, as surely besotted as he'd once poked fun at his friends for being.

Perusing the betting book, he firmed his lips and traced Renishaw's scrawl. Bold as brass, the arse. He'd made no effort to hide Jeremy's identity or Lucan's, for that matter. Peterson was no more subtle.

~*~

Ld R bets Mr. Peterson 20g to 5 a certain idiot brother of HG the Duke of Harcourt will be jailed for trespass by Yuletide.

~*~

A grim smile bent Lucan's mouth.

Not hardly, you unmitigated asslings.

With the safeguards Lucan had put in place, a gnat couldn't sneak onto or off Chattsworth property. Lucan tapped the book with his forefinger. "He'll lose the bet, the dolt."

"He's an idiot. Is the man incapable of declining a bet?" the Marquis of Bretheridge pointed to four other entries on the page with Renishaw's name inscribed. "He's lost at least ten more wagers here, and most are against Bellary. Not at all wise on Renishaw's part. Bellary's notoriously hot-tempered and doesn't take kindly to swindlers."

Thumbing through a few previous pages, Bretheridge scratched his forehead. "In the last six months, he's fought two duels against men owing less than Renishaw. Killed one, maimed the other. Renishaw had best pay up, or he'll be looking down the nozzle of a pistol himself."

Lucan rubbed his jaw and pointed to the ledger. "Wonder if I can buy Peterson's bet? Ever been done?"

"No. You cannot alter the books or change the wagers—not even to scratch or black them out—" Bretheridge drew in a harsh, hissing breath. "By God, the damnable cur."

Seldom did Bretheridge become angry or curse.

"What?" Lucan glanced at the scribbled entries again.

His mouth pressed into a stern line, Bretheridge stabbed the book with his manicured finger. "Just there."

~*~

Ld R bets Ld. Craven a hundred to fifty, the gypsy AA will be compromised or disgraced before Season's end. Two hundred to fifty if Ld R succeeds in seeing the deed done personally.

~*~

Alexa's initials leaped from the page before rage blurred Lucan's vision and blood whooshed in his ears so loud, it muted the din in White's. He balled his hands until his nails cut crescents his palms.

"Ruddy bastard." Lip curled, he practically snarled. "I'll kill him."

By God. Renishaw's coming across Alexa at the bookstore hadn't been by chance. He'd sought her and created a public spectacle intentionally. The unconscionable churl intended to ruin her for sport and profit.

Money passed through Renishaw's fingers faster than piss through a drunkard. If he masterminded the fire in Derbyshire—and Lucan would wager his title Renishaw had—the thugs who started the blaze wouldn't wait for payment.

With pockets to let, Renishaw would have to procure funds. And fast. Their sort didn't take kindly to being bilked any more than Bellary did. The viscount might find himself with a broken arm. Or worse.

Far past time the members of White's blackballed Renishaw and threw him into the gutter where he belonged. Lucan would pursue that another day. Right now, however, a cold sweat engulfed him as concern for Alexa and Jeremy formed a shriveled knot in his gut.

Men of Renishaw's ilk possessed no honor, a truth Lucan knew too well. Harvey rested in the family cemetery these many years as a result of a Renishaw's unscrupulousness. The bugger would use any means to ensure he collected his wagers.

Lucan shoved his right-hand fingers into his glove. Best have a word with Needham and warn him of the danger to Alexa. Wise, also, to send a note round to Chattsworth, advising Genny to use extra diligence regarding Jeremy.

"Placing a bet, Harcourt?" Renishaw's overly loud, nasally voice penetrated Lucan's ire-induced haze.

Lucan spared him an indirect glance and crammed on his other glove. "Sod off, Renishaw."

"Tsk, tsk. No need to be boorish. Cannot imagine why you are so tetchy." A shrewd smile teased the viscount's mouth. "The question was innocent enough."

Nothing the fiend did was innocent.

Renishaw ambled closer and peered at the ledger. His mouth twisted into a full smirk when he saw the page Lucan and Bretheridge studied. "Thought you were above such mundane pursuits."

"You know bloody well, I place an occasional wager." Always entirely harmless.

"Hmm, true." Renishaw touched his chin and

affected a contemplative pose. "Wait, it is duels your *maman* won't let her little boy participate in."

"For you, I'm sorely tempted to make an exception and send you straight to hell's lowest level to burn for eternity." Sending a covert glance around the room, Lucan pointedly edged away from the viscount. He'd like to place something in the betting-book, all right.

Renishaw's smug face.

"How *is* your mother?" Renishaw jibed. "Heard her health was failing. Tut. Tut. Whoever will care for your imbecilic brother—?"

"Stubble it, Renishaw," Bretheridge warned, slamming the betting ledger closed.

"Speaking of my brother, you sodding piece of..." Lucan mustered every ounce of control he possessed and smothered the vulgar oath tapping behind his teeth. "Harm Jeremy, even look at him unkindly, and you'll rue the day you returned to England."

The din and conversations dwindled as regulars noticed the tense exchange and stilled to listen.

A satisfied glint entered Renishaw's narrowed eyes.

He was enjoying this.

Lucan wouldn't have thought it possible, but Maurice Renishaw was even more arrogant and loathsome than his older brother.

"After our exchange earlier today, Renishaw, any man claiming a *whit* of common sense, or the faintest intelligence, would've steered clear of me." Catching Bretheridge's attention, Lucan slapped his hat atop his head and jutted his chin toward the door. "Let's go. I find the air has grown most offensive."

"I'll say. Positively vile." Bretheridge followed suit with his hat. "We can continue our conversation later."

"That gypsy wench is a tasty little morsel I mean to have." Renishaw licked his lips and cupped his crotch, making a lewd motion.

Holding his breath, Lucan closed his eyes and clenched his jaw.

He's goading you.

He curled his toes in his boots and fisted his hands, picturing Alexa's lovely face, then his mother's frail features.

Don't react.

Lucan tried to recall one of the many scriptures he'd heard during Sunday sermons on patience and being slow to anger.

Nope. That didn't help one iota.

Oh, to hell with it.

He seized the shorter man's lapels and jerked Renishaw near so their noses practically touched. God, he wanted to pulverize the prick.

"I don't know what warped game you're playing at, but if you harm one hair on either Miss Atterberry's or my brother's head, if there are *any* more mysterious fires or suspicious occurrences within five miles of *anything* I own, if you place another bet which affects me or mine, I promise you—" Lucan lifted the viscount another pair of inches and shook him until his teeth clacked—"you will regret ever having been born. I shall ruin you."

"Harcourt." Bretheridge laid a calming hand on Lucan's arm. "Let him go. You have an appointment. Remember?"

Lucan released Renishaw and, resisting the urge to slug the bastard to next Christmas, shoved him away. "Bother Miss Atterberry again, murmur her name—even in a dream or your perverse thoughts—and you'll answer to me. Feel free to wager on *that*."

Renishaw stumbled backward a few paces, a flush darkening his countenance. His livid gaze roved the room as he straightened his rumpled clothing. "Awfully protective of the chit. Makes a man wonder why, if you have designs on her yourself."

A thread of truth there. Lucan must convince Alexa to marry him. Soon. Once she bore his name, she'd be safe. None dared risk his wrath or the power his position afforded him. More than one man had experienced absolute destruction due to an offended, high-ranking peer.

He hadn't ever gone that route before, preferring not to abuse his title. However, for Renishaw, he would gladly make an exception.

"Or"—Renishaw winked at a couple of his already half-foxed cronies—"perhaps you've already sampled the little vixen's charms yourself."

Outraged objections mixed with a smattering of lewd chuckles exploded around the room until Lucan elevated a brow and stared down a handful of men.

"What was she like? Wild, I'll bet." Renishaw licked his lips, lust glazing his eyes. "Does she know any heathen tricks?"

That bloody well does it.

"I beg your pardon, Bretheridge." Lucan handed his cane and hat to Bretheridge. "I'm afraid I have to delay our departure for a few moments."

"You're an utter imbecile, Renishaw." Bretheridge shook his head and stepped to the side. "Just don't know when to leave off, do you?"

Confident everyone's attention focused on him, Renishaw grinned and raised his voice. "I heard she likes her swiving rough and willingly spread her legs for her brutish captor—"

Lucan swung—a fierce right hook straight to Renishaw's beak-like nose.

Bone crunched, and Renishaw crumpled to the floor.

"Here now, Your Grace," said the manager as he and waiter carrying a linen serviette rushed over. "I cannot permit ungentlemanly behavior in this establishment. I'm afraid that I must ask you to take your leave."

The waiter knelt to attend an unconscious Renishaw. He half-heartedly daubed at the blood oozing from the viscount's nose.

"My apologies, Mr. Raggett." Lucan accepted his possessions from Bretheridge. "I was but defending a lady's honor."

Raggett gave a sage nod, slinging Renishaw a contemptuous glance. "Indeed. Such a thing shouldn't be necessary amongst White's gentlemen."

Lucan flexed his hand.

Might've broken a knuckle.

After swiping his hair off his forehead, he slapped his hat atop his head before addressing the other patrons.

"I strongly suggest that in the future, no one agree

to any sort of wager with this blackguard." He veered his attention to Renishaw, now moving his head back and forth and groaning. Swiveling to the door, Lucan bumped into a newcomer. "Beg your pardon."

"Not to worry, Harcourt." Bellary's stern countenance remained unchanged until his attention lit on Renishaw. The planes of his face hardened to granite, his eyes slits of wrath. He stamped to the moaning man.

"You can expect more of the same, or worse, if I wait much longer for you to honor your wagers, Renishaw." He nudged the viscount with his boot, a sneer contorting his face. "You have two weeks, then I'd choose my seconds if I were you."

As Lucan exited the club, he turned to Bretheridge. "My man of business is out of town for an extended period. Might I impose upon you to have yours inquire at every gaming hell, card room, and club in London and purchase Renishaw's vowels? Anyone he owes a farthing to, I want to buy out."

Bretheridge cocked his head, his acute gaze probing. He gave a half-nod and fell into step beside Lucan. "Yes, I'll see to it today. I shall also see if Warrick can aid me. Perhaps even Devaux-Rousset. He's returned to England for an extended stay."

"Devaux-Rousset? Isn't he the chap who helped protect Lady Bretheridge? He visited Craiglocky, didn't he?" Lucan adjusted his hat and nodded at an acquaintance.

"Yes." Bretheridge nodded a greeting too. "He has quite a network of men who specialize at covert sorts of things."

Gratification tempered Lucan's heated blood. "Do request Devaux's aid. I intend to crush Renishaw."

"I gathered as much."

They skirted a pair of young women peering into a shop window. The ladies burst into giggles when Lucan and Bretheridge strode past.

Thank God, Alexa didn't giggle. At least not a high-pitched bird-witted tittering that set his teeth on edge, crossed his eyeballs, wilted his staff, and made him crave a bracing gulp of whisky.

"Harcourt, might I ask why you are so infuriated?" Bretheridge eyed him speculatively. "Renishaw's an unmitigated arse."

Yes. He is.

"And, what he said about Miss Atterberry was undeniably reprehensible."

Inexcusable.

"But, by George, you lost your temper and broke his nose."

Most satisfying.

"Not the least typical for you, my friend. And now you're hell-bent on revenge. Why?"

Lucan spared Bretheridge a sidelong glance. "He deserved what I dealt him and more, truth to tell. I stopped him from striking her at the Temple of the Muses this morning."

He swung his cane and set a brisk pace. He'd promised to call upon Alexa, and Needham must be warned of Renishaw's ill-intent.

"God rot him then. Cannot say I blame you in the least." Bretheridge heaved a sigh. "He'll call you out. I would bet on it."

Lucan shook his head. "No, he won't. Not when I possess every I.O.U. he owes and spread the word that if he challenges me, anyone who lends him a groat or extends him credit, will experience my ire."

His ears still rang with Renishaw's filthy suggestions. He wanted to punch the bastard again. And again.

He would give Renishaw a choice.

Lucan would pay Renishaw's debts if he signed an agreement to leave England and never return, or he would demand payment for Renishaw's vowels, which everyone knew the bugger couldn't pay. He'd bankrupt him, make sure every door and resource was closed to the cur. *If* the thugs he owed money to didn't get to him first.

Bretheridge stopped and gripped Lucan's arm. "This isn't like you, to abuse your position. You didn't after Harvey's death, and you bloody well had good reason to then. Why now?"

Lucan met Bretheridge's green-eyed gaze. No condemnation or accusation shone there—merely concern and confusion.

"I intend to marry Alexa, Flynn, and I need your help." Shutting his eyes, he strove to regain his self-control as another wave of ire overcame him.

"*Marry her*?"

Lucan almost smiled at the incredulous expression distorting Bretheridge's face and the way his voice rose to a schoolboy's squeak at the end.

"After that"—Lucan jerked his thumb in the

direction of White's as he resumed walking—"she must have the protection of my name as swiftly as possible. *Le bon ton* will take after her now like the devil himself."

"There's truth to that, unfortunately." Bretheridge stepped behind Lucan to allow a couple to pass.

Lucan checked his watch.

Blast and damn. He'd be late if he didn't hasten. He should've ridden.

"Please inform our friends of my intent and my wish for their support," he said, lengthening his stride. "Our circle must rally around her, show their acceptance, and act as a buffer until I can convince her to accept my suit."

"Why wouldn't she?" Bretheridge crooked his mouth and winked. "Doesn't every woman aspire to marry brilliantly?"

"Not Alexa. She doesn't want to be a duchess. Doesn't want the life of a peeress or the *ton's* trappings." Lucan slowed his pace.

Would marriage to him make her miserable, destroy the fiery gypsy who captivated him, and transform her into a bored, bitter woman?

God, no.

He'd move them to a crofter's cottage in the Highlands first.

"Forget about titles, reputations, scandal, and gossip." Bretheridge nudged Lucan's upper arm. "*You* need to convince her to marry you as a man who loves her, adores her, and cannot fathom a day in his life without her. Nothing else matters to a woman."

"Waxing poetic, Bretheridge?" Lucan tipped his mouth into a lopsided smile. "What's this nonsense about love? Much too soon to toddle along that nonsensical trail."

Grinning broadly, Bretheridge slapped Lucan's shoulder. "I just witnessed a man defending the woman he loves. You, my friend, are, tit over arse, head in the wool-pile, smitten."

Am I?

On horseback and waving like demented hags, Sir Howard and Lord Craven clattered across the pavement, making straight for Lucan. Craven reined in his horse, and his constant shadow followed suit.

Was Howard capable of independent thought or action?

Did he piss when Craven did too?

Lucan kept walking, not trusting himself not to yank Craven from the saddle. Only betting against Renishaw saved the fop from the same fate as the viscount.

"You left the Needhams' too soon, Harcourt." Craven toyed with his reins, anticipation lighting his nondescript eyes. "Missed quite an entertaining spectacle."

"Don't know when I've been more amused." Sir Howard chuckled and scratched his chafed chin. "Indeed, I don't."

Lucan turned around and furrowed his eyebrows. "What are you blathering on about? I didn't see either of you earlier when I dropped Miss Atterberry and her servants at home."

Wise to make sure anyone eavesdropping knew he and Alexa hadn't been alone in his carriage. He'd deemed it prudent to leave before he'd been forced to acknowledge Alexa's family. He didn't trust them—particularly Peterson—and he didn't trust himself to remain civil around the bounder.

Several passersby slowed to listen to their exchange.

"Came up behind you. Recognized your crest, of course." Craven's horse pranced in a circle. "Didn't know who the other carriage belonged to until The Dowager Lady Atterberry thrust her head out. Furious as a hellcat. Actually gave my heart a terrible start, she was so incensed."

Craven patted his chest over his heart.

Sir Howard nodded or attempted to until his over-starched cravat brought him up short. "Cannot blame her. Her stepdaughter seduced Lord Renishaw—in public, at that."

21

*E**scape.*
Alexa forced her legs to move, to put one foot in front of the other and turn toward the doors. Both her fathers had betrayed her, each claiming their actions were for her benefit. Gut-wrenching pain, so forceful she feared she would vomit, tore through her middle.

Stoicism be damned.

Unused to such extreme emotions, she desperately sought privacy to digest what she'd learned. After a final glance at the solicitor, she spun on her heel. Head bowed, she hurried to the entrance.

Before she grasped the handle, the door flew open, and she careened into Katrina and Shona.

"Alexa, what is it?" Peering beyond Alexa's shoulder, Katrina reached for her. "My God, what has happened?"

Shona tentatively touched Alexa's arm. "Alexa? You're pale as milk."

Alexa shook off their hands, grasped her skirts, and sprinted along the corridor. She must reach her room before she cast up her accounts or wailed like an infant.

Double betrayal.

Dat had lied.

He'd known her identity and then pretended he didn't.

Why hadn't Steafan sent her to live with the Needhams if he worried for her safety? Surely, sequestering her with family members, rather than strangers secreting her away, made more sense.

Tears burning her eyes, she lowered her head and darted around a corner. She rarely cried and never did so in public.

She skidded to a halt at the stairway's bottom.

On the entry's other side stood Mr. Mortimer, the Duke of Harcourt, an elegant dame, and an austere gentleman. She'd seen the latter two at the bookstore, hadn't she?

Concern etched their faces and filled their eyes.

Lucan surged forward. "Alexa, what has happened?"

With one hand, Alexa shielded her face, hiding her watery eyes. Not caring if those below viewed her calves, she lifted her gown higher and raced up the risers two at a time.

Was she never to be given a reprieve?

Not even within her home?

She couldn't make it to her chamber without others witnessing her devastation and giving rise to more speculation?

My God.

She'd been a tattlemonger's delight—one abysmal episode of succulent scandal after another.

Skirts at her knees and gasping for breath, she bolted up the stairway.

Let Shona have the blasted title. Alexa didn't want it or the troubles invariably accompanying positions of that nature. She wanted to go home, to the security and obscurity of Scotland and the tinker's camp.

But she couldn't.

Not anymore.

She hadn't a place to escape to, and that frightened her more than this ill-fated trek into High Society or the ongoing gossip dogging her. She was done over, good and stuck until this inheritance and title business sorted itself out.

How long did those proceedings take?

Weeks? Months? *Years*?

Impossible.

She couldn't endure the chaos for so long. She must be away from here, the sooner, the better. Hot tears spilled onto her cheeks. Swiping at them, she darted the wide corridor's length as Mr. Ponsby's words echoed over and over in her mind.

Your father arranged…paid…hide you.

Reaching her bedchamber, Alexa fumbled with the handle, tears blurring her vision. The latch finally gave way, and she rushed inside. She kicked the door shut behind her and sucked in a shuddery breath. More tears blinded her as she crawled onto the window seat. She angrily swiped at her damp cheeks.

Infants and weaklings cried.

It shouldn't matter.

But it does, her heart cried.

She'd been well-cared for. Had been loved. She'd known nothing different and lived contentedly as a humble traveller.

Who else knew of Steafan's arrangement?

Someone took her to the travellers after he died. Someone Steafan trusted and who kept silent, though whether from fear or loyalty, Alexa couldn't determine. Or perhaps, whomever Steafan chose to aid him had betrayed him too.

Except Mr. Ponsby hadn't said travellers.

Mayhap...

Was her presence with the tinkers a colossal mistake?

Hugging her knees, she buried her face against them and at last gave way to the sorrow hounding her from the moment she'd discovered she wasn't Tasara Faas. As much as she abhorred waterworks, her reserves, her self-control, the fortitude she prided herself in, were depleted to a nutshell's worth, scarcely enough to keep her from shrieking and railing like a common fishwife.

The door whisked open.

Aunt Bridget or Katrina?

God above.

If He had the slightest morsel of mercy, He would spare her Minerva or Shona. Those two she couldn't face at present.

"Please go away. Let me be." Between sobs, Alexa sucked in a ragged breath, her face pressed to her knees. "I do not wish to talk to anyone right now."

"Then don't talk, Kitten. Just weep. You can tell me what's wrong afterward." An instant later, strong arms scooped her against a solid chest before settling her atop a very manly lap.

"Lucan?" She tilted her head against his shoulder. "You oughtn't to be here. It's most unseemly. Think of the gossip."

More spiteful natter—a handcart load if he is caught.

"You've been the object of more than your share of tattle, haven't you?" He kissed her forehead and adjusted her more securely against him. "I've left the door ajar, but I couldn't ignore you when you fled upstairs that distressed."

Alexa let her eyelashes flutter shut and snuggled closer.

He smelled divine. Spicy cologne, coffee, and—she sniffed—yes, a touch of heather.

She'd not been comforted in a tender embrace for a long time. Right now, she didn't know who else to trust, and his sturdy arms encircling her soothed her wounded soul, although it wasn't her soul that an intense burst of heat surged through.

"Lucan, do you realize this is the fourth time you've come to my rescue or defense? The Blackhalls, the ball, the bookstore, and now?"

"Actually, it's the sixth, but it is the fourth time today."

She loved how his chest rumbled when he spoke, his voice a rich, melodious baritone. She slipped her arms about his waist and his muscles bunched. "Good heavens, truly? I am becoming a nuisance for you, aren't I?"

"Never." He hugged her, whispering fiercely against her hair. "I would sacrifice my body, give my life to protect you."

His words, ringing sincerely, brought about another round of tears. Alexa blinked them back. "How can you say that? You barely know me."

"I'm of a mind that the length of acquaintance doesn't necessarily equate to how well you know someone. I believe similar spirits recognize one another." He rested his chin atop her head, his breath warming her scalp.

True. In mere weeks, Katrina and Seonaid had become sisterly to Alexa.

"I've known some coves decades, and couldn't tell you a single personal detail about them. Turns out, I didn't know my own father that well either." A depth of melancholy she hadn't heard before etched his voice.

Alexa acknowledged a similar truth. She grazed her fingers along the curve of Lucan's ribs. Lean, rippled firmness. Not given to stoutness at all. A foreign, although not unpleasant, twinge vibrated her woman's center.

"What happened while we were apart? Only a couple of hours passed." The folds of his neckcloth muffled her question.

"I broke Renishaw's nose and informed Lord Craven in the most succinct terms what he ought to do with his flapping tongue." Lucan's torso shook when he laughed while rubbing her shoulders in a slow, soothing pattern. "Physically impossible for the chap to do as I proposed he should, but made me feel somewhat better for having suggested it."

"Oh?" She opened her eyes, her gaze fixed upon the slope of his lips. Why did he have to have such a lovely mouth, not thin, wet lips like the rat? "Do I want to know why you felt the need to protect me?"

"No, but Renishaw is not to be trusted." A serious glint entered Lucan's pewter eyes. "He's placed a bet to see you disgraced. And since they arrived in Town, White's betting book has been peppered with his and Peterson's name."

"I'll bet Harrison is behind Renishaw's wager. He revealed his true nature today." She wanted to arch into Lucan's palm skimming her spine.

"Wouldn't surprise me at all." His breath warmed her scalp as he tucked her nearer. "Those two castoffs taint the earth with their presence."

She feared them and what they were capable of.

The arc of Lucan's mouth grew before he dropped a kiss upon her nose, though his gaze caressed her lips. "It's imperative we marry, and hastily."

"Still bent on that, are you?" She arched a sardonic eyebrow. "The answer remains no. I'd make you miserable, Lucan."

He was as unyielding as an oak, and if their circumstances permitted, she might've been charmed.

"I disagree. I think we'd get on very well."

She toyed with the buttons of his coat. Besides, she'd lose her inheritance and with it, any hope of independence or helping the Highland travellers. "Hasn't what's occurred these past twenty-four hours been proof enough for you? I am not duchess material.

I'd bring you disgrace, and in time you'd come to resent me."

"No, I wouldn't." He dropped another kiss atop her nose. "What do you take me for? Some kind of ogre who expects perfection?"

She slumped in his arms. "Think of your family. I doubt they'd welcome a black tinker with a scandalous trail a league long into their midst."

"You'd be sorely wrong, and you've no dishonor attached to you. Except that which snobs have taken upon themselves to pass judgment upon and thus found you wanting."

If only she could believe him, that he didn't care what his peers thought, wouldn't care as time whispered onward. Nevertheless, often with the noblest and most honorable of intentions, people frequently found themselves regretting impetuous decisions.

"I'll not quit until you agree." He brushed her cheek with his thumb. "I'd be far more miserable without you and cannot imagine ever resenting you. I've become most attached to you, my little gypsy."

She shook her head. "Do not, I beg you."

"We can talk of this later." His arms tightened the merest bit. "What has you distraught? How can I help?"

Ominous clouds blanketed the sun, and the rays warming her through the beveled glass disappeared into bleak grayness.

Alexa sighed and shifted from Lucan's lap. Pure foolishness to continue sitting atop his marbled thighs. Indulging in fantasies of him kissing her, and what life as his duchess might be like, had her almost forgetting the travesty in the salon minutes ago.

Her woman's core pulsed again.

Yes, indeed, gossip was the least of her worries.

He released her, but stayed close, his thigh touching hers. Tilting her chin until her gaze met his, he smiled. "What happened, Kitten?"

She explained what had occurred from the moment he left her at the curb to her bolting into the entry.

"I'm glad for Shona's sake, but truthfully have no idea where this leaves me. My father's will names me as his heir, but if I understand correctly, Shona's petition for the title is valid. She's welcome to it too." She wrinkled her nose and stared into space for a moment. "I may have that portion wrong. In truth, I don't understand most of this title business. I know Harrison would see me gone in a flash. Shona would've inherited my portion if I hadn't returned in another two years. I'm sure that chaps their bums red and raw as the Highland winds in January."

"You honestly don't care about the title?" The penetrating look Lucan gave her set her heart aflutter. "Most women in your position would."

Alexa plucked at the delicate lace covering her gown until Lucan wrapped his palm around her hand. She didn't care about the title, but she'd be a colossal liar if she denied caring about the money. She'd spent eighteen years surviving on next to nothing and didn't relish returning to a pauper's state.

"No, I don't, Lucan. In fact, it's almost a relief to think Shona may be awarded it. If I have my own funds, I would prefer she does."

What Alexa would do if that proved true, she hadn't determined. She hovered in limbo between worlds, not wanted by or fitting into either. At least she would have the means to support herself.

She offered an apologetic glance. "I know that may be hard for you to understand. I wanted the power and monetary benefits to help the tinkers, but I'm not even sure they'd accept my aid now."

He drew little circles in her palm with his forefinger, sending more of those tantalizing sensations along her nerves. "I have a foundling hospital along with other charities I support. Perhaps you might start there with your benevolent work. I believe those of us born into wealth and power have an obligation to ease the misery of those who weren't as fortunate."

"Hmm, perhaps. If I stay for any length of time, which I don't foresee."

Underneath her window, a charcoal-brown bird hopped about in the garden in search of insects.

Alexa lifted a shoulder, then slouched against the casement.

"I...Lucan, I don't belong here. I can never relax and be myself. I feel as if I'm acting, playing a role I'm expected to perform, but this"—she swept her hand over herself—"isn't the real me. Yes, these are lovely trappings, and I've enjoyed having nice clothes and pin money, I cannot deny that. But it feels like a holiday which must eventually end."

"Who is the real you?" Lucan tucked a tendril behind her ear, then traced his finger along her jaw. "I see an extraordinarily beautiful, intelligent woman, who's brave beyond belief, one I would be honored to spend the rest of my life with."

He bent near and brushed his lips across hers.

A heady sensation enveloped her, similar to the time she'd imbibed too much wine during Hogmanay.

The urge to press her lips against his molded mouth, to feel the warmth of his lips, overwhelmed her. Before she considered the rashness of her actions, she cupped his nape, drew him to her, and kissed him.

Most unduchess-like.

The tender sweetness exceeded anything she'd imagined, and for the briefest of moments, she yearned to be his wife, to know him as a woman knows a man, to carry his children in her womb, to risk everything to be his.

To say *yes* to his proposal.

She didn't have the courage.

Or stupidity.

Turning her head away, she covered his lips with two fingers. "We cannot."

He caressed her nape, his forehead pressed to hers. "I wish you would trust me. I want to marry you and no other."

Alexa remained silent.

In truth, it wasn't him she didn't trust.

She might fall in love with Lucan, perhaps halfway had already. Handsome, rich, educated, funny, kind. The sort of man a woman dreamed of loving. Yet, her love might destroy her. She'd have to turn her back on her identity and become something she never wanted to be.

Something she disdained and the thing he—his

elevated position in society—required in a wife. She couldn't risk that, and couldn't jeopardize her inheritance for what might become a wretchedly unhappy existence.

"Marry me. I would strive every day, for as long as I lived, to make you happy." Cupping her face, he placed a reverent kiss on her forehead.

This must stop before Alexa lost what little reserve she still possessed. She blurted the first thing springing to mind. "The solicitor said my father feared for his life as well as mine, and that's why he sent me into hiding."

Lucan stiffened and angled away, the planes of his face growing tense. "Then, you might still be in danger?"

"I honestly do not know. None of this makes sense to me. Why would my father suspect someone wanted him dead? What happened to make him think such a vile thing and take the extreme of hiding me with strangers rather than with my family?"

A dog barked, and she cast a disinterested glance into the garden.

Sir Pugsley snuffled around the grass.

The others must've found their way to the drawing room. How many callers had arrived since she'd dashed to her room? What excuse had Aunt Bridget given for her absence?

Pray God Minerva and Harrison had left for Dorthea Hinton's.

"Lucan?" She searched his dear face. "I cannot believe my aunt and uncle knew of this. They've been nothing but the epitome of kindness since they arrived at

Craiglocky."

"What did your uncle say when you asked him if he knew your father sent you to the gypsies?"

"I left before he answered." Puffing her cheeks, she blew out a breath and looked beyond the window again. "You know, Mr. Ponsby didn't say gypsies. He said my father made arrangements, and in my distress, I assumed he meant the travellers."

Sitting at the awkward angle caused the toes of one foot to fall asleep, and she kicked off her slipper to wiggle them.

Did duchesses go about in their stockings?

Likely not.

If she trotted around barefoot, the ladies of *le beau monde* would collapse into a swooning frenzy. Sure as rain fell in Scotland, none of them had ever stepped in goat or horse dung while shoeless.

The mental image brought a budding smile to her mouth.

"I wish I knew the truth, but to know for certain, I must speak to Balcomb." She pressed her palm against the warm glass. "You met him at Dounnich House."

Lucan glanced at the door as if he'd heard something. "Well, then, that's what we shall do. Find Balcomb and ask him. Do you know where the tinkers are this time of year?"

Alexa turned to Lucan.

To know precisely what *Dat* knew would bring her great peace of mind and might answer the other questions this afternoon had sparked. "They generally venture near Inverness from October to January or

February, depending upon the weather."

He made a contemplative sound in the back of his throat.

She folded her arms against a chill.

"Will we travel there? It's not the best time of year for a journey to Scotland." Frowning, she worried her lower lip. "But I don't think he would come to London. Scottish Highland travellers are quite different from the Roma frequenting Gypsy Hill."

"Hmm, let me think about it. Unless we're married, we cannot travel together. Right now, Kitten, we need to present ourselves below—"

A soft rap preceded the entrance of the grand dame from the entry, leaning on her walking cane. "Forgive me for intruding, but we must make sure the young lady's reputation remains untarnished." She delivered a friendly smile and glided farther into the chamber, her deep scarlet gown rustling with the elderly woman's stiff movements.

"Harcourt, dear boy, introduce us."

Lucan rose and extended his hand to Alexa. Once she stood as well, he grinned. "My lady—"

"Speak up." The elderly woman thrust her cane at him. "My hearing isn't what it used to be."

Lucan dutifully raised his voice a notch. "May I present Miss Alexandra Atterberry? Alexa, please meet my grandaunt Kathryn, the Dowager Marchioness of Middleton."

The dowager angled her white head, her dove gray eyes twinkling and a smile hovering on her mouth. "Did I hear something about marriage? Are felicitations in order at last, Nephew?"

Elbow on the settee's arm, Lucan took a sip of the fine cognac Needham had poured while they waited in the drawing room for the women to join them for their jaunt to the theater.

Yesterday afternoon, when Lucan had extended the invitation to the Needhams to join him in his box, they'd decided to share a carriage as well. Mrs. Needham swiftly agreed. In fact, he couldn't help but think she'd deciphered Lucan's interest in Alexa and welcomed it. Good to know. He might enlist her aid in winning her niece over.

He'd half expected Alexa to beg off after yesterday.

Her emotional upheaval, his grandaunt's not-so-subtle hint, and the strain of entertaining a dozen callers for two hours would take the wind from the sails of a more robust person than his petite gypsy.

Again, she'd surprised him, informing his grandaunt the marriage business she'd overheard pertained to Alexa helping him find a suitable bride, and she'd also enchanted the Needhams' visitors with her ready wit and graciousness.

Every guest left utterly entranced, and another mark in Alexa's favor, sure to dilute the poison spread by less benevolent souls. Not generally given to smugness, nevertheless, he'd been hard put not to puff out his chest as she played the brilliant hostess.

Alexa might not know it, but she already possessed the qualities of a quintessential duchess—a decent, caring character, a frequent, kind smile, keen intelligence, and an instinctive ability to put others at ease.

And the most unusual, seductive laugh to ever tickle his ears. Low and throaty, it caused him to speculate what noises she'd make in the midst of passion and created the most disconcerting reaction in his pantaloons.

~*~

Yesterday, Grandaunt Kathryn had pulled him aside as Alexa bid the other callers farewell. He steered his elderly relative into an alcove, lest she raise her voice— as those hard of hearing tended to do—and her words carry to the others.

"That gel is a diamond of the first water, if there ever was one, Harcourt. She's got a sensible head on her lovely shoulders and spirit in her blood." She poked his arm with a swollen, arthritic finger while pointing her weak gaze at Alexa. "I like her. I do, indeed."

Doddering Sir Baldwin kissed Alexa's hand and found himself stuck in the half-bent position. He grimaced and grabbed his lower back. Smiling sweetly,

Alexa said something that sent the old fellow to chuckling as she helped him stand upright once more.

Grandaunt Kathryn whacked Lucan's leg with her cane.

Lucan wiggled his brows. *Feisty old bird.* "Did you want something?"

"Pay attention, young scamp."

She threatened him with the confounded rod again, and he gave her a mocking salute. "Yes, ma'am."

Gripping the carved ivory handle of her walking cane, she leaned heavily on the black cherry length. "Raised by Scottish gypsies and kin to the Atterberrys. What's her stepmother's name again?"

"Minerva Atterberry."

"No, no. Her name before she married Atterberry. Widowed, wasn't she? And she's Scots too?"

"I believe so, but I have no idea what her name was prior to marriage. Perhaps Hugo Needham knows."

Needham chatted amiably with Mr. Mortimer.

Giving her cane an emphatic thump, she murmured, "It will come to me. Always does. Hmm, *Minerva.* Minerva Atterberry. I know her name sounds familiar. Cannot recollect where I heard it before, though."

Despite her advanced years, Grandaunt Kathryn possessed an astonishing ability to recall details others forgot or dismissed as unimportant. She'd ponder on Minerva's name until she remembered.

"The dowager seems like a kind enough woman, perhaps not altogether competent, but her stepbrother, Harrison Peterson," Lucan couldn't prevent his lip from twisting as he spat Peterson's name, "he's not worthy to wipe your shoes on."

"Best make an offer before one of these other infatuated fops does. Trust me, that beauty will not stay available long, although from the smitten spark in your eye . . ." Grandaunt Kathryn gave him a rather wicked, knowing smile—one that reminded him she'd been quite the outrageous widow in her prime.

"That rubbish she spouted about helping you find a bride, meant to put me off the trail, wasn't it? Want to keep it a secret for now, do you?"

"I've already asked her—thrice—and she turned me down neatly each time." His attention strayed to Alexa again. Such an unassuming thing as watching her brought him such joy. "I mean to keep at it until she consents, however."

Lucan would woo her, assault her senses, and ask her every day to become his wife until she argued no more.

"Humph. Don't dawdle for too long." Grandaunt Kathryn shrugged and angled half-way toward the door. "Didn't you promise your mother to have the deed done by the holiday?"

"Heard about that, did you?" Lucan drew his hand across his mouth.

Issuing a rude noise, she thumped the floor with her cane again, drawing several departing guests' scrutiny. "My God, boy, who hasn't? I also heard you planted Renishaw a facer yesterday and told Craven to stuff his tongue up his arse."

"Er, yes." His grandaunt's ears and eyes were everywhere, it seemed.

"Help an old woman to her carriage. I'll want my usual seat at the theater tomorrow night, and make sure that delightful young woman sits next to me."

"Of course.' Grinning, Lucan took her frail elbow. "Anything else, Your Majesty?"

She chuckled. "Impudent pup."

~*~

Now, eagerly anticipating the evening before him, Lucan enjoyed another mouthful of the superior brandy and smiled at the antics of what appeared to be a fawn-colored, fur-covered piglet with a black mashed-in face, attempting to climb onto the matching floral settee.

"Needham, Renishaw placed a bet at White's that Alexa will be disgraced by Season's end. He vows to do the deed himself. She needs to be protected and on her guard."

Needham's eyes rounded before narrowing. He flicked a piece of lint from his trousers. "Never did like that scapegrace. Or Peterson either. Both are cast from the same tainted mold."

"I want to marry Alexandra. I can keep her safe."
Damned fine way to announce it, man.
 Blurt it out like a drunk casting up his accounts.
Needham set his glass aside and, after assisting the dog onto the couch, folded his hands across his middle. For an extended moment, he scrutinized Lucan.
"Why?"
The dog turned in circles, snuffling and snarfing as he situated himself beside his owner. A pink tongue

appeared from amongst the fat folds as the creature set about noisily grooming himself.

"Why? I could name dozens of reasons." Lucan flicked his forefinger, and his gaze, to the ceiling. "How long do we have before the women arrive?"

"Why don't you start with one? The one reason you think will convince me of your sincerity?" Needham lifted his glass once more. Elevating his beetled brows, almost in a challenge, he took a generous swallow.

Lucan stared into the amber liquid remaining in his glass. "She captivated me from the moment I sneaked into her chamber at Dounnich House to rescue her, and she brandished a dagger to protect her sister and brother."

In an instant, she'd stormed his defenses, circumvented his objections, and burrowed her way into his mind—*no*—anchored herself and those unfathomable purple eyes to his soul. He gave a sideways smile and pointed to his eye. "She punched me soundly. I sported a bruise for weeks."

Needham's features relaxed marginally, and the corners of his mouth quirked. A spark of humor gleamed in the depths of his eyes as well. "Alexa's not your typical female, to be sure. She may be a Scottish noblewoman by birth, but she is a Highland gypsy at heart."

"And that's precisely what fascinated me about her. She's a refreshing change, unpretentious, genuine, and I cannot stop thinking about her. Since the business about her life being in danger came to light, my gut's been a tangled knot." Which is why he'd set Darley to hiring a man to tail Alexa whenever she left the house. Something dark and nefarious lurked, or he didn't favor coffee.

Lucan took a quaff of the remaining cognac, then fingered the glass, a poor substitute for the velvety, ivory skin he longed to caress.

Alexa consumed his thoughts. Reprieve from the mental onslaught occurred when he slept; *if* he managed to fall asleep. Even then, she invaded his dreams, many so erotic, a painfully hard erection awoke him and plagued him throughout the day.

No other woman held his interest half as long, particularly one he hadn't bedded.

A log in the fireplace fell, sending a shower of orange-red sparks spiraling up the chimney and drawing Needham's and the dog's attention.

"What of your promise to your mother to marry by Christmastide, Harcourt? There are those who will insist your wish to marry Alexa is simply the fulfillment of a promise to a dying woman." The gimlet-eye Needham directed at Lucan was clearly of a man sincerely worried for his niece's welfare.

Nonetheless, as Lucan learned from his father's deceptiveness, his ability to judge character or outward appearances needed honing. He could thank his sire for his intuitive, distrustful instincts.

His cautious nature served him well on the few Diplomatic Corps missions for which Yancy enlisted his help. Usually, it took tremendous effort on Lucan's part to put aside his reservations, but with Alexa, he held no misgivings.

All the more reason to marry her.

"Others might speculate Alexa's fortune entices you." Needham steepled his fingers. A master at luring and waiting.

Lucan sent him a dark scowl. "Preposterous. I have my own fortune."

"Don't get your wind up. I'm saying what others will, so you had best be prepared. Would you be as interested in Alexa if she didn't have a groat to her name?"

"Yes. I would. I'd take her bare as the day she came into the world."

And treasure each day spent in her company.

Lucan quite liked the idea of her naked. On his bed. Her glorious hair fanned across his pillows as he made love to her at dawn. He redirected his musings before forced to explain a raging erection to his host.

A tight sound echoed in the rear of Needham's throat. "I mean no disrespect, Your Grace, but you've not exactly kept your aversion to matrimony a secret."

Lucan slowly nodded. "True, I hadn't intended to pursue a bride yet, but when I saw her at the ball, I knew in an instant, even if I hadn't made that confounded promise to my mother, I wanted to wed Alexa."

No sincerer words had he spoken. In their short acquaintance, Alexa had managed to wiggle her way into his heart, and if he had become this mesmerized after such a brief period, how enthralled would he be as time ticked onward?

He set his glass aside. "Did you know of her father's arrangements with the gypsies?"

Needham's face fell for an instant, and he firmed his lips, the lines framing his mouth, deepening to thick grooves.

Lucan savored a mouthful of brandy as he awaited a reply.

"No. She should've been with Bridget and me. We are Alexa's godparents, and we would've treated her like our Katrina." He stared across the room, uncertainty shadowing his eyes. "I can only speculate Steafan feared Alexa wouldn't be safe with us either. I wish I knew why, and before you assume it's because she'd come to harm by my hand or my wife's, let me dispel the absurd notion. For months, we tore Scotland apart, searching for her. I'd like to have a word with Balcomb Faas, I'll tell you."

Lucan didn't expect to hear anything from Darley regarding Faas for at least a fortnight. "So would Alexa. You've no idea why Steafan secreted her off? Do you think his death unintentional?"

Angling his head, he studied the older man. Bankers didn't usually possess the most integrity, but Needham, renowned for his honor, boasted a pristine reputation.

Needham blinked and released a deep breath before giving a partial shake of his head. "I don't, to both of your questions. And I don't trust Minerva or her brother. Something's queer there. Something I cannot put my finger on but raises my hackles every time I see either of them."

That makes two of us.

Glancing to the door, Needham's countenance grew guarded. "I would prefer to keep that from the women, however."

"I'm in agreement with you. No sense stirring their qualms. You should know I've sent my man in search of Faas. I believe he knows more than he's revealed." Lucan leaned forward. "Do I have your permission to court Alexa then?"

"She's of age. So giving my permission means nothing. Nevertheless, I do not believe you'd abandon your quest if I denied my consent."

The mantel clock chimed the half-hour. They'd be late, perhaps missing the first act, if the ladies didn't appear soon. Theater traffic was always horrendous, but opening night tested the patience of a saint.

Needham rubbed beneath his chin. "You are a man used to setting his own course and getting what you want, Your Grace. And I suspect you rarely, if ever, find yourself dissuaded or thwarted."

"True, I have lived a privileged life, but I've also striven to be honorable and beyond reproach. I would be faithful to Alexa and put her interests above my own." Unlike his father. Alexa would never know the betrayal his mother had. "She's confused, unsure, and given the disturbing events of this afternoon, she's understandably wary."

He raised a hand to drag it through his hair but caught himself. Smythe would scalp him if he disturbed a single, carefully groomed strand. His valet took more pride in Lucan's appearance than he did.

Instead, he examined his fingernails. "She refused my offer three times yesterday. I haven't had the opportunity to propose today, but there's always this evening."

He sent a covert glance to the open doors.

Anyone might overhear their conversation.

How trustworthy were the staff?

More than Lucan's bufflehead of an outrider, he hoped. A word of reprimand to the chap this afternoon resulted in the fellow taking his leave along with several valuable items from the carriage house. He wasn't the first hireling to acquire a position intent on stealing from his employer.

"Indeed?" Needham released a low laugh. "Alexa won't be easily won, I'm afraid. She has much at stake."

"At stake?" Lucan frowned.

Needham fingered one side of his mustache. "Alexa is in a difficult place at present. The title may well be awarded to Shona, but Alexa has inherited everything unentailed. Did she share that with you?"

"Yes," Lucan nodded. "She did, and that, along with the scurrilous gossip regarding her presently flooding the upper salons, is yet another reason why I'd like to wed her at the earliest convenience. Making her my duchess is the best way to protect her."

The pudgy little dog flopped onto his back, presenting his rounded stomach for a rub.

When Needham didn't oblige him, the dog maneuvered onto his haunches and cast his soulful gaze upon Lucan.

Not a chance, my furry friend.

"If she marries you, Harcourt, she loses her inheritance. She must marry a Scot to keep it. That's her father's last directive."

Lucan's gaze swung to the other man. "She didn't mention that detail."

His little wild gypsy didn't want to lose her funds.

He didn't blame her.

Few women possessed funds of their own or enjoyed the freedom financial independence afforded. "Easily remedied. I'll settle a portion on Alexa and have a contract drawn to prevent doubts."

"Have you discussed this with her? It's her decision to make. I'd welcome the match. I believe you a decent sort, and you'd do well by her." Needham ran a hand over the dog's back. "And I think you capable of defending her. Which, although women stubbornly refuse to admit, they do need and welcome."

"I appreciate your support." The smile Lucan gave him held equal parts relief and pleasure.

Uncrossing his legs, Needham examined the clock. "By Jove, we shall be late if they don't put in an appearance soon."

Lucan grinned when the determined dog crawled, dragging his hind legs, into his master's lap.

"No, Pugsley. I do not need dog hair covering me." Needham set the dog on the floor, then pushed to stand. "Alexa's rather like a feral horse. You might be able to tame her, teach her to accept a saddle and bridle, but her heart will always crave freedom to run wild, and if you deny her that, force her to fit into the mold you believe a duchess should conform to, you will destroy her—break her spirit."

Definitely not the words of a man bent on harming her.

Lucan rose as well. "I have no intention of—"

"Here we are. Do forgive our tardiness, but I'm sure you'll agree our lateness is well worth it." Mrs. Needham sailed into the room, Miss Needham, Seonaid Ferguson, and Alexa in her wake.

A young buck at his first ball possessed more aplomb than Lucan at the moment. His blasted tongue refused to form words, his lungs stalled, and his eyes wouldn't heed his command to blink at the vision of Alexa in a royal blue and gold gown, glittering sapphire combs adoring her silky curls with more jewels gracing her ears and neck, and a playful smile curving her rouged mouth.

"Harcourt, old man, you're gaping. Do shut your mouth and bow before an albatross alights inside." Needham whispered sotto voce from the side of his mouth, his voice riddled with humor.

Lucan clamped his mouth closed and hid the telltale flush heating his ears by sweeping the women a courtier's bow. "Ladies, I don't know when I've ever beheld a lovelier foursome. I'm overcome with admiration."

As one, the women curtsied, murmuring, "Thank you."

"Miss Ferguson, I didn't realize you'd arrived in Town," Lucan said.

Miss Ferguson bestowed one of her gentle smiles on Lucan. "Just this morning, Your Grace. My brother and his wife send their greetings."

"My dear, you are ravishing." Needham kissed his wife's hand, and she dimpled, coloring like a schoolgirl.

How long had they been married?

Any fool could see they still adored each other. Had Needham ever strayed?

Most married men did, with the exception of Sethwick, Warrick, Clarendon, Yancy, and Bretheridge, Lucan's five giddily married chums.

Lucan skirted the marble-topped rosewood table, and as he did, the pug jumped from the settee.

Beaming, Mrs. Needham looped her arm through her husband's proffered elbow. "Shall we? I'm quite looking forward to seeing the play from your box in the first gallery, Your Grace. I've not enjoyed such a spectacular view before."

"I'm to have the honor of escorting these goddesses?" Lucan extended both elbows and winked. "How did I, a mere mortal, earn such a privilege?"

"A bit overdone, don't you think, cousin dear? Seonaid?" Katrina chuckled and peeked around him to see both Alexa and Miss Ferguson grinning.

"Yes, quite." Alexa tilted her head, precociousness causing the gold flecks in her eyes to flash. "As for your good fortune, Your Grace, it's nothing of the sort. You have the larger carriage. Therefore, it's logical we make use of it. Else one of us would be compelled to sit upon the other."

Alexa laid her hand atop his arm, and though her glove, and his shirt, and cutaway coat separated their skin, a jolt seared him just the same. From her little start and half-gasp, she'd felt it too.

Lucan would endure the lot, piled in a chaise's close confines, if it provided the opportunity to hold her. He lowered his head and whispered in her ear. "Alas, I shouldn't have offered the use of mine, and I might've enjoyed the privilege of your plump bum atop my lap once more."

23

orty minutes later, Alexa descended from the plush interior of Lucan's carriage parked along Catherine Street before the Theatre Royal, Drury Lane. It took nearly the entire ride for her skittish pulse to calm and her body temperature to return to normal after his wicked remark.

Sit on his lap, indeed.

Sounds wonderful.

Her buttocks still tingled where the bulge of his manhood had pressed against them yesterday.

Accepting his outstretched hand, she permitted him to tuck hers into his side and braced herself for the now familiar jarring sensation his touch caused.

A dank breeze wafted by, and she shivered, settling her velvet cloak more tightly about her shoulders. The weather had taken an abrupt turn for the worse, and the sky, which had glowed a vibrant cerulean yesterday morning, now threatened to unleash an ugly gale upon them.

A hint of Lucan's woodsy cologne lingered in the air. He was quite the most delicious smelling man she'd ever met. She furtively eyed him from beneath her lashes.

Dressed in his evening finery, stark black except for a ruby and diamond stickpin in his neckcloth, the man exuded male perfection.

When had she become intrigued with him?

When Alexa left London, she feared she'd leave her heart behind. Which, quite naturally, thoroughly botched her future plans of marrying and having a family.

"Oh, it's become quite brisk, hasn't it?" Aunt Bridget hustled past, expertly steering Katrina and Miss Ferguson through the throng, like a schooner parting the sea.

Shaking his head in bemusement, Uncle Hugo followed, leaving Alexa and Lucan to trail at the rear.

"Alexa, we shall go straight to my box rather than mill about and chat. Better, I think, to distance you from the gutter-minds for now. I have several friends I'm anxious to introduce you to. They have promised to visit our box, and my aunt specifically requested you be seated beside her." His lips twitched, and he winked. "She'll undoubtedly say something scandalous."

She gave him a mischievous grin. "I do hope so."

"Hmm, perhaps I ought to keep you two apart. No telling what sort of a conundrum the pair of you might dredge up together." Lucan guided her past two couples animatedly chatting at the stairway's base.

Upon spying Alexa, they ceased conversing and presented their rigid backs.

Cut direct.

Her smile faded.

The injustice rankled, and fury fired in his veins.

She lifted her chin as they ascended the stairs. "This is what you'd have to endure if I were your duchess. Constant shunning and ridicule. Is that what you want?"

"If you were *my* duchess, those inferior cods' heads would grovel and beg for a kind word from you. They're not fit to wait upon you." Lucan directed the quartet a black look.

At his profession, the sting from their scorn evaporated.

He slipped an arm about her waist. "Marry me."

"No." She would give him credit for persistence, but edged away, heedful of the impropriety of his touch.

She might easily become enamored of Lucan, but to what avail? Alexa intended to depart in a short while—wanted to leave upon settling the inheritance hullabaloo—and she doubted she'd ever return to London.

Or England, for that matter.

Encountering him every now and again was simply too painful to contemplate. She mightn't be the stuff of which duchesses were cast, but that didn't mean she relished seeing him with another woman. Even if it was the wisest course and would make him happier in the end.

Perhaps she'd hire a companion and travel the continent. Yes, that might do nicely. If she could afford the distraction. Mr. Ponsby hadn't disclosed her actual allowance.

Why did her father stipulate she must marry a Scot?

Confounded inconvenient.

Never mind that for now.

Finding Balcomb topped her list, and when she knew the facts, the whole of everything behind her tenure with the travellers, she could move forward and plot a course for the rest of her life.

Wait.

What about the letter from my father?

Where had it got to?

Amongst the drama yesterday, she'd forgotten about the note. Uncle Hugo or Aunt Bridget must've secreted the missive away.

When they returned home tonight, she'd ask about it.

Once inside the theater, Alexa surrendered her cloak and put aside the previous ugliness as the evening's excitement took hold. After yesterday, she was determined to enjoy her time with Lucan, brief though it may be, and glean whatever pleasure she might from her short Season.

Travellers always chose to view their circumstances through optimism's lenses.

She looked this way and that, taking in the theater and the grandiose patrons. She'd never seen a performance indoors before, although she'd enjoyed several at summer fairs upon outdoor stages. On occasion, she'd played her violin with other tinker musicians for entertainment and coin.

"It's quite something, isn't it, and larger than I'd anticipated." She almost strained her neck, gawking at the ceiling's painted angelic beings. Was the ornate plasterwork's gilding actual gold?

"The theater seats more than three thousand, and now that gas light illuminates much of it, it's far safer than candles." Smiling and nodding, Lucan propelled her around a passel of tittering misses, each virginally attired in white, including their slippers and hair fripperies.

Craning her neck, Alexa looked for the others in their party. There they were, chatting with several other elegantly attired people near the bottom of an imposing carpeted staircase. They turned and smiled as she and Lucan approached.

"Isn't it magnificent, Alexa?" Katrina glowed with excitement.

Unlike Alexa, she thrived in crowds and the *tonnish* hubbub.

Seonaid's astute gaze vacillated between Alexa and Lucan. "It can be a bit much for those not accustomed to the pomp."

Alexa nodded. "Yes, it's grand, and yes, it's a bit much, but I'm quite anticipating the performance."

"Shall we make our way to my box?" Lucan extended his free arm, indicating they should precede him.

From the corner of her eye, she saw Harrison leaning languidly against a column, arms folded, and a brooding expression warping his sullen countenance.

Damnation.

Why did he have to be here tonight?

Most assuredly, Minerva and Shona attended as well then. Alexa hadn't completely sorted her feelings, hence when she received a note today asking her to call upon Minerva, she'd sent her regrets.

In the missive, her stepmother implored Alexa to reconcile the differences between them, but something rang insincere in her overdone plea. The letter lay on Alexa's dressing table where she had tossed it.

What differences did Minerva mean?

That she thought her daughter was entitled to the entire estate and inheritance?

That there remained no doubt, she resented Alexa's reappearance?

That she and her bounder brother might've had something to do with Steafan's death?

One thing had become clear as Loch Arkaig's pristine waters. Alexa couldn't live with them, and honestly, she didn't trust Minerva, even if motherly fear for her daughter's future motivated her actions.

Moments later, Alexa sat in the front row of Lucan's box, him to her right and the delightful Lady Middleton to her left. The remainder of their party sat behind them.

What a splendid view of the stage.

She angled forward to better see.

"Here, Alexa." Katrina tapped Alexa's back. "Use my opera glasses. I'll borrow Mama's or Seonaid's." She dipped her head close to Alexa's ear. "Mama always falls asleep after the intermission. I pray she doesn't start snoring again as she did at the opera."

Katrina rolled her eyes. "She's not a delicate snorer either. Rather sounds like a bull snorting or choking. Several guests hissed their annoyance when she rattled particularly loudly during an aria."

"Thank you." Grinning, Alexa accepted the pair.

With the extent of shopping they'd done these past weeks, she couldn't believe Aunt Bridget had overlooked purchasing additional opera glasses.

"I brought mine." Seonaid produced a mother-of-pearl embellished set. "I purchased them while in Paris visiting my aunt."

To the rear of the box, Seonaid raised her glasses and peered around the theater. She gasped and stiffened, her jaw sagging open. She snapped her mouth closed before abruptly lowering her theater glasses.

"Are you all right, Seonaid?" Nothing untoward caught Alexa's attention in the sea of unfamiliar faces tilted toward their box.

"Yes, I'm fine." Seonaid offered a wan smile. "I didn't know Lord Devaux-Rousset had returned to London, is all. I also met him in Paris."

Judging from the tense set of her mouth, their association hadn't been altogether pleasant.

"Miss Atterberry, you've drawn the attention of several theater-goers." Smiling and occasionally waving, the dowager inclined her neatly coiffed silver head toward the other stalls. The turquoise ostrich feather atop her head dipped and bobbed with her exaggerated movements, as did her spectacular diamond earrings.

"Those Hinton windbags are sharing that cow, Clutterbuck's box." She inclined her head and gave a little finger wave their way. "Yes, I'm talking about you too, you pernicious chinwags."

Suppressing a giggle, Alexa set the opera glasses to her eyes and instantly regretted the impulse when she encountered a myriad of attendees pointing their attention in the direction of Lucan's box.

Mr. Morton waved exuberantly, earning him a glower and the smack of her fan from the lady beside him.

Lucan edged closer to Alexa and lifted her hand. He kissed the back for a lingering moment. Given the surge in whispers nippily following his kiss, several sets of theater glasses likely dipped to focus upon their hands.

"Please, *please*, marry me, Kitten," Lucan whispered in her ear.

Alexa swung round to admonish him, but her mouth dropped open at the heat radiating from his granite eyes.

If I were tinder, I'd burst into flames.

The scorching temperature permeating her was hot enough to incinerate. She flipped her fan open. Heaven above, what this man did to her…

What she'd *like* him to do to her.

He lowered his lashes partway, a seductive smile teasing one side of his too-tempting mouth, the blasted dimple in his cheek mesmerizing her. "Smile and nod, then give me a look of besotted adoration. You may flutter your eyelashes and giggle to make your infatuation more believable if you wish."

"Foolish man, I'll do no such thing." Alexa chuckled, the tension easing from her.

"Then say yes to my suit."

"No." She released another tense laugh. "Have you always been this obstinate, or do you not understand the simple word?"

Hadn't she thought the same thing about him when

they'd first met? Only now, she found his pigheadedness charming and amusing.

He winked and set her hand upon his sculpted thigh, holding it there by placing his hand atop hers. "My ploy worked, didn't it? Aren't you more relaxed now?"

"Uh-hum." She was.

The dowager nudged Alexa with her fan.

"Yes, my lady?"

Alexa tried to ease her hand free, but Lucan firmly pressed her palm into his leg, giving a brief squeeze and another wicked flash of white teeth.

At this rate, she might be the one to ravish him. She clenched her teeth against the desire to trail her fingertips along the sculpted muscle.

Surveying the audience, he patted her hand as if he knew perfectly well how he affected her.

Probably did.

The earlier cacophony filling the auditorium filtered to a muted buzz as the audience quieted in readiness for the performance.

Dowager Lady Middleton all but bellowed into the stillness, "Tell me, my dear, why on earth did you refuse my nephew's proposals?"

24

Three weeks later

Standing before her bedchamber window, Alexa fastened the frog at the neck of her redingote before gathering her muff and umbrella. Fog engulfed the garden, and intricate frost patterns etched the perimeters of her windows.

Autumn had, at last, descended in full force and appeared intent on remedying her previous temperate weather by skipping straight to soggy and freezing, making this the most frigid November in Londoners' memories.

The Highlands would be bitterly cold.

How did her family fare?

Certainly, with a thousand pounds at their disposal, more comfortably than in previous years.

"Hyde Park today again?" Katrina flopped onto her back atop Alexa's bed.

"Yes. His grace is teaching me to drive, and afterward, we're going to a tea house to warm ourselves." Alexa smiled faintly. "He'll have coffee, of course."

She'd never known anyone who preferred the beverage more.

Katrina rolled onto her stomach, exchanging a pleased—almost smug—look with Seonaid. "'Twould seem the duke is courting my cousin."

"And most diligently at that," Seonaid agreed, curled in a chair before the fire, Sir Pugsley fast asleep in her lap.

Alexa laughed and pointed her umbrella in turn at both women.

"Stop it, you two. The duke and I enjoy each other's company. He merely seeks my advice about which damsel he should turn his attention to for a bride. You are welcome to join us and lend your expertise. I'm sure his grace would appreciate it, given he's made a complete muddle of finding a spouse on his own."

"Go outside? *In that*?" Katrina fluttered her fingers above her head in the window's general vicinity. "I'll eschew the experience, thank you very kindly. I shouldn't want to take a chill before the ball tonight. Major Domont requested I save a waltz for him."

A dreamy smile tilting her pink mouth, she released a long sigh.

"Ah, yes, the major. He seems to appear wherever you are. Happenstance, I'm sure." Alexa winked, and Katrina grinned unabashedly.

At this rate, Katrina would be betrothed well before the Season's end.

Seonaid had encountered Lord Devaux-Rousset a number of times too. However, their encounters proved far less cordial. When he'd taken a seat beside her at the Featherspoon's musical last week, she'd stabbed him a glare fierce enough to singe the feathers from a goose before jumping up, fists clenched, and stomped away muttering, "Insufferable, handsome toad."

"Isn't the duke's time to select a bride running short? Christmastide is but a few weeks away, and the banns need to be read for three Sundays unless he purchases a special license." Seonaid's doe-like eyes regarded Alexa innocently, yet Alexa also detected the merest bit of amusement shining in their russet depths.

"That's 'cause he's made his decision already." Cupping the side of her mouth while slicing an exaggerated look toward Alexa, Katrina said in sotto voce, "Only the lady he's chosen isn't cooperating."

"He most assuredly has not made his decision." Alexa knew full well what her precocious cousin hinted. "And I am too cooperating. I'm helping him choose a duchess, aren't I?"

Katrina and Seonaid snorted in unison, then burst into gales of laughter, waking Pugsley.

He gave them a drowsy look before smacking his chops, closing his eyes, and resuming his gentle snores.

Let them have their fun.

Alexa *was* helping Lucan, except *he* wouldn't cooperate. To date, he'd found some fault or other with every lady Alexa suggested he show an interest in, and he continued to ask her to marry him each time they met, although with a chaperone present, he'd resorted to some creative measures.

Yesterday, he'd slipped a note into her glove when

Bindy stopped to pet a dog. The caress of his fingers as he secreted the paper against Alexa's palm caused all manner of disconcerting thoughts and sensations.

The day before, he'd persuaded her to extend their outing and indulge in a hot chocolate in order to discuss which miss he should dance with at the Bremerton's ball that night. Tucked away in a corner nook, he used his knife to write *wed me* on his pastry plate.

Wholly incorrigible.

He'd laughed when she wrote *no* in strawberry preserves with her finger, then he had the audacity to lick her fingertip clean.

She'd nearly slithered onto the floor and would've made a cake of herself if the waiter hadn't brought fresh scones to their table a moment later.

At her insistence, Lucan danced with eligible damsels at each ball they attended, but it became his habit to claim two dances from her, including the supper waltz, each time. As a result of his expert tutelage on the dance floor, she'd become passably good at keeping off his toes.

Over the weeks, they'd slipped into a comfortable companionship and become the greatest of friends. Lucan knew more about her life as a gypsy and her concerns about her present situation than Katrina or Seonaid. With him, she talked freely about almost anything.

"Hmm." Katrina flipped over once more and, hands in the air, spread her fingers. "Three weeks of daily excursions to Hyde Park—even in the rain and sleet. Two theater performances, one opera, a day spent at

Bullock's Museum." She wiggled four fingers before continuing her catalog. "Four balls, a musical—"

"Don't forget dinner here thrice, a visit to Gypsy Hill, two card parties, and several heather bouquets," Seonaid said with a saucy wink.

Has it really been that many?

"Hush, you two." Alexa shook her gloved finger at them. "I've told you before, nothing can come of it. Honestly, I do not want to be a duchess. I've tolerated the public excursions because of your presence and his. In case you hadn't noticed, *la beau monde* hasn't exactly embraced me."

With Lucan at her side, she'd met the *ton's* scorn head-on. True to his word, his friends rallied around her and buffered her from the worst of the *le beau monde's* reproof, yet snubs and rebuffs continued out of his view.

Although grateful for their support, she'd determined the time to depart was nigh. Within a fortnight, she'd leave London and wouldn't return. "Have you forgotten I'm planning to leave as soon as my funds are transferred?"

Her monies hadn't been deposited yet, something to do with auditing the trust transactions for the past two decades, having taken longer than Mr. Ponsby anticipated. He'd discovered Harrison and Minerva had accumulated a formidable amount of debt, and his ailing partner had allowed them to borrow against Shona's trust.

It appeared they'd tampered with hers as well.

Irritation raised sharp little claws and scratched a path of annoyance along Alexa's nerves upon learning that disagreeable news. Given Harrison's seedy character, the revelation didn't astound her.

"Well," Katrina drew circle-eights atop the counterpane, "you haven't managed to dissuade the duke from pursuing you with your protestations, have you?"

Big mistake, telling her pert cousin that tidbit.

Katrina slid Alexa a sly glance before grabbing a pillow and stuffing it beneath her head. "Do you think he'll ask you to marry him *again* today?"

Undoubtedly.

Which was one reason Alexa had decided to leave. Lucan wouldn't seriously seek a wife with her about, which meant breaking his word to his mother. Not something a man of his caliber took lightly.

The other motivation to move ahead with her life had resulted from Shona unexpectedly receiving the Lord of Parliament title the day before yesterday.

Calling her to his study, Uncle Hugo gently informed Alexa of the committee's decision. Although unexpected, and the ruling had incensed her aunt and uncle, Alexa's initial reaction was of profound relief.

Except for when their paths crossed at social events, she purposely hadn't sought her stepmother or sister since the day of Mr. Ponsby's visit. Minerva, nevertheless, persistently tried to see Alexa.

She and Harrison called twice the first week, but after Aunt Bridget's frosty reception and Alexa's non-appearance in the drawing room, Minerva resorted to sending Alexa invitations to call almost daily. When those efforts proved unsuccessful, she persuaded Shona to pen a few as well.

Alexa didn't intend to be unkind or uncongenial, but she dreaded Harrison's company to such an extent, she avoided the others as well. Truth to tell, after learning her father worried about their safety, Alexa didn't trust Minerva either.

Perhaps the letter from him would clarify his concerns, if she unearthed its whereabouts.

"You're sure you didn't spot an unopened letter near the tea tray in the salon the day Mr. Ponsby came? Steafan wrote it to me, and neither Auntie nor Uncle has seen it. I saw the solicitor lay it on the table, but as you know, I left the room in quite a dither and forgot about it until the next day."

"No." Katrina shook her head. "But then, things were quite chaotic when Shona and I entered. Perhaps a servant misplaced it. Have you asked the housekeeper or butler?"

"Yes, both, and I searched the room myself, including beneath the cushions and settees."

Alexa closed her eyes for a moment, picturing the salon. Harrison sat at that end of the settee.

Had the cur pocketed the note?

Alexa wouldn't put it past him.

Before she returned to Scotland to seek her father, purchase a modest cottage, and attempt to set a new course for her life, she intended to bid Shona farewell and wish her success in her new position. The life of a peeress suited Shona better. She'd do well as Lady Atterberry and, hopefully, she'd attract the interest of more suitable beaux than Renishaw and make a proper match.

The dreaded visit to confront Harrison about the letter must be scheduled. Alexa would drag Aunt Bridget or Katrina with her to ask the snake if he'd helped himself to her letter, not that he could form a truthful word with his forked tongue.

After one more meeting with Mr. Ponsby to receive her funds, she would be off. She had to wait until November fifteenth when he returned from Edinburgh, or she would've departed sooner. Each day she spent with Lucan, it became more difficult to contemplate leaving. But depart she must, for both their sakes.

She scrunched her nose.

Where had she put her reticule?

A person needed an extra hand to tote the paraphernalia a gentlewoman required for an outing.

"Why don't you want to marry the Duke of Harcourt, Alexa?" Echoing the question the dowager had hollered at the theater, Seonaid leaned her chestnut head against the floral damask chair's high back.

Alexa thought back to that night and wanted to groan. Thank God the orchestra had launched into the overture, preventing Alexa from having to answer Lady Middleton. Nonetheless, she'd been keenly aware of the looks directed her and Lucan's way, many speculative, a few envious, plus a passel of outraged scowls.

She met Seonaid's inquisitive, yet kind, gaze.

Alexa might as well share the truth. Seonaid doubtlessly knew it already. Having a friend with the second sight made it devilishly hard to keep secrets.

"The duke needs a refined wife, one who knows

how to assume the role of a duchess. Not an awkward Highlander who'd rather wade barefoot in streams."

Within the tedious constraints of propriety—a noblewoman's tightly laced emotional corset—Alexa would shrivel and die from boredom. "And besides, I cannot be sure his persistence isn't only because he finds me less objectionable than the other candidates, not from a great desire for me personally. Socially, we're worlds apart, and I fear, in the end, we'd despise one another, or at the very least, our resentment would lead to avoidance."

Ah, there's my reticule.

She scooped the bag from beneath a discarded fichu.

Far worse to have disappointment and disillusionment ferment for years until affection turned to bitter antagonism, or worse, indifference, than to depart with a marginally cracked heart. The latter she might eventually recover from. But the former? Well, she'd bear that scar for a lifetime.

"It's not such a difficult thing to overcome, Alexa. You're intelligent and can readily learn what is required of a duchess. His grace seems a patient, undemanding man." Katrina turned onto her side and propped her head with her palm. She pointed at Alexa. "Forgive me, my dear, but in my opinion, it's a pathetically feeble excuse, and you are not a coward."

"She's right, you know. You're conceding defeat before you've tried. I'm rather surprised, given your resilient nature." An indirect challenge tinged Seonaid's words.

"What about love?" Alexa rested her hip against her dressing table and toyed with a silver-overlaid perfume bottle. She searched their faces before returning to fidget with the bottle. "Your parents love each other, and my Scottish parents do too. Would you marry someone who needs to procure a wife in a rush to satisfy a vow, but who doesn't love you?"

Rounded, solemn gazes and grave silence met her question.

"I thought not." She replaced the bottle atop the table. "I don't wish to either, even if his reasons *are* honorable and unselfish."

Katrina sat up, concern replacing her giddiness. She cast Seonaid a desperate look. "Alexa, I had hoped… What I mean to say is, I thought by you marrying his grace some of the sting from…"

Seonaid cocked her head, her eyes warm with empathy. "What are your plans now that Shona is Lady Atterberry?"

~*~

Lucan patted his pocket as he descended from his coach in front of the Needhams' manor and inhaled a calming breath. Another couple of weeks and Achilles ought to be fully mended. Silly, how much he missed his horse.

Did Alexa ride?

Astride mayhap, but sidesaddle?

No, he'd bet Prinny's tubby toes she didn't, and knowing her, she wouldn't want to learn, though she'd been eager to learn to drive a team.

The weather had conspired against him, and he couldn't use his landau with its convertible top anymore, though ensconced in a carriage with her at his side didn't cause the usual phobic reaction.

Lucan rehearsed, again, how he intended to propose to Alexa today. Yes, she'd refused him each previous time, but last evening as he brooded before a crackling fire in his study, pondering her reluctance, an epiphany rocked him.

Prepared this time with a ring in his pocket—straight from the jeweler's, as a matter of fact—and armed with what Bretheridge and Warrick assured him women wanted to hear, he intended to finally win her consent.

Over the past weeks, his fascination and admiration—and yes, his lust—evolved into the most intense, confusing, wholly mind-altering emotion he'd ever experienced.

Love.

He loved Alexa.

Loved her enough to appoint a proxy to vote for him in Parliament and bustle her to the country if she despised living in Town. Devil it, after Mother died, they'd move to Scotland if Alexa couldn't abide Chattsworth Park House.

Another surprise awaited her too, which was why he decided they'd forgo their usual jaunt through Hyde Park—too bitterly cold to toddle about outdoors today, in any event. Frost covered the ground, and the boldest streak of sunlight couldn't penetrate the dense cloud cover.

Still, the oppressive elements couldn't damper his jovial mood.

A half-past seven this morning, pounding at the door had interrupted Lucan's morning coffee.

Darley brought welcome news.

Bellary had saved Lucan the inconvenience of ruining Renishaw by putting a lead ball in the cawker at dawn. As Bretheridge had predicted, Bellary grew impatient waiting for his monies and had challenged the viscount to a duel.

In typical cowardly fashion, Renishaw fired early, nicking Bellary's shoulder. Bellary's aim hit home and dropped Renishaw in his tracks. Now Lucan would never know if the viscount was responsible for the factory fire.

Nevertheless, relief for Jeremy and Alexa filled him. The one morsel of empathy he mustered existed for the Dowager Viscountess Renishaw. She'd lost both of her wastrel sons in duels, and with no other children, was at the new heir's mercy. Lucan prayed the next Viscount Renishaw possessed a modicum of decency his predecessors had lacked.

Whistling, he dashed up the Needhams' steps, his weighty navy-blue greatcoat flapping about his ankles. The door swung open before he lifted the knocker.

"Good morning, Lucan," Alexa fairly chirped.

The door frame swallowed her petite form as she stood inside, grinning. Bundled in a scarlet coat trimmed in ermine, her hair was tucked into a matching hat, except for a few silky, ebony curls at her temples. That adorable beauty mark beside her plump lips taunted, daring him to press his lips against the enticing speck.

Eyes sparkling, she shoved a hand into a fur muff.

Had she watched for him at the window?

The knowledge further ignited the warmth in his heart. Despite her adamant refusals to marry him, she anticipated their excursions as much as he.

"Good morning, Kitten. Are you ready?" He perused the empty entry. "Is Bindy accompanying us again today?"

"No, she has a fierce cold, poor dear." Alexa looped her reticule onto her wrist. "Jules is coming instead. He'll ride above with the driver, else you two long shanks will knock knees the entire time."

Not the most appropriate of places for proper chaperonage. No matter. Lucan's house lay but a half dozen blocks away. "I have a surprise for you. Two, actually."

"Oh? What kind of surprise?" Tossing him a saucy smile, she slipped past.

Minx.

She clambered into the carriage without waiting for assistance.

The footman exchanged a bemused look with him, and Lucan notched a shoulder. "She's an independent little thing, isn't she?"

"Indeed, sir, she is." Jules grinned as he shut the door behind Lucan.

Once settled, Lucan draped a thick lap robe across their knees. "Renishaw died in a duel this morning."

Poorly done. You might've warned her instead of blurting the news.

Fidgeting with her reticule's satin straps, Alexa remained silent for an extended moment. "I cannot rejoice in his death, for I know it grieves his family. Nevertheless, I'm grateful he won't harass me any longer."

Her inflection, and the disconcerted glint in her eye, revealed Renishaw's death shook her, despite him having been her nemesis.

A change of subject was in order.

The dismal skies outside dimmed the carriage's interior. "We don't usually have such severe frost this early."

"Aren't we beyond discussing the weather, Your Grace?" Shivering, Alexa laughed, the sultry, tantalizing sound driving him mad with lustful musings.

God, he loved her laugh.

Loved to make her smile and giggle and adored the impish glint in her lilac eyes. Lucan chuckled and took her gloved hand in his. "Way beyond, and we're also far beyond the 'Your Grace' silliness too."

She stared at their entwined fingers for a moment before burrowing closer to his side. "I'm leaving London."

25

"**L**eaving? For how long?"

Lucan's heart skipped a beat, or perhaps the carriage lurching forward as they left the curb launched the organ to his throat. He'd gulped twice before managing to form a coherent sound.

Alexa slid him an unreadable glance, the gold shards in her eyes glittering. "Forever, Lucan."

Her face blurred, and he blinked away stinging moisture.

She might as well have ripped his heart from his chest and pitched it underneath the horses' tramping hooves. Tiny black spots wavered before his eyes, and a cold sweat engulfed him as the carriage's sides shuddered and gradually closed in, suffocating him.

Breathe.

You're fine.

Look at Alexa.

He forced his gaze to her eyes and gulped air into his lungs. "Why?"

He'd waited too long to tell her he loved her.

Her bowed mouth bent downward, and she rested

her head against his shoulder as if she couldn't bear to look at him.

"Because you will never seriously seek a wife as long as I remain here, and I cannot marry you. I've been selfish these past days." She wiggled the fingers he held encased in his hand. "I am selfish even now, but it's unfair to you. The longer I stay, the less time you have to find a bride and honor your promise to your mother."

Lucan grasped her chin, gently turning her face to his. He searched her eyes. Shadowed with turmoil, they appeared almost black. "I want no other, will wed no other, even if it means breaking my word. Even if it means my title passes to my wastrel cousin."

Something between a sigh and a sob escaped her, and she raised torment-laden violet eyes to his. "Oh, Lucan. You cannot make such a sacrifice."

"Of course, I can. I shall, if it means you'll marry me."

He would too. In a blink. He couldn't contemplate enduring the remainder of his days without seeing her. Or worse yet, seeing her occasionally and knowing she'd never be his.

Angling her head away, Alexa presented her profile. "If I thought I could make you proud, perform the duties of a duchess with a modicum of success, I'd be sorely tempted. Though, if I'm honest, Lucan, the notion terrifies me. I'd commit gaffes and *faux pas*, bring ridicule and shame upon you and the duchy."

"I do not care! Run naked through Almack's Assembly Rooms or turn cartwheels and expose your stockings at Vauxhall Gardens. I shall do both with you." Lucan kissed the top of her head, the ermine tickling his nose.

"Preposterous. Imagine what Lady Jersey or Countess Esterházy would say." She gave a watery chuckle before her countenance became grave once more.

"You need to be serious, Lucan. We both know you and your friends' influence contributed to my acceptance these past weeks. Even then, the reception has been scant more than stilted politeness to my face and disparaging behind my back."

"Fine, we shall shun the lot." He swept his hand in the air. "Bugger them all. You never have to host or attend a single event. We shall retire to the country, change our names and the color of our hair, don masquerade masks when we go out—"

She jabbed his side with her pointed elbow. "Will you stop blathering and listen to reason, please?"

"Must I?" Had she eaten berries this morning, or were her lips rosy from the cold?

He'd like to taste them to find out.

"Lucan!" Frustration radiated from her.

He exhaled and forced his attention away from the bewitching mole taunting him. "Say your piece, my lady."

"You must maintain a presence in the House of Lords in order to help those less fortunate than you. You said so yourself. Those born into privilege have a responsibility to help others."

He lifted her hand and touched it to his mouth. Pressing his lips to her knuckles for an extended moment, he breathed in her refreshing heather scent.

"I know you will lose your inheritance if you don't marry a Scot, but have you forgotten, my little gypsy, I have Scots blood?"

Alexa whipped her head up, cracking his chin soundly. "How did you learn about that?"

"Ouch." He grabbed his jaw. "Your uncle told me."

"Yes, I had forgotten." Gaze contemplative, Alexa nibbled her lower lip and rubbed the top of her head.

He almost heard the cogs in her brain clacking and grinding as they revolved round and round.

"Mr. Ponsby didn't say how much Scottish blood my husband needed, only that he has to be Scots." She squinted at him intently.

Ought to have donned a kilt and tam o'shanter.

Bare arsed in this weather?

Nae.

His ballocks shriveled to prune-sized, like the fruit he'd eaten for breakfast, didn't appeal.

Alexa poked his arm. "You can prove your lineage?"

Was she considering accepting?

Lucan pretended to be put upon. "I suppose, if I *must.* I can dig through the family archives and find the connection."

Pages and pages of musty documents.

It might take days.

Weeks.

He snapped his fingers. "Or better yet, we shall call on Grandaunt Kathryn. She'll know. That woman doesn't forget a thing."

Alexa clasped his hand tighter. "You must think me horridly mercenary for caring about the inheritance. I don't want the money for myself, but for the black tinkers and other impoverished Scots."

"I think no such thing. The law affords women little power or independence, and as my wife, you'd be stepping into a foreign realm. Having your own funds surely must bring you a degree of security and peace." He brushed her jawline with a bent finger. "Rest assured, I would see you provided your own monies to do with what you will."

Slumping against the squabs, she shut her eyes, her thick midnight lashes fanning her ivory cheeks. "I'm afraid I'd disappoint you, that in time you'd come to begrudge me. Regret marrying me."

She spoke softly, and he strained to hear her above the horses' clopping hooves, the creaking carriage, and the wheels clattering upon the cobblestones.

"Never." In one deft movement, he lifted her onto his lap.

A tiny squeal escaped Alexa as her eyelids sprang open, and she clutched his shoulders. She twisted to look beyond either window. "Put me down. Someone will see."

He waggled his eyebrows and gave her a wolfish grin. "Would that make you marry me?"

"No, you dolt." Her upturned lips belied her name-calling.

Holding her securely around the waist, Lucan hastily lowered both window coverings. "There, now no one can see a thing."

"And when we emerge with the windows covered?" She gestured at the shades. "No one will speculate as to what transpired inside the carriage? Rumors will abound that we coupled throughout Berkley Square like springtime rabbits."

He mentally measured the seat.

After they married, he might try to persuade her to do exactly that. He might even wear a kilt for the occasion. An avalanche of lust ripped through him. Thank God, Alexa's thick redingote and his weighty greatcoat hid his giddy member's reaction.

"Well, I hope by then we shall be betrothed." He shifted her to reach inside his coat. He withdrew the jewelry box.

Her delicate brows rose as she eyed the petite cube dubiously before lifting her wary gaze. "Oh, Lucan. What have you done?"

Not exactly ecstatic.

"Open it." He set the violet velvet box atop her lap, then set about removing her left glove. "I had it designed for you."

Alexa tilted the lid and gasped. "A thistle ring? Is this an amethyst?" Emotion clogged her voice. "It's my favorite stone. How did you know?"

Lucan nodded as he plucked the ring from its nest. "It's the same shade as your eyes, and it's set in gold because you have gold flecks around your irises."

"I...I don't know what to say, Lucan."

"Say, yes. You'll marry me, and together we shall help the travellers, cock a snook at the upper ten thousand, and live happily ever after like sweethearts in a fairytale." He slipped the band onto her finger. "I love you, Alexa."

"You do?" A tear trickled from one eye as she gazed at him in wide-eyed wonder.

He wrapped her in his embrace. "Yes, I do, and I shall do whatever it takes to make you love me too."

Giving him a tremulous smile, she laid her palm against his cheek. "I already do, foolish man. Why do you think I refused to bring dishonor to your title?" Alexa raised herself up and brushed her lips against his. "I know I'm going to regret this someday."

"No. You won't." Lucan nuzzled her ear, and her breath rushed from her on a sigh.

"It makes absolutely no sense." She nipped his lower lip before her tongue flicked the edge of his mouth.

Where had she learned that trick?

His manhood surged.

"It makes *perfect* sense, Kitten." He skimmed his palm the length of her narrow ribs until he met the fullness of her breast. The plump mound nestled perfectly in his cupped hand. Another errant tremor pulsed in his groin.

"We don't suit." She twined her arms around his neck, her breathing soft, wispy pants.

"We suit perfectly."

Lucan grazed her lips, returning again and again for little tastes of their sweetness and to tease the mole gracing her lower lip, which had driven him mad for weeks.

"See, we cannot even agree on this."

He rubbed his thumb across her breast's tip, and she arched into his hand, another sultry moan escaping her.

"Oh, but we do agree on *this*." He captured her mouth in a searing kiss, born of weeks of restraint, unprofessed love, and adoration.

No reticent miss, Alexa met his onslaught, their tongues tangling and dueling, raising his passion to a dangerous degree outside the privacy of a bedchamber.

Caught in sensation, it took Lucan a moment to realize the carriage had shuddered to a stop and rocked as the driver and footman alighted.

"We've arrived." He shifted Alexa onto the seat beside him.

Cheeks flushed and lips glowing, she hastily straightened her skirts as he put a respectable distance between them.

"Arrived? Where?"

The door swung open, and she eased forward to peer outside.

"My house. Remember, I have a surprise for you."

"What kind of surprise?" She peeked at him as she accepted Jules's hand and exited the carriage.

"Thister!"

26

Alexa whipped around, tramping Jules's toes in her haste and almost falling.

"I'm sorry," she gasped, trying to regain her balance and stamping his foot once more.

A strong hand at her elbow steadied her. "Careful, there."

Humor feathered the edges of Lucan's mouth and eyes.

Laughing, their sweet faces scrunched with glee, György and Lala bolted down the steps.

In the doorway beside a beaming butler, Father and Edeena stood smiling.

Not caring she would soil her coat, Alexa knelt and opened her arms. Her brother and sister crashed into her, nearly tumbling them to the ground.

Again, Lucan's strong arm kept her upright.

He'd arranged this, though how he convinced her father to leave Scotland for London would make for interesting telling.

Tears clouding her eyes, she smiled her gratitude. "How? When?"

György pointed at Lucan. "His grace let us ride in his carriage all the way from Scotland."

Lucan extended his hand. "Here, let me help you. We shall go inside, and I'll tell you everything."

Several curious spectators paused to gawp. Yes, it was best to continue the reunion indoors.

She accepted his help, then lifted Lala onto her hip. "Yes, let's do. I have so many questions."

"I lost a tooth. Now I am talkin' like Lala." György grinned and exposed the gap in his upper teeth as they climbed the risers.

"I've missed you so." She wrapped her other arm around his slender shoulder. "How have you been?"

He scampered up the last two steps and opened his arms wide. "We are sailin' on a big ship to America."

"*America*? Why?" She met her father's understanding gaze. So far away. She mightn't ever see them again. "You love Scotland."

Alexa tossed Lucan a bewildered look.

What did he know of this nonsense?

"We shall discuss it once we're settled in the salon." His lips bent into a smile, and he clasped György's hand. "Do you like hot chocolate and biscuits? I bet I can get Cook to find some."

György nodded enthusiastically.

A few minutes later, after Alexa hugged her parents and brother and sister again, Jules led the children to the kitchen for the promised hot chocolate, and Houston delivered a generously laden tray to the salon.

The butler removed her redingote while she curiously peered around the functional, though inarguably austere-in-its-maleness, room. The plain, heavy furniture reflected Lucan's stark taste.

Beeswax, linseed oil, and the aroma of burning wood lent a hospitable ambiance to the chamber. A family portrait provided a hint of color amongst the neutral browns and grays. From the bright canvas, Lucan peered at her, a glint of mischievousness in the depths of his youthful, pewter gaze.

He didn't seem to prefer bright hues or embellishment as she did.

Another incongruity between them?

"Would you please, Alexa?" Indicating the service, Lucan then prodded the fire with a poker, encouraging the flames higher.

"Of course." She poured coffee into the four eggshell thin teacups. A smile quirking her lips, she raised the pot. "Most un-English-like."

Everyone chuckled, and the tension eased a trifle from Father's and Edeena's features. Although, Edeena still gingerly cradled her cup and saucer as if afraid the china would shatter merely from being touched.

Offering her father a plate of assorted biscuits, Alexa's nerves unexpectedly overcame her. As much as she wanted to know the truth of how she came to be with the Highland travellers, part of her longed for the blissful ignorance that had protected her these many years.

"Mr. Faas—"

"Please, Yer Grace, call me Balcomb."

Lucan inclined his head a degree. "Balcomb, the tickets are in my study. *The Morning Star*—" He twisted to address Alexa. "She's part of Stapleton's Shipping and Supplies fleet which Lady Sethwick owns. Of course, you remember her from your stay at Craiglocky Keep."

"Yes." Alexa managed a partial nod.

Lucan had purchased the tickets?

Why?

"As I was saying"—Lucan brushed a shortbread crumb from his leg—"*The Morning Star* sails with the tide two nights hence."

She sucked in a startled breath and, hands shaking, set her teacup aside, the china clanking until she brought her shaking hands under control. "That soon?"

"*Aye*, Tasara." After exchanging a glance with Edeena, Father abandoned his cup too. "His grace has generously paid for our passage to Boston and given me a letter of reference for a position at Lady Sethwick's shippin' office there. He also insists I accept a sum from him so that we"—he glanced at Edeena—"can begin again in the colonies."

"But why are you leaving the travellers?" Alexa gestured to Edeena, then Father. "You've only known the black tinker's way of life. I thought you loved it."

She swallowed the grief tearing at her throat. She'd borne the banishment from her clan, but her family moving to a different continent?

To never see György or Lala again?

"Times are changin', lass. It is becomin' harder and harder for the tinkers to find places we are welcome, and harder yet to earn coin. Speakin' of which." He gave her a sheepish half-smile. "Jamie forced me to accept the reward money from yer uncle."

"Why?" She pushed a stray lock of hair off her forehead.

"He said he and the brethren were owed it for keepin' silent. Ye *ken* travellin' is a hard life and a thousand pounds? Well…" Father shrugged his thin shoulders. "I *canna* begrudge Jamie for bein' a bit greedy."

Alexa couldn't either. Many a traveller took advantage of opportunities when presented. Knowing Father hadn't sought the money for himself did much to heal the rift in her heart.

"Within our tribe there is more and more discord as well. We're no' the first family to leave, lass."

"I know." But America? Why so blasted far away? "Why don't you stay in England with me? Or better yet, I have an inheritance. We could live on that."

"*Nae*, lass. I make my own way, ye *ken* that. In America, we'll have opportunities we can never hope to have in Scotland or England. Lala and György can make somethin' of themselves there."

Hope lit his tired features, revealing the handsome man he'd once been before a lifetime of want and hard work ravaged his face and body. Father rose and looked toward the entrance. "With yer permission, Yer Grace, may I shut the door?"

"By all means." Lucan took Alexa's hand and gave it a comforting squeeze.

Searching his eyes, she pressed a palm to her stomach. "Do you know what this is about?"

"I do. He told me last night when they arrived, but

you should hear it from him." He squeezed her hand again.

Father stood before the fireplace, hands clasped behind him, and stared at the carpet. The lines of his face deepened as he furrowed his brow and flattened his mouth. He struggled to form the words, as she wrestled with the urge to flee the room.

At last, he regarded her. "It is true ye were found in the forest. But, what I havena told ye, havena told a soul, except the duke and Edeena recently is that Forba found ye hidin'—beaten and bleedin'—inside a hollow log."

Why would someone assault a toddler?

"I became worried and went searchin' for her." Pausing, he scraped a hand through his hair, an untamed look in his eye. "I came upon her tryin' to defend herself, and ye, from a monstrous brute. A small knife meant for cuttin' plants was all she had."

Lucan patted Alexa's hand before standing. He strode to the bell pull and, a moment later, Houston entered.

"Yes, Your Grace?"

"Please bring a bottle of Scotch and four tumblers."

"At once." The butler remained stone-faced at being asked to procure spirits at half-past ten in the morning.

When the door closed behind Houston, Father resumed his tale. "He charged me, knocked me to the ground, and nearly choked my life from me before Forba bashed him in the head with a rock."

Edeena looked around nervously, as if afraid Father would be overheard.

He flicked Lucan an uneasy glance. "I swear he

would've killed me if she hadna acted quickly, Yer Grace."

"I don't doubt it in the least." Lucan returned to his seat beside Alexa. "Are you all right, Alexa? I know this must be trying for you."

His presence gave her strength. She needed to know everything. She nodded. "Yes. Go on, Father."

"We stuffed his body as far into the hollow log as we could, intendin' to return at night and bury him. Only we never returned. The *bairn* was delivered while we were away, and when Jamie saw ye, lass"—Father gestured at Alexa—"even though we told him we found ye alone, he gave orders to break camp immediately."

"Jamie is nae man's fool. He *ken* somethin' was afoot and feared for the safety of his people." Edeena ducked her head at her boldness before taking a careful sip of coffee.

"*Aye*, and when he asked why I was bloodied and my clothes torn, I lied, claimin' to have slipped and fallen. Easy enough to do in the Highlands."

Drawing in a steadying breath, Alexa wet her lips. "And this man, do you have any idea who he was?"

"*Aye*, by accident, I stumbled across the bugger at Dounnich House. Forba hadna killed him, only knocked him unconscious."

"Good God." Alexa couldn't suppress the shudder ravaging her at the mention of the Blackhall fortress or the brutes who imprisoned her.

Lucan boldly draped an arm across her shoulders. The heat of his fingers radiated through the fabric, branding her as his.

"His name?" She'd already guessed what Father would say.

"Angus Blackhall." Father shook his head and stared into the distance. "He remembered me, after all those years, and must've realized exactly who he'd captured. Though his clan was under attack, he headed straight for the staircase, the bloody sod."

Would Angus have killed her if he'd known her identity earlier?

A sinister grin skewed her father's mouth. "The other travellers and I ensured he dinna make it to ye, lass."

Alexa calmly took a drink of her coffee. Not the reaction a peeress should have if she'd heard her father confess to killing a man, but she wouldn't feign faintness or upset she didn't feel.

More of a wild beast than civilized human, Angus Blackhall's violent ending didn't produce an ounce of remorse in her. Taking another sip of the dark brew, she hid a grimace. A mite too strong for Alexa's taste. She added a dab more milk to her coffee. "Why didn't he search for me?"

Father shrugged. "I *canna* say for certain. There are dozens of black tinker tribes, and we are always movin'. Besides, I'd guess he dinna want whoever hired him to kill ye to ken he'd failed all those years ago."

That sent a frisson of dread sluicing through her. Now chilled, despite the cheery fire cavorting in the hearth and the hot coffee warming her, Alexa relaxed into Lucan's heat, grateful she'd chosen to wear a long-sleeved wool spencer over her gown.

"Blackhall didn't tell you who hired him? Not a hint?" Lucan withdrew his arm and bent forward, anticipation radiating from his taut form.

Alexa felt strangely bereft without his arm's comforting weight.

"There wasna time for an interrogation, Yer Grace. Ye were there and *ken* it was chaos in the beginnin'. But I would bet my boots he told someone else. His kind are braggarts."

"That might explain Harrison's knowledge of my captivity." Premonition scratched her sharp talons down Alexa's spine.

Lucan nodded and rubbed his nape, his face settling into harsh lines. "Yes, it's quite feasible he knew someone there. His stepsister is Scots, after all."

"But wouldn't that mean he also be aware she'd been abducted?" A puzzled frown wrinkled Edeena's plump face as she looked from person to person.

"*Aye*, it—"

A brisk rap interrupted Balcomb and preceded Houston's entrance, bearing the requested spirits in one hand, and guiding Lady Middleton with the other. "Sir, Lady Middleton has arrived."

"Forgive me for calling unannounced, Nephew, but I have urgent news." She faltered upon spying Father and Edeena.

Cautious around gentry and noblemen, and hesitant of her reception, they eyed her uncertainly.

"Houston, please leave the Scotch beside the coffee." Lucan indicated an empty spot atop the tea table.

"Shall I pour you each a finger's worth, Your Grace?"

"No, that's not necessary, but please fetch my grandaunt a teacup and tumbler too."

That did earn a subtle eyebrow and lip twitch from the butler. "Indeed."

He faced Alexa's father. "Mr. Faas, your children would like permission to visit the coach house next door. They've been extended an invitation to play with a litter of six-week-old beagle pups. Naturally, Jules will accompany them and keep them from harm and mischief."

Poor Jules, playing nursemaid. Not what he'd expected today when he'd agreed to act as a chaperone.

Father smiled. "*Aye*, they would enjoy that. Thank ye."

With a regal nod of his head, the butler slipped from the room.

Lucan strode to his aunt. "Grandaunt Kathryn, this is a surprise."

She pointed her cane at Alexa's parents and squinted. "Are you the couple who raised Miss Atterberry?"

"*Aye*, m'lady," Father murmured, bending into a stiff bow as Edeena attempted a clumsy curtsy.

"Lud, none of that m'lady falderal. We're practically family. Come. Let me have a look at you." The dowager marchioness drummed her cane upon the floor, and Alexa's parents swapped disconcerted looks.

Quite obvious where Lucan had acquired his tenacity. If his mother possessed her aunt's resolve, the poor man hadn't stood a chance when she demanded he find himself a wife.

Lucan released a tolerant chuckle. "Why don't you have a seat on the divan, and Mr. and Mrs. Faas can sit on either side of you? Then you can tell us why we have the pleasure of your company before the stroke of noon."

"Hush, boy." The dowager silenced him with a flip of her bony hand and limped toward Alexa. "Alexandra, dear. Looking as lovely as always."

Only Lucan's Grandaunt Kathryn would dare to shush a duke.

Alexa scooted over and patted the seat beside her. "Please, have a seat, and permit me to introduce you to my parents."

The elderly woman paused, seemingly disoriented and dazed for a moment. "Parents. Yes, yes. That's why I'm here."

"To meet my parents?" Alexa slid Lucan a questioning look.

With an imperceptible shake, he canted his head, apparently sharing her puzzlement.

Father and Edeena sat tensely on the edge of the facing divan, their expressions carefully impassive.

"No. That can wait. This cannot." Dowager Lady Middleton seized Lucan's arm, her face alarmingly pale.

Concern creased the corners of his eyes and between his brows. "Is something amiss? Are you unwell? Should I call for a physician?"

"Pooh, I'm not about to cock up my toes." With her saucy retort, a bit of color returned to her papery cheeks.

"I told you I'd heard the name before. It took me weeks of pondering. But when I awoke this morning, I suddenly remembered, clear as a bell, as if it happened yesterday."

Name?

"Here, take a seat." Lucan eased her onto the divan as Alexa tipped a few drops of amber spirit into a glass, then handed it to the shaken woman.

He squatted next to his grandaunt and tenderly took her delicate hand in his. Darkish hair covered his knuckles.

Alexa had never noticed the smattering before.

However, the consideration he showed his grandaunt caused her heart to swell. A decent man— strong, yet gentle and considerate.

"What has you flustered, Grandaunt Kathryn?" He winked at Alexa, his dimple mocking her. "She's usually the stoic one. When everyone else is running about in a scatter-brained dither, Grandaunt Kathryn remains calm as a lily floating atop a pond on a windless day."

The dowager quaffed the Scotch in one gulp, earning her goggle-eyed looks from everyone. She bent frontward and banged the glass on the table before removing her gloves. "Don't look at me like that. When I'm done telling you what I remembered, you'll be reaching for a bottle. Trust me."

"You've remembered something which has upset you? Can we help?" Alexa took the dame's gloves and, after straightening the fingers, laid them on the divan's arm.

"Minerva Atterberry." The dowager pointed a finger and waved it beside her temple. "I knew I'd heard her name before, but I couldn't put my finger on where. Niggled at me and kept me awake at night for weeks." Her voice wobbled, and she trembled noticeably. Her keen gaze flew to Father and Edeena, then darted to Alexa. "Harcourt and I—that side of our family—are part Scots too."

Alexa sent him a loving glance. "That was one of the first things I learned about him."

No need to share precisely how she came by the knowledge. Fingering the somewhat loose ring she'd forgotten in the tumult since arriving, she offered him a promise-filled smile. She hadn't responded to his umpteenth proposal either.

His answering provocative tilt of lips propelled a jolt to her center. Even in the midst of a crisis, he sent her pulse cavorting. Lucan eased onto the divan, holding his elderly aunt's hand.

"Years ago, the same Season my Elizabeth came out—God rest her sweet soul—Minerva, a backward Scots lass, came to London. Elizabeth befriended the poor, awkward girl, and we grew to know her rather well, or at least better than most. Others couldn't move beyond her oddness." The dowager grew silent for a long moment, renewed sorrow shadowing her lined face.

"I still miss my Elizabeth. Quite dreadfully at times."

"She died after birthing a stillborn son," Lucan explained, for the others' benefit.

Alexa gave the woman a hug. "How tragic. I'm

truly sorry."

Drawing a trembling breath, Lucan's aunt blinked and gave a little shake of her silvery head. "If I recall correctly, Minerva is related to the Hintons, and they sponsored her come out."

That explained Minerva's comment about visiting Dorthea Hinton the day Mr. Ponsby descended upon them.

"In any event, she caused quite a bumblebroth when she eloped to Gretna Green with Byron Severson, and they remained in Scotland afterward." The dowager shook her head again. "The boy couldn't have been more than eighteen."

"Didn't his parents' object?" Lucan recalled his own headstrong behavior at eighteen, but he'd heeded his mother's wisdom.

The Dowager Lady Middleton nodded, her gray eyebrows twitching. "Naturally. They were furious and threatened to cut him off, but it was said he didn't care. He'd inherited a tidy purse from his maternal grandmother and threw funds about with a youth's abandon, promising to pay his debts when he turned one and twenty and the trust was his."

"Likely, that's what drew Minerva's interest. If I've learned one thing about my stepmother, it's that she watches out for herself. How long were they married?" Alexa folded her hands in her lap.

"So they lived on credit?" Lucan scratched his temple. "Seems unlikely they didn't have some help."

Eyeing the Scotch longingly, Lady Middleton pulled a face. "Rumor has it, mere weeks after their joining, Severson petitioned for a divorce. Cannot do that in England—a woman has to be an adulteress—but Scottish laws are different.”

“So the Dowager Lady Atterberry’s first husband divorced her? Do you know why?” Light streaming through a window cast a vague aura about Lucan’s tilted head.

“No, no.” His aunt pressed a quivering hand to her throat. “He died before the divorce was granted. Runaway carriage. Plummeted off a cliff, killing the driver and team too.”

Alexa’s breath hitched, suspended painfully between inhaling and exhaling as her gaze hurled to Lucan’s.

Too eerily coincidental.

“But what I wanted to tell you, what gave me the shivers and curdled my blood like tainted milk in coffee, is that…” The dowager marchioness drew in a shuddery breath and, voice raspy, blurted, “Minerva’s maiden name was Blackhall.”

If Lucan hadn't been sitting, Grandaunt Kathryn's revelation would've knocked him on his arse. He almost shook his head and stuck fingers in his ears to unclog them.

Other than compressing her lips and stuffing her hands beneath her legs, as she did when anxious, Alexa appeared composed. Nonetheless, the tempest raging in her pansy gaze belied her outward mien.

Flawless duchess.

"God Almighty." Fat droplets spilled down Mrs. Faas's cheeks as she fumbled for her husband's hand.

Face crestfallen and his shoulders slumping, Balcomb wilted, horror clouding his eyes. "Right into the vipers' nest, we sent ye. Forgive us, lass."

His wife rummaged in her ample bodice, eventually withdrawing a vivid scrap of cloth to blot at her streaming eyes.

Blackhall.

The reviled name epitomized deceit, ruthlessness, and greed, and to not assume Minerva guilty of every suspicion directed her way thus far took a stalwart act of

Lucan's will.

Houston returned with the extra glass and teacup, and after considering everyone's countenances, took it upon himself to unstop the crystal decanter and pour generous splashes into the tumblers.

The minuscule portion would do nothing to dispel the shock Lucan and the others had received.

Returning the Scotch to the table, Houston gave a sage nod. "My hallowed mother always said, 'Nothing like a hearty swig to chase a fiery path to your gut and eliminate your cares.'"

Hadn't his mother died from liver failure?

After indulging in a stinging swallow, Lucan touched Grandaunt Kathryn's elbow. "May I have a few minutes alone with Miss Atterberry?"

His instincts told him—no, shouted—Alexa remained unsafe. Thank God he had her followed whenever she left her aunt and uncle's house.

"Indeed. I need to be on my way at once. I have an appointment at the milliners, but I did want to impart what I'd remembered. By the by, heard Renishaw's breathed his last." Grandaunt Kathryn rendered him a grave look. "Cannot say I'm sorry to see such rabble snoring soil."

With Lucan's assistance, she struggled to stand. Near the entrance, she adjusted her bonnet then retied the ribbons as Alexa collected his aunt's gloves.

She and her parents stood as well.

"Trust an old woman's intuition, Nephew. Mine's finely honed and has served me well for nigh on six and seventy years." She tapped his arm. "Something's off with Minerva Atterberry."

As off as a purple-butted duck.

"We are goin' to collect on our wee ones. Excuse us, please." Balcomb angled toward the door, but he swung around and pointed to a bundle lying on the polished walnut window seat. "Yer violin is there, Tasara. I *ken* how ye enjoyed it."

Lucan's soon-to-be-wife was full of surprises.

Delight lit Alexa's face, and she rushed to embrace him in the doorway. "Thank you. I've missed playing these past weeks."

"We'll no' sail before sayin' goodbye, Tasara." Balcomb enfolded her in a firm hug.

"I know," emotion choked her voice, but she smiled bravely.

She hadn't said a word about going with them.

A thought slid, serpent-like, into Lucan's mind and curled around his confidence, mercilessly squeezing the frail glint of hope.

She hasn't agreed to marry me.

He vehemently booted the unwelcome notion aside.

True, but she hasn't said no this time, either.

"Thank you." Smiling serenely, Alexa bussed his grandaunt's cheek. "I cannot tell you how helpful you've been. Knowing Minerva's history sheds light on my situation. I wish I knew how her stepbrother fits into all of this."

Attempting to tug on her glove, Grandaunt Kathryn's face folded into a frown.

"Here, let me." Alexa took it from her.

"Thank you, dearest." His aunt lifted her chin and

gave Lucan such a penetrating stare, he felt she'd opened his skull and peered inside. *Marry her,* she mouthed above the top of Alexa's bowed head.

"That's another irregular thing." Giving Alexa a grateful smile, she extended her other gnarled hand.

"What is?" Alexa slipped the second kid glove onto his grandaunt's stiff fingers.

"The stepbrother." Bundled warmly against the unwelcoming outdoors, Grandaunt Kathryn pursed her lips. "Minerva's an only child. Her parents died, and her barbarian uncle raised her. Harrison Peterson is no more her stepbrother than the Prince Regent is."

Alexa jerked as if struck.

Her confounded gaze sought Lucan. "Another lie?"

"So it would appear." Not the last deception either, Lucan would bet.

Skimming a hand across her forehead, a brittle laugh escaped Alexa. "What else have they fabricated? I cannot begin to sift fact from fallacy where they are concerned."

His aunt patted Alexa's cheek. "You trust my nephew to see this conundrum sorted, and stay far away from those hobgoblins in the meanwhile."

Lucan encircled his grandaunt's elbow in a supportive grasp. Wanness etched her features. Done in, poor dear. "I'll be but a moment, Alexa. I have some thoughts I'd like to discuss with you regarding what we've learned today."

"Certainly. I'll wait here. I'm eager to examine my violin and adjust the pegs." Alexa glided to the window seat, where she lovingly lifted the instrument from its humble nest.

He saw his grandaunt on her way, and upon returning to the salon, found Alexa sitting at the window, playing a haunting melody. Eyes closed, she whisked the bow across the strings with the familiarity of a lover's touch.

Loath to interrupt her and the soothing music flowing from the strings, he inched farther into the room. He must've made a sound, or else her intuition told her someone intruded.

Her thick lashes eased open, and she self-consciously lowered the bow. Holding the violin by the neck, she raised it a fraction. "It belonged to my first gypsy mother. The one who found me in the woods."

Laying the instrument beside her, she directed her attention outside once more and gazed at the passersby, daring the bleak weather.

The heavens had darkened to a pinkish-slate, and from the coolness dogging the salon, the temperature had plummeted as well. Snow by nightfall?

Adding another hefty log to the fire, he gauged her.

Shoulders slightly slumped, sadness, or perhaps resignation, sharpened her pert profile.

What he wouldn't give to relieve her of the yoke she'd been burdened with.

"Do you think Minerva and Harrison are behind my abduction as a child?" She rested her forehead against the glass.

Brushing specks of dirt and bark from his hands, Lucan strode to her, the Aubusson carpet buffering his steps. He laid the violin on a nearby chair before pushing Alexa's skirts aside and taking the instrument's place. "It seems highly probable."

Her lips parted on a wispy sigh.

He took her delicate hand and, turning it over, ran his forefinger along each digit. "Kitten, with your permission, I'd like to send a message to a friend of mine—a Bow Street Runner—and have him and a couple of other runners meet us at your stepmother's. I don't want her to know we're coming, however."

Alexa faced him, her indecision apparent. "Is that wise, confronting them? They'll just lie. Without proof, there's nothing to be done, is there?"

"What did the letter your father left for you say?" Lucan hoped there might be something helpful in the contents.

"I don't know. It disappeared, and no one has seen it since Mr. Ponsby set it on the table. I think Harrison might've filched it."

He would, the sneaky blackguard. "Or Minerva. If so, it's undoubtedly been destroyed."

Along with any incriminating evidence against the pair.

"True." Alexa dragged in a breath, holding it for an instant before gradually exhaling.

A stronger, more self-controlled, and resilient woman he'd never met. He knew men with less fortitude, but he needed to comfort and reassure Alexa, her resilience be damned.

Lucan drew her unresisting form into his arms. Inhaling her unique spicy scent, he rested his head atop hers. Contentment, unlike anything he'd ever known, engulfed him.

Encircling his waist, she melded against him and issued a soft, happy sigh, which flew straight to his already full heart.

He thought he knew passion and want, but this burning in his blood, aching of his soul, surpassed desire and the base need for physical release.

Why, amongst the ladies he'd known, many of whom he'd shared the ultimate carnal pleasure with, had this petite, spirited Highlander been the woman to crack his carefully constructed barriers?

Lucan's burgeoning love squashed his cynical outlook regarding marriage until making Alexa his consumed him. He could almost be persuaded to believe in fate and destiny, or that a higher force brought them together. What other explanation sufficed for their paths having crossed?

Alexa snuggled closer, her head nestled against the curve of his shoulder.

A commotion echoed in outside the door, and they guiltily sprang apart. A moment later, Baron Devaux-Rousset, then Miss Needham and Miss Ferguson, bearing a bloodied and bedraggled Miss Atterberry, swarmed into the room.

The latter struggled free of their grasps and stumbled forward a pair of tottering steps. "Alexa, Mama means to see you dead."

28

"What in heaven's name has happened?" Chagrin, coupled with alarm, propelled Alexa from the window seat. "Shona, have you been assaulted?"

Her sister lurched across the room. Sobbing, she threw herself into Alexa's arms.

Alexa staggered backward several paces. Thank goodness no one seemed to notice the untoward position she and Lucan were in when the others plowed into the salon unannounced.

Shona's words registered at last.

Minerva wants me dead?

No.

Means to see me dead.

Alexa squeezed her eyes shut against nauseating fear.

"Forgive me. I should have come to you when I first suspected something nefarious, but I was confused. And afraid." Mouth quivering and eyes red-rimmed, Shona dashed at the tears skimming down her rounded cheeks.

She's afraid too?

Shona clasped Alexa's forearm, her gaze

beseeching. "Please understand, Alexa, although thrilled to have a sister, I was terrified Mama's well-laid plans for my life had been disrupted. She doesn't respond well when she doesn't have her way."

So Alexa had determined.

Shona gingerly touched her battered face. "She has a vicious, *vicious* temper when thwarted."

"Did she strike you?" How else had Shona acquired her swollen lip and bruises?

Nodding, her sister sniffed rather pathetically. "Yes, although it's not the first time. I missed last Season due to a severe beating." She jutted her round chin upward. "I refused to marry an ancient lecher with a fat purse."

Shona's life hadn't been at all what Alexa assumed, and remorse tightened her throat.

"Here, my lady, dry your tears and tell us what has happened." Lucan appeared at Alexa's side and produced his kerchief. "Devaux, I presume you escorted the ladies?"

Alexa veered a covert glance in Seonaid's direction and found her taking in the room's decor while pointedly avoiding looking in the baron's direction. Whatever had occurred between them to cause such a palpable rift?

"*Oui*. I needed to discuss a pressing business matter with Mr. Needham. When I didn't find him at the bank, I called at their home." Lord Devaux-Rousset clasped his hands behind his back, his attention focused on Seonaid once more. "Most fortunate that I did so."

"I suppose it depends on one's idea of fortunate, no?" Seonaid murmured with a falsely sweet smile.

Lord Devaux-Rousset's raven brows rose in a challenge, and he nonchalantly smoothed his neat mustache. Male appreciation glinted in his dark eyes even as his lips moved the merest bit.

Wrapping an arm about Shona's waist, Alexa guided her to a divan. "Sit dear, and let me have a good look at your injuries."

Katrina tossed her bonnet and gloves on a table beside a bronze stag statue before plopping beside Shona. "Mama and Papa have gone to pay their respects to the family of one of Papa's former clerks who passed yesterday. When Shona arrived disheveled, babbling hysterically, and begging to speak with you, Seonaid and I knew at once we must find you."

"How *did* you find me?" Alexa tilted Shona's face and suppressed a gasp upon spying partial reddish-purple fingermarks encircling her neck.

Minerva or Harrison?

"When the duke came for you, he told our butler where you'd be in case someone sought you at Hyde Park." A naughty smirk teased Katrina's mouth.

Minx.

Houston rapped upon the doorjamb before announcing in unflappable tones, "I have taken the liberty of ordering fresh tea and a light repast as well as have asked for cold water, ointment, and cloths for the young lady."

"Excellent." Lucan pulled the window covering aside and perused the street.

What exactly did he seek?

"Should I send for a physician?" Expression

concerned, the majordomo's troubled regard hovered on Shona.

Alexa blinked.

Why, his stuffy exterior hides a gallant's heart.

"Nae, nae." Shona shook her head, slipping into Scots. "Nothing's broken this time." *This time? Oh, my God.* "Just a few cuts and bruises."

Lucan glanced behind him to Shona, huddled on the couch, and frowned. "Houston, please send for Mr. Thaddaeus Palmer of the Bow Street Runners. If he's not available, request another runner come in his stead. Make sure they are aware the matter is urgent, and discretion is mandated."

Shoulders squared with self-importance, Houston inclined his regal head. "At once, Your Grace."

Lucan turned away from the window and straightened his askew waistcoat. Nothing to be done about his awry neckcloth, however.

Had anyone noticed?

Renewed desire spurred Alexa to lower her lashes and focus her wayward thoughts elsewhere, lest someone detect her secret.

Black Hessians appeared in her line of vision.

Lord Devaux-Rousset?

He would do nicely to distract her from her carnal thoughts.

She tilted her chin. "My lord, you felt the need to accompany my sister?"

That Seonaid consented to ride in the same carriage as the baron without smacking him with her umbrella indicated much.

"Yes, his lordship *insisted* on assuming the role of our protector." Seonaid glided to an armchair and gracefully sank onto the cushion, all the while regarding the Frenchman with an undefinable expression.

Devaux-Rousset's hawk-like gaze swept over her before his lips inched upward, and he swung his attention to Alexa.

"Lady Atterberry vowed you were in extreme jeopardy," he said with the slightest French accent. "Given her distress and unkempt state, I concluded her concern was valid. I couldn't permit the ladies to venture outdoors without an armed escort, no?"

He pushed aside his Spanish-brown greatcoat to reveal a sleek pistol tucked into his waistband.

Shona gave a little gasp, her plump fingers fluttering to her ample bosom.

Lucan perched a hip on the divan's arm and laid a hand upon Alexa's shoulder. "Lady Atterberry, why did you think Alexa was in danger?" he asked, speaking in a gentle tone one might use to soothe a skittish horse or an abused dog.

Shona darted him a shy glance before her gaze skittered away, and she lifted one shoulder. "I've known for some time that Mama and Uncle are involved in something... *untoward*. I overheard snatches of conversations, which made no sense, and more than once..." Her face glowed crimson. "I saw Uncle Harrison sneaking from Mama's bedchamber."

"Harrison in *Minerva's* chamber?" Alexa couldn't keep astonishment from pitching her voice high as her gaze collided with Lucan's before careening to Katrina's and Seonaid's mutually flabbergasted expressions.

"Yes." Shona tittered, pinkening. Her embarrassed snigger ended abruptly, and she touched a finger to her injured lip. "Mama often sent me to bed without supper. I'm too plump, you see."

All women were too plump compared to Minerva's pole-thin figure.

Katrina made a tsking sound, her robin's-egg blue eyes sparking angrily.

Shona grimaced, then scowled at her rounded middle. "I learned to pick the lock and often sneaked to the kitchen when my hunger grew too awful to bear."

"You poor dear. How often did she lock you in your bedchamber?" Katrina grasped Shona's hand, and the girl bestowed a grateful smile on her.

"Oh, Mama locked me in every night." Shona winked, or at least tried to. Her reddened, puffed-up eye scarcely moved. "But once I learned to escape, I prowled the house, spying on them. I became rather good at it too."

Her sister possessed more mettle than Alexa had credited her.

"How clever and daring. I'm sure your excursions proved interesting." Lucan grazed Alexa's shoulder with his fingertips.

Shona nodded, so eager for approval that Alexa's heart ached in compassion.

A shadow passed across Shona's face, and she pursed her lips, her focus fixed upon her tattered slippers.

"Forgive me, Alexa, for not saying anything sooner.

I saw Mama steal the letter to you from your papa when no one was paying attention. She stuffed it into her reticule. What's more, the instant we arrived home, she and Uncle Harrison sequestered themselves in the study. I'm sure they read it together."

I'll just be they did.

"Mercy, the row they had." Shona twisted her lips and wrinkled her nose. "The worst I ever heard between them. Their oaths fairly blistering my ears, they both stormed from the study, and I crept in afterward."

Houston re-entered the room and, after setting a tray of medicinal supplies down, offered a neatly folded piece of linen to Shona. "Here, miss. It's ice cold."

She gratefully accepted the damp cloth Houston extended and patted at her discolored face.

"How did you learn they intended to hurt your sister, Miss Atterberry?" Lord Devaux-Rousset asked, standing behind Seonaid's chair.

She looked anything but pleased at his near proximity.

"I know I'm wicked through and through," Shona said, looking appropriately guilty. "But in their rage, they'd forgotten the letter atop the desk. I slipped it into a hidden pocket I use to conceal food, and after racing to my chamber, I...I read it." Pink swept up her plump cheeks. "Then I hid it where they'd *never* find it."

"That was very brave of you," Alexa told her. "I'm so proud of you."

A grateful, nascent smile tipping the corners of her mouth, Shona inhaled a ragged breath. "Your nurse had been Steafan's too, Alexa. According to what I overheard, eavesdropping on Mama, he trusted her more than anyone else. She said Harrison and her cousin Angus caught Nurse trying to sneak you away."

The doll's shoe beneath the willow.

"That beastly cousin killed the poor thing and dumped her body, heaven knows where." Tears swam in Shona's eyes.

Oh, God.

Such evil boggled Alexa's mind. "Probably in the same area where my mother found me hiding."

She scarcely believed what Shona had revealed. At great risk to herself, her sister had sought Alexa to protect her.

"The letter?" Lucan prompted, kindly.

"They beat me, but I wouldn't tell them where I concealed it. I knew you'd need it as evidence, Alexa." Pride colored her words as she opened her reticule. She handed Alexa the badly crumpled paper. "Here. Read it."

"Thank you." Alexa turned the missive over. A long, jagged tear bore witness to the missive's violent opening.

"When they left the house today, I picked the lock and practically ran the distance to the Needhams' to warn you." Shoulders sagging, Shona drooped against the divan, dejection crumpling her face. Biting her lips and wringing her hands, tears trickled from her eyes.

"Mama plans to hire someone to kill you. For your inheritance."

Katrina choked on a ragged gasp.

"The devil, you say!" Lucan sprang to his feet, his

nostrils flared and eyes glinting threateningly.

"I'm a despicable daughter for betraying my mother, but I couldn't let them harm you." Giving a wobbly smile, Shona winced when her lip's dried blood cracked anew. "I'm sure you must hate me, Alexa, because the committee awarded me the title. I'm not sure who was more surprised, Mama, Uncle Harrison, or me."

"You are not a despicable daughter, and I don't hate you. You risked so much to deliver the truth to me, which says a great deal about your honorable character." Alexa squeezed Shona's hand. "I much prefer you have the title."

"Truly?" Doubt warred with hope in her eyes. "Mama said it went to me because the Hinton sisters' cousin was on the committee, and he absolutely abhors Scots and gypsies. He persuaded the others to vote against you."

Well, at least Alexa knew the why of it now.

Shona dropped her gaze and fiddled with her cuff's torn lace. "I feel just dreadful, Alexa. The barony should've gone to you."

"Miss Shona, you'll have to tell the runner what you've seen and heard." Though softly spoken, the gravity of Lucan's words struck home. "The scandal will be immense, perchance even insurmountable, but your mother and Harrison cannot be allowed to commit murder or remain free."

"I know." Shona sucked her lower lip into her mouth, fresh tears balancing on her lashes. "I...I don't want to be like *her*."

"You're not, Shona. You've already proven that." Alexa embraced her. "You have me now, and my family."

Teary-eyed, Katrina nodded and hugged Shona. "Yes, we shall pretend to be sisters too."

Bracing herself, Alexa unfolded the wrinkled mess that had once been a tidy letter.

Neat writing covered the page, and she tried to smooth the creases. She couldn't read the lone communication she'd ever receive from her father while observed by others, keen interest riddling their gazes as they gauged her reaction.

"Excuse me, please." She retreated to the window seat once more.

The day's gloom had deepened further, and an occasional snowflake sifted from the sky onto the deserted street. Angling her back to the room, she read and reread the words.

~*~

If you are reading this, my beloved Alexa, then I'm dead.

Forgive me for sending you away, but I had to be positive you were safe. That Minerva couldn't find you until you were old enough to read this and know the danger she presents to you.

Whatever you do, my darling daughter, do not trust her. Ever. I learned too late that I had been taken in by the scheming witch...

~*~

After refolding the letter, Alexandra held it to her chest. How her heart could ache this much for a man she barely remembered astonished her, but the biting pain throbbed fiercely.

"I think we should return home and tell Mama and Papa what has occurred." Katrina's soft voice yanked Alexa back to the salon.

Sighing, she stood. "That's wise."

Sliding on her gloves, Katrina tilted her head. "Shona, I'm sure they will want you to stay with us until this, er, situation is sorted out."

Until Minerva and Harrison are apprehended and jailed, you mean.

Alexa caught Lucan regarding her, concern shimmering in his eyes, the same shade of deep gray as the leaden skies. "Alexa, I'd like you to remain until the Bow Street Runner arrives, then we'll also return to the Needhams', and Miss Shona can tell the runner what she knows."

"Of course." If she'd an inkling of today's impending events, Alexa would've remained abed, her head firmly buried beneath her pillows. Pasting a smile on her face, she bid the others farewell. "I'll be home after I've given the runner a statement. Katrina, please make sure Shona has a bath and meal. She can share my chamber."

Lucan shook the baron's hand. "Devaux, are you able to stay at the Needhams' until the authorities arrive, in case the dowager or Peterson dare to call? They are not to be admitted."

Lord Devaux-Rousset gave a short nod. "*Oui.* I must wait to speak to Needham in any event."

Seonaid sent a martyred look ceiling-ward as they filed from the room.

Alexa would have that tale from her friend someday.

Lucan closed the door behind them.

"How long do you think it will take for the authorities to find and arrest Minerva and Harrison?" Alexa stood before the fire warming her hands. An emotionally and physically numbing chill engulfed her.

Lucan encircled her from behind and dropped a kiss on her crown. "Knowing Palmer, today."

"That soon?" She angled her head to meet his eyes. "Is there enough evidence to convict them?"

"With Shona's testimony, more than enough." He grinned and kissed her nose. He was always doing that. "She has pluck."

"Do you think she's truly Steafan's offspring?" Facing the crackling fire once more, Alexa leaned into his embrace, relishing his touch.

"I think he was a decent man who worried about a young girl's future once he discovered how corrupt her mother was. I believe that's why he claimed her as his." He rested his chin atop her head. "However, I'm positive he never expected Shona to receive the title. I suspect he intended to expose Minerva, if not while alive, then certainly after his death."

"Yes, that does make sense. He was a wise man."

He pressed his lips to her crown. "Will you contest

the title now?"

"No. It's all Shona has left." Alexa covered his hands encircling her waist, entwining their fingers. Remorse tempered her speech. "I would like to have known my father, yet I wouldn't have met Balcomb and the others, never have lived as a traveller. I cannot regret that."

"I don't regret it for an instant. I'd never have met the gypsy termagant intent on skewering me." He brushed aside the curls at her nape and gently bit the flesh.

Alexa shuddered, but not from cold.

She wanted this man, wanted him in her bed, to father her children, to hold her hand as they ran across the heather-covered moors, to see his face first thing upon wakening every morning and last thing at night until the end of her days.

Life without him?

Utterly unbearable.

A smile played around the edges of her mouth as she unfastened her spencer. The Lord had made her a Scottish Highland traveller. She could endure everything else. For him, she'd learn to host *haut ton* gatherings, ignore snobbish set downs, try to be a wife, a duchess, he would be proud of.

"Lucan." She lifted her hand, turning it this way and that, the purple gem flashing in the fire's light. "I never thanked you for the ring."

~*~

Lucan's pulse quickened in anticipation, and he rotated Alexa in his arms, searching her eyes. The golden shards shimmered with something he'd not seen before.

"Dare I hope you intend to accept it? Me?"

Her sweet mouth crept upward. "Well, you did have the ring designed especially for me, and the gem *is* my favorite."

"Are you saying yes?" Lucan spanned her narrow ribs with his hands, brushing her lips with his.

Nothing ever mattered as much as her answer.

"Promise you'll have no regrets?" Biting her lower lip, she trailed a finger across the seam of his mouth.

Raining feather-light kisses over her face and alabaster neck, he pulled her tight against him. "Not now, or in a month, or a decade, or fifty years."

"Not if a half-century passes, and I've grown fat and wrinkled? And toothless and bald?" Alexa skimmed her fingertips across his forehead before sliding her hand into the hair above his ear.

He chuckled as he palmed her cheek, his nose touching hers. "Not if time ceases."

"What if I prove a bumbling, inadequate duchess?"

Rubbing his thumb along her fine jawbone, he whispered fervently, "None of those things matters a whit. Having you at my side until I draw my final breath is what I care about."

She touched the tip of her pink tongue to her upper lip. "And you love me?"

"Yes, my gypsy witch. I love you. Now hush and kiss me." Lucan gave her a fierce squeeze, earning him a breathless giggle.

Alexa's mouth parted, and he plundered the sweet cavern. Their breath mingled as they kissed, tongues thrusting, retreating, and plunging again and again, a tantalizing dance of sensation and exploration.

He poured his love into the simple act, binding her to him—his Highland-Gypsy-turned-lady—across eternity and beyond. Lucan pressed his mouth to the mole gracing her mouth, then the pulse throbbing at the juncture of her throat.

Alexa arched her neck, her breasts thrusting upward with the movement, and her fingers biting into his shoulders.

Theirs would be no tame joining.

His groin surged with lustful expectancy, and he sucked her lower lip. How soon might they wed?

Lucan crushed her to him. "I love you."

A siren's smile curved her mouth as she reached for the buttons of his falls. "Why don't you show me how much?"

"Now?" Dashing a fervent glance to the closed door, he wavered. "I cannot take the time I'd like to—"

"We can go slowly next time." Alexa shrugged off her spencer as she folded to the floor. Reclining upon the carpet, she drew her skirts up her shapely thighs before bunching the fabric around her waist.

Mother of God.

A saint couldn't have resisted the luscious display. Firelight glinted over her satiny flesh, and the raven curls nested between her thighs beckoned.

Dropping to his knees, Lucan freed his rigid member. "I don't want to hurt you, but we haven't time for me to properly prepare you. The runner could arrive at any moment."

Alexa spread her legs and raised her arms. "Silly man. I've been wet with want for weeks."

Nipping her collarbone, Lucan positioned himself between her legs, his penis teasing her moist entrance.

Arching, she urged him to her.

"Hungry little thing, aren't you, darling?"

"Uh-hum." She opened her mouth and gyrated her hips in invitation. "Hurry."

Plunging his tongue into her sweet mouth, the same instant he sank home, breaking through her maidenhead, he fought to keep from exploding into her tightness.

He needn't have worried.

Alexa's violet eyes widened, and an incredulous expression swept her face. "Lucan. Oh, God, Lucan."

Clutching his shoulders, she wrapped her legs around his waist and surged against him, convulsing so violently, he burst.

Gripping her full buttocks, Lucan threw his head back and let bliss carry him away. When he could think coherently again, he rocked against her, still ensconced within her honeyed depths. "Kitten, you didn't answer."

Breathless, her eyes passion-glazed, Alexa whispered, "Can we marry before my family sails?"

Praise God and hallelujah.

"Yes. I already have a special license." He'd acquired it the day after his grandaunt admonished him to marry Alexa, post haste.

Alexa chuckled. "Confident I'd change my mind, were you?"

"No, desperately hopeful you would." He nuzzled her neck, and she slanted her head to give him better access. "I would've been a miserable, cranky, old curmudgeon for the next fifty years if I hadn't been successful."

Alexa grew pensive, doubt dimming her vibrant eyes. "Lucan, is our love enough to make our union work? Strong enough to last and persevere? We are so very different, you and I."

His father's stern visage hovered before his face for an instant. If his sire had loved his mother the way Lucan adored Alexa, no seductress's wiles could have tempted him to abandon his vows.

"Love is why our union will work and be joyous beyond our greatest dreams. If we're committed to the end, no matter what providence sends our way, we can endure anything together." He pressed a kiss to her nose. "All else matters naught. I give you my pledge, as long as life's blood flows through my veins, I shall love you above everything else, upon my honor."

The smile Alexa bestowed upon him surely came straight from heaven, for his soul shouted for joy as it recognized the answering love shining from her radiant face.

"Then, my answer is yes."

Epilogue

Chattsworth Park House
24 December 1818

Alexa tucked her toes farther beneath her nightgown as she wrapped the quilt tighter about her shoulders. This far from the hearth, the room retained a stubborn chill. Yet, she'd been unable to resist watching the snowfall. As a child, she'd been captivated by the mystery and, as an adult, the phenomenon's majesty and tranquility mesmerized her still.

She'd awoken a bit ago to the mysterious silence foretelling a thick blanket of white. Slipping from Lucan's warm embrace, she snatched a covering from the bed and now lay curled onto the window seat. Intoxicated with happiness unlike anything she'd ever conceived, she hummed a Scottish lullaby and rotated her wedding ring.

Mere weeks ago, she'd become Her Grace, the Duchess of Harcourt, and tomorrow she'd experience the British holiest of holidays with Lucan's charming family. Scots didn't observe Christmastide, but

Hogmanay?

That was a different tale entirely.

The Scottish celebrated with merriment and gusto only a Highlander fully appreciated. The Dowager Duchess of Harcourt, the sweet lady, expressed delight when Alexa suggested they plan a Hogmanay New Year's, and she wanted to introduce Alexa to Boxing Day too.

Goodness, so many festivities.

Though frail and tiring easily, Lucan's mother's health hadn't worsened. The dowager hinted, often, that she'd like to live long enough to see Lucan's son.

His brother's reaction upon spotting the beagle pup they'd brought him made Alexa chuckle softly again. Nothing, this side of heaven, ever shined more joyfully than Jeremy's face at that moment. Weeping, he'd fallen to his knees, and Baron—Jeremy's name for the four-legged, needle-toothed terror—scampered onto his thighs and proceeded to lick Jeremy's face until he collapsed in a fit of giggles.

Minerva and Harrison maintained their innocence, but with the overwhelming evidence against them, as well as Shona's testimony, their trials had been pathetically brief. Their deportation sentence, rather than hanging, was attributed to the Hintons' generous greasing of a few palms. Alexa last saw them dragged from the courtroom, spewing curses and damning Alexa and Shona to hell.

God help her, but Alexa couldn't extend them a jot of compassion, and the injustice that they should be extended mercy when they'd been so ruthless and prepared to murder her, rankled.

The Needhams graciously took Shona into their fold, and she was far better for it. She would receive the love and acceptance she'd lacked most of her life.

Alexa's parting with her Highland family had been bittersweet. The New World offered them opportunities they'd never have as black tinkers. With a promise to visit in the next couple of years, she'd tearfully bid them farewell.

"Come back to bed, Duchess. I'm cold without you beside me." Grogginess weighted Lucan's deep baritone as he rested on one elbow. He stared at her hungrily, the bedcoverings gathered at his waist, revealing his sculpted torso lightly covered in hair.

"*Och,* that's what I'm good for, keeping you warm?" Alexa swung her feet to the floor and shivered as icy tendrils snaked up her calf. Scampering to the bed, she jumped onto the mattress, only to have her husband pin her beneath his muscular frame.

"No, lass, I can think of a thing or two more you are especially good for." He dipped his fair head and suckled her breast through the fabric of her gown.

Pleasure speared to her core, and she raised her hips in invitation.

He reared upward. "Off with this."

In one deft movement, he peeled the gown over her head.

"Brr, Lucan, it's freezing." Alexa burrowed under the covers, then giggled when he pounced atop her again, this time flesh to flesh, his sinewy hardness against her rounded softness.

"Let me warm you." His hands everywhere, caressing and arousing her, he lathered hot kisses across her breasts and collarbone, his penis nudging the apex of her thighs.

Reaching between them, she curled her hand around his thick length, grinning when he issued a guttural groan. She stroked him, reveling in how her touch affected him.

He groaned again and grasped her hand. "Careful or the deed will be done before we start."

"We cannot have that. I shan't be cheated." Spreading her legs, Alexa guided him to her center, moaning when he slid home.

As the snow blanketed the earth outside, the wonder of their joining worked its mystical magic until, as one, they crested ecstasy's peak.

Later, satiated and drowsy with contentment, she lay with her back cradled against the hard expanse of his chest and his strong thigh wrapped around her legs. She skimmed her nails along his forearm. "Tell me again when you knew you loved me."

He rocked his hips into her buttocks and nipped her shoulder. "When you looked back at me at Dounnich House, my heart became yours."

"When did you know you loved me?" Lucan lifted her thigh and eased into her warmth once more.

Alexa arched into his thrust. "When I looked back at you at Dounnich House."

SCANDAL'S SPLENDOR

Highland Heather Romancing a Scot, Book Four

She can see the future.
But she never saw him coming…

Seonaid Ferguson gave up on the Marriage Mart long ago. Spinsterhood is *far* preferable to allowing the *haut ton* to exploit her second sight. But thankfully, she has a plan to rid herself of her accursed abilities—a plan she'd be well on her way to enacting if a snowstorm hadn't stranded her with the very *last* man she ever wanted to see again. It's just her misfortune that she might actually *need* the handsome devil.

Jacques, Monsieur le baron de Devaux-Rousset, is running out of time. If his Scottish silver mine doesn't turn a profit sizable enough to save his estate, he'll be forced to search for an heiress to wed. And unfortunately, the mine seems doomed to fail. The *last* thing he needs is to fall for the lovely and spirited Seonaid. He mustn't even *consider* helping her with her risqué plan—even though he'd love nothing more…

Is it chance or dark design that brought these opposites together? Only time will tell. But if they want their happily ever after, Seonaid and Jacques better get ready to fight for it…

USA Today Bestselling, award-winning author COLLETTE CAMERON® scribbles Scottish and Regency historical romance novels featuring dashing rogues, rakes, and scoundrels and the strong heroines who reform them. Blessed with an overactive and witty muse that won't stop whispering new romantic romps in her ear, she's lived in Oregon her entire life. Although she dreams of living in Scotland part-time. A confessed Cadbury chocoholic, you'll always find a dash of inspiration and a pinch of humor in her sweet-to-spicy timeless romances®.

Explore **Collette's worlds** at
collettecameron.com!

Join her **VIP Reader Club** and **FREE newsletter**.
Giggles guaranteed!

FREE BOOK: Join Collette's The Regency Rose® VIP Reader Club to get updates on book releases, cover reveals, contests and giveaways she reserves exclusively for email and newsletter followers. Also, any deals, sales, or special promotions are offered to club members first. She will not share your name or email, nor will she spam you.

http://bit.ly/TheRegencyRoseGift

Dearest Reader,

Thank you for reading HEARTBREAK AND HONOR.

So many of my readers kept asking me when Lucan would get his book and also hoped Tasara would have one too. When I first introduced them in other romances, I didn't know they'd end up sweethearts. They did, though!

Shona has her own story too, THE ROGUE AND THE WALLFLOWER, The Honorable Rogues®. She also makes an appearance in a few of my other The Honorable Rogues® stories.

Highland travellers (yes, that is the correct spelling) were Scottish gypsies, also known as black tinkers. Though some claimed Roma blood, many did not, and gypsy refers to their nomadic like lifestyle rather than their ethnicity.

Please consider telling other readers why you enjoyed this book by reviewing it. I also truly adore hearing from my readers. You can contact me on my website and while you are there, explore my author world. I also have a fabulous VIP Reader Group on Facebook (http://facebook.com/groups/CollettesCheris). If you're a fan of my books and historical romance, I'd love to have you join me.

If you enjoyed reading Alexa and Lucan's story, be sure to check out the other books in my HIGHLAND HEATHER ROMANCING A SCOT series. The series is a spin-off of my CASTLE BRIDES series, where you'll see many of the same characters.

Hugs,

Collette